T0077995

Momas baby
Papa's maybe
THE *Secrets out*

Pyre Kabu Ajamu

authorHOUSE·

AuthorHouse™
1663 Liberty Drive
Bloomington, IN 47403
www.authorhouse.com
Phone: 833-262-8899

This is a work of fiction. All of the characters, names, incidents, organizations, and dialogue
in this novel are either the products of the author's imagination or are used fictitiously.

Published by AuthorHouse 05/25/2022

ISBN: 978-1-6655-3169-6 (sc)
ISBN: 978-1-6655-3168-9 (e)

Library of Congress Control Number: 2021914170

Print information available on the last page.

This book is printed on acid-free paper.

Contents

The Ribellyon &
Rebella Rez

Get Right or
Get Behind

Beautiful Disaster
by
King Vengeance

Chapter 1

The Day My Heart Broke

Early in the peak of the morning as the Sun rises to position.

Andreah lightly and slowly awakens to the piercing Sun bleeding through the blinds of the room of her childhood love Jeff.

She yawns as she wipes the Cole out of her eyes, and frowns a pleasurable smile across her face reminiscing about the erotic performance last night of the mid-morning when her and Jeff arrived safely back to his house and released pint of love, aggression, deprivation, and pure lust in his bedroom

A masculine arm wrapped around her petite thick young frame. She is loaded with blush and raw indescribable emotions. As she turns her body around to greet her love with a kiss. But she receives the most lethal death grip across her mouth to prevent her from screaming "AHHHHHHHHHHHHHHHHH." The angel grip of death serves its purpose mulling her cries to the circumference of the small size-bedroom.

Her eyes were bug eyed as she matched the pair of soul snatching reaper eyes that was all too identical to hers.

She practically pissed herself when the voice that has been considered Satan to her since…. she was 12 howled in a murderous whisper "He'll O puppet I've been looking all over for you."

Her bowls beyond her control relaxed as she through accidental fear soiled her lover's bedspread from the sound of her father's voice.

She wined through profusely spilled tears begging her father for forgiveness. To show her mercy. But with his hand still firmly clamped around her mouth he whispered "SHOOOOOOSSSSSHHHHH Puppet it's OK Daddies hear now sweet pea.

You know me, and your umi (Arabic for mother) was worried sick about you. I believe this is the first time since I've came home, years ago

1

that you missed early Morning Prayer Hmmmmm "he sighed deeply as he looked at his once innocent daughter's pure flesh. Outside of his own perverted deeds she has befouled him, and it angered him as he relived his daughter's shirk (Arabic for sinful deeds).

Orchestrated out in front of him as he grips her hair atrociously, causing serious pain. As he barked in a whisper "we better get going now before your umi gets worried about us. I wouldn't want her to witness the state of disgust you're in as a Muslim in the name of Father Allah you have 30 seconds to get dressed if you make one peep... "he allowed his hand that once gripped her flawless locks and now placed it around her throat crushing her windpipe; her nose began to bleed as she struggled for air to plead with her father to stop because she was slipping out of consciousness

She nodded her head and patted his forearm frantically. To inform him of her compliance with her father Stretch, who smiled Devilishly and said, "Ha Ha I knew you would see things daddies' way puppet...Smack." She yelped loudly from the impact of his hand, slapping her across her youthful face as he growled "lil bitch shut the fuck up and get dressed (he spits on her then says) hurry up:

Meanwhile a few blocks away at the neighborhood local convenient store Jeff with a smile says, "ok so lemme make sure I got this right you said I take 2 eggs fry them on the skillet allow 2 minutes on each side."

Jeff with excitement carried on as he asked Ms. Haskins an elderly woman that's been in the hood forever instructions on how to cook an egg & cheese bacon omelet for him, his love, and first Lady (Mother).

Ms. Haskins smiled as she attentively listened to the young man ask away with such a glare of joy in his eyes.

She was so enthralled with the joy exuberant off of Jeff that it reminded her back in her day when she was young, and head over heels over her childhood love whom after 30 years plus and counting they were still married.

She answered his questions wisely, and with warming gestures even suggests ingredients she uses to warm her husband's soul with her cooking,

As Jeff gave, an open ear with a smile his pager went off, and he reached for it and look at the numbers to see whom it was he peeped the sequence of numbers that read "4316" his once warming smile, and charm decease, and worry soiled his mood. He dropped the groceries from his hands, and politely brush past Ms. Haskins and said "I'm sorry ma'am 11 I have to go."

He darts for the exit of the convenient store, and peeps Baltimore Finest and the Fire Department flew down the block. His heart rate increases sporadically as he whispers a prayer under his breath "Lord God please keep going straight don't turn right." As the Fire Truck and Baltimore Police Department in tow behind the truck ease on the brake and hooked a sharp right. Jeff's heart fell to his gut as he screamed a gut-wrenching cry "Mom Maaa Noooooooo".

Six blocks away in front of his house was a thick entourage of damn there the whole neighborhood gathered around in worry and fear praying that the Thompson household made it out alive.

Jeff's older brother sadly got eliminated from the streets a long time ago. So, the only residence of the household was Jeff and his mother. His father was a wealthy man that sadly wanted nothing to do with the likes of him and his mother. So, at a young age Jeff stepped up to the honor of becoming the man of the house and never looked back. Years of being a child was over and as he sprints like a track star back to his residence.

His comrade Freddy, and the rest of the Jaama boys snapped as one solider growled "Yo Gee where the fuck is Jay at Cho."

Freddy shot back with "Nigga if I knew that do you think I would be out cheere right now with you fools did you page the comrade."

The lil solider with attitude growled back with "man Gee you know I paged the comrade he ain't hit back yo.

Four fire fighters in tow on cache end of the stretcher had Jeff's moms Ms. Clara Thompson laid flat on her back strapped to an air-mask as the firefighters in the front yelled "make room people come on let's go make room."

Freddie's voice cracked up as he seen the women who was like a second mom to him come out on the stretcher unconscious, and barely hanging on strings of her lifeline.

He snapped as he barked at the Firefighters and said "you motherfucka's better make sure Ms. T pulls through you hear me shit....u think I'm playing. Ms. T hold on Ms. T. please we need you to hold on, and stay strong La Jaama is here."

Jeff muscles his way through the crowd screaming at the top of his lungs "mama mama I'm here, right here yall niggas move the fuck out of my way MAMA."

As the crowd parted like the Red Sea Jeff's knees almost gave out. As soon as he seen from five feet away his mother was on a stretcher, barely clinging to life. When he yelped with teary eyed pain "Ma Ma Mama Nooo 00000" he stormed over to her with every bit of energy he could muster and collapsed to his knees as the firefighters loaded her in the back of an Ambulance Truck.

"Excuse me Sir you can't be on the truck" a Caucasian with dirty blonde hair with forest green eyes mid-age women protested Jeff blacked on the poor woman as he spazzed out saying "Bitch this is my motherfucking Mother I'm not going no fucking were."

The Caucasian Surgeon instantly grew intimidated, but rationally through protocol and professionally told Jeff Sir I'm not gonna began to try to describe what your going through, but your mother Sir her pulse is weak, and has a strong chance if you get off, and follow us: I'm sorry Sir but are policy doesn't allow residents to ride...

"Jeff growing irate pulled one of his guns pressed it against her forehead and growled" BITCH FUCK yo policy this is my mother yo now ya cracka ass is gon... "Out of his peripheral he spotted a teary eyed mess of a familiar face!

They locked eyes for a split second until Jeff gone mad, and howled under his breath "YOU..." In a flash, he darted off the truck in pursuit of the familiar face unaware his comrades were hot on his tail.

The familiar face jumped out of her heels, and high tailed as fast as she could. But sadly to no avail she was captured by a young solider. Who appeared from the cut, and gripped her up by her top half as the young comrade growled "Bitch where you think you going."

The voice with a thick accent screamed, "Lemme go punjietas I didn't do nothing what the fuck can't a bitch walk or run as she please."

Jeff cut her off and growled, "Not when that bitch is one of the faces I've seen last night then hours later my mother is on life support. "Freddy overtly excited yelled "Yo Gee that's that Ho from last night who was with that other Ho with the crazy father."

Jeff hearing his comrade and brother n arms mention his love as a Ho instantly made him worry about her. Wondering if she was still trapped in the burning house. But him being quick at the draw with thought he sounded off on Freddy with "Freddy take my car, and a couple of the young Jays and follow that ambulance truck to the hospital."

Freddy protested as he said "nah Gee let me handle this bitch yo go tend to mom... "Jeff snapped as he growled back" Motherfucka #1...."I was not asking".... now go NOW!!!

Freddy looked at him with a crooked look then ice grilled shorta before he assembled some comrades, and yelled aloud "come on y'all lets go MOVE."

A couple of younger Jaama boys stayed back with him as he began to interrogate Tatiana who cried out "please Jeff you have to believe me there was nothing I can do he had the drop on me when y'all... "She screamed in pain as he snatched her up by her long jet black Latino hair, and growled "BITCH there's a lot you could of done..... now save the sob story and tell me what you know...."

Mean while.....3-Blocks away somewhere around the corner

Agonizing screams escape off the lips of the warrant less soul of

Andreah whom was position erect from the knees up ass-naked, bound and held by the wrist her entire body covered in welts, bruises, cuts, and blood. Her speech was muted from the unbearable treatment she suffered by her father. Whose sick and perverted ass took pleasure in whipping her like Jesus on the mantle before crucifixion! When he purred in Arabic "Allah uh Akbar uh Akbar a Shendu wa had illa had n Allah I la salaat wa lad coma ta salaat wa lad coma ta salaat Allah uh Akbar Allah uh Akbar lad n la had n la Allah" he was calling what Muslims in the Islamic world call the Dun ya which is the open part of prayer Muslims recite before offering there salaat.

Andreah's mother Khadeejah could be heard outside of the room in the hallway banging on the door screaming to Stretch "Baby stop in the name of Allah, I beg you please this is my baby our baby for the love of God STOOOPPPPPP AHHHHH. Khadeejah bangs and claws at the locked door with hopes to gain access, but to no avail, its sealed shut. When Andreah tried to scream for help, her father backhanded the piss out of her leaving her slumped unconscious as he mumbled in her ear "Lad puppet no one can save you from the wrath of Allah not even myself."

He kissed her forehead, and sickly began licking down her face to her chin ending at her lips parting them with his tongue as he began passionately trying to kiss her. He screamed like a school-girl as she grabbed a hold of his tongue with her teeth. She then tried with all the energy she could muster to gain her freedom.

However, he stopped her with a sharp jab to the ribs that caved her right side in. This sent her crashing to the floor in excruciating pain. Her arms dangled and still bound and constrained in her restraints as Stretch her father barked "you stupid crazy little bitch look what you made me do."

He roared with a blood-filled speech as he hiked Andreah to position by the hips, and moved behind her and barked, "The hellfire has special places for little whores like you." While meanwhile at the front door of the Bey Residence, knocks at the door "Dreah, Dreah baby are you in there."

Jeff continues to loudly knock on the door awaiting entry praying, and hoping Andreah's father would answer the door, so he could blow his motherfucking head off, from all the trouble, he has caused. After hearing the spill from Tatiana how he had abducted her the following night after Jeff and Andreah dropped her off.

He did terrible things to her, to make her spill the whereabouts of Andreah. Jeff was in disbelief and appalled to encounter across such evil. Tatiana was visibly shaking in the company of the young and wild BGF boys she feared that they would kill her because of unleashing the whereabouts of Jeff's residence to a monster like Stretch She was in shock and warming towards Jeff who told his younger comrades to let her go, and for them to go join Freddy at the hospital with his mother. When some protested to him in battle, he denied them with thanks for their courage, but simply ended with "I'm taking the gloves off on this one G… now go please."

From there he sprinted up the block in the direction of Andreah's house, with one reason in mind, which was free, his love from captivity and murk what was left of the Bey residence. Frustrated outside of the Bey's front door battling the urge of kicking down the door. His thoughts eating at him, as he revisited all that happened from the wrath of this man's hands, he said aloud to himself how sick of a bastard Stretch was, but all of a sudden he heard a faint scream in the distance of a distressed women.

Then he screamed while shooting and kicking the front door down "Dre AAAHH baby hold on I'm coming." He fired through the house like a Sergeant of Arms, in search for Andreah, the eerie smell and feeling of death lingered thickly in the air, but unafraid Jeff searched through each room in the house screaming Andreah's name. Then followed the voice of the battered woman who was still on the second floor of the hallway.

A hysterical mess at the door clawing away screaming "Stretch please honey stop she did not mean it. Oh God Oh Allah please no no no no no have mercy." Seeing this Jeff snapped into action, and rushed over to Ms.

Bey and yelled "Ms. K Ms. K were is Andreah." Ms. Khadeejah, Andreah's mother looked like she seen a ghost when she stared into Jeff's eyes.

Who now shook her violently and growled, "Ms. K I'm going to ask you one more time where the fuck is Andreah, and that perverted piece of shit..." Jeff paused as he heard moans and groans of a young women crying in the next room beyond the locked door. Ms. Khadeejah was three feet away crying.

He retrieved his guns and now positioned himself in front of the door, where the moans and groans where coming from and increasing louder in sound.

Jeff trembled as he tried to fathom the worst that could be happening beyond that door. He took a deep breath, then clutched on his burner and fired two shots before he kicked the door down and said "DREEE. AAAAHHHH!" Andreah sweetie "Ah Ah huh wh wh WHAT." Andreah finally awoke out of her hypnotism, gasping vigorously fighting for air. Frantically looking around the psyche doctor's office trying to place everything back to perspective.

As to what occurred until her psychiatrist calmly said "Ms. Phillips, Ms. Phillips it's ok Ms. Phillips relax, it's just me Honey look at me me me look at me come on." Andreah began to relax a little, and focus in back on her psyche. An elderly age Caucasian women with graying hair, glasses, and a secret crush on red bottom heels and Michael Kohrs accessories. As she calmly stated to Ms. Andreah Phillips "there you go darling you almost gave me a scare there, when you broke connection Honey are you ok."

Andreah blinks her eyes fervently adjusting them back to reality. Where in the physical, she is now a 41-year-old black women who has relocated now in D.C., for over a decade and a half plus. She changed her last name to try to erase the past of a bloody mortifying History of sexual and physical abuse from her biological father. She is on the run from a dangerous criminal organization known as the Black Guerrilla Family.

That green-lighted a bounty on her head for the fall of there beloved comrade Jeff 24 years ago. She worked as a receptionist for the Federal District Courts in D.C. now for 10 years. For a large portion of those years she has lived in fear until recently, she started having nightmares. Which explains her reasoning for the urgent appointment? "Iii uhhhhhh I did it again didn't l" Andreah said aloud sounding defeated.

The psychiatrist scooted closer to her and took her hand into hers and consoled it gently and said "I'm afraid so Ms. Phillips, but not to worry my dear where making progress quite well. but remember we never made it this far before." Andreah somewhat still shaken sighed deeply and said "it's never gonna get better, D.O.C. it's gonna just keep getting worst and worst."

Doctor Gasper warmly said, "Well Ms. Phillips with a negative outlook on your growth and Development acting like that you sadly might be right. However, if you really wanna tackle this thing it first starts with believing in yourself. Andreah shook her head irritated with her doctor for lecturing her, although she did not dispute what she said.

Not to be sure with her philosophy was easier said than done. No way in hell would she expect someone as fortunate as Doctor Victoria Gasper to truly understand? Andreah rose to her feet that where elevated in 4 in royal blackish purple with fox fur the same color wrapped around the huff made by Manko Tran heels and said "maybe your right Doc I guess...(she paused looked around then said) sometimes it's just easier to give up. "I mean death's got to be easier right."

Doctor Gasper also rose to her feet and went over to one of the counters that was locked. opened it then walked back with Andreah's prescription slip, and said "Death is certain and Life is not my dear so before you consider to yourself what's easier look to others fate and count your blessings, because it could be much worst."

Andreah having heard enough reached for her prescription slip smiled then said with a sigh "huhhhh maybe your right Doc I should get going. I have many errands to run thank you again for everything, as always I am greatly appreciative of your time." Doctor Victoria Gasper inched closer towards Andreah, gave her a warming hug, and said, "My pleasure Ms. Phillips, but seriously, please take care, I caution you to consider what I'm saying dear I mean no harm to you just concern, holistic healing out trumps any capsule prescribed in a pill form."

Andreah now with the slip in her hand continued to smile at her, but wonder for a brief second "No way does this ole hag know what my pure intentions are with these pills." She was prescribed psyche meds called Remeron and Trazodone, but outside of that, she was able to get prescribed Oxycontin 80's and Roxy 15's which were a substitute for Percocet which was stemming from when she got into a bizarre car accident years back when she was still living in Baltimore City.

Cutting and weaving through traffic trying to get away from her BGF captors who green lighted a bounty on her head over the fall of there comrade Jeff. In the thick of the heat she was struck hard by a School Bus who wasn't paying attention, and caused her to be in a induced coma for three months. The young comrades believing she was dead, and the U.S. Government in fear of catching a suit against the comatose patient if she were ever to awaken thought quick and wisely an did there homework.

Three months later as she pulled through hooked up to Life Support machines. Outside of Baltimore City in a hospital in Laurel, Maryland. She was visited by a doctor who informed her of her full recovery then later in the day two Federal Agents that played there role to the T. When they spun a web, of a drawn out story of events that caused her accident.

Spiraled from reckless driving from young Radical Black Militant gang-bangers who tailgated her, and rear-ended her vehicle into the line of travel of a Baltimore City School Bus. For her safety she recalled one agent saying we can relocate you, employ, and provide schooling and a home plus transportation and a change of name if you agree to cooperate against the monsters who attempted to kill you.

Andreah thought long and hard about what he said, she remembered telling them "Ah Ah Ah I mean honestly I don't know how I can be of any help officers, outside of them trying to kill me I really don't know.." One thirsty agent edged on "Well Ms. Smith-Bey what about Jeffrey Thompson AKA Ramu he was your boyfriend wasn't he, "She fought back the tears because at the time it had only been a few months since his death so the wound was still fresh when she muttered "Na Na Nooo he was not my boyfriend but I loved Jeff very much."

The agent edged on deeper then said, "So what you're telling me is he was not your boyfriend, but you where in love with him, so what! You were in love with a ghost or something, come on Ms. Smith-Bey, Pretty young fine thing like yourself, I'm pretty sure you pillow talked occasionally." Andreah faced frowned up when she said "Excuse Me!" The agent kept on refusing to let up when he said "Seriously Ms. Smith-Bey make this make sense to us your birthed by a notorious lowlife from New Jersey gets caught up spend 13 years of your 18 years of existence in one of our tax paying U.S. pens.

Is marked as a high ranking Islamic Black Intelligent Extremist in our U.S. Federal Database. Don't you find it odd how one could think your full of shit when you tell us you know nothing when the man that raised you is amongst the same walk of life the man you just finished telling us you love is identical to young lady where trying to help you here.

"Andreah snapped when she shot back with "#1 ain't nobody ask y'all pasty face ass for help and #2 no matter how many times you ask me the question in different tones the answer is still going to be the same. I don't know nothing. I was too busy getting my ass molested and beat by the same motherfucka you think y'all know outside of y'all penal system."

The agents paused as they keyed in on Andreah as her Life Support machines rattled outta control triggering she was getting a little worked up. Surgeons stormed in immediately to assist Andreah as she began to wined down for a little bit from the excitement. The other agent that didn't speak only when spoken to simply removed a card from his vests jacket pocket placed it at her feet on the bed, and said "Ms. Smith-Bey our apologizes for the forwardness.

Were just trying to do our jobs the best way possible. Now unfortunately sometimes it calls for acts that go way outside our protocol were supposed to follow nevertheless the cause is always for the betterment of the people. The surgeons were telling the agents that they had to go due to the immediate 047 (hands on deck) patient that needed the entire focus.

As the one surgeon was escorting the agents out Andreah's room the agent that continued to talk had now retrieved a picture from his pants pocket of her love Jeff Thompson and said "Ms. Smith-Bey you can think whatever you want to think about us, but at the end of it all your opinions is your own personal conception it has nothing to do with what our job detail is which is protecting all including you from monsters like what your boyfriend used to be before he valued life and began to assist us in the takedown of the BGF."

Finally out the door the agent made one last statement to Andreah saying "the choice is yours Ms. Smith-Bey by God we pray you make the right one please consider, and will offer you the same thing we were gonna offer Jeff." Slipping in and out of it suffering from a heart attack she dwelled, and marinated on the Agents last comment.

She couldn't come to terms in believing Jeff was a confidential informant for the same government that worked holidays to dismantle the structure of the militant Black Guerrilla Family that was his right to membership by birth. She quickly drifted off allowing the thought to fly freely as it came, but what stuck with her was the brisk conversation after their sexcapades Jeff had with her about skipping town, and never looking back just him, and her on the open road.

"BEEEEEEEEEPPPPPPPPPP escapes loudly out of the Life Support machines over the commotions of surgeons performing surgery" back into reality" the ringtone It ain't Tricking Less you Got it by new southern rappers that recently just blessed the scene." It rung loudly out front of the

Psychiatrist Victoria Gaspers building in Andreah's peacoat pocket as she fumbled trying to get it with a smile knowing exactly who it was.

Andreah said sarcastically with a smile over the phone "Damn bitch what you got Spidey senses or something all up in my cobwebs knowing what's missing who you working for. "The women on the other side of the receiver name was Celeste, and she was in stitches as she responded with "HONEY. STOP. you know who I work for, and I must be doing damn good sense I'm able to detect when ya Ho ass gotta itch that needs scratched."

They both laughed together in unison letting their guard down now a little more after their interrogational humorous intervals. Andreah responded back "Wow and itch that's what you Madams and Pimps call a bitch needing some dick now dear God "she snickered, but then Celeste added "Call it what chu want boo, but before I forget check it out what you got plan for the night Honey tell me your free.

"Andreah sighed before she said "girl you know I got a hot date tonight with some red wine some hoes name Oxy and Roxy taking tums with my King Kong (her black dildo) at home. Celeste giggled and said "Awwweeee you poor thing" Andreah shot back with "Bitch; fuck you King Kong got more stamina than them weak ass boy toys dis pussy then ran through."

Celeste shot back with "I'm sorry somebody seems dismissive about my service if that's the case miss thang why do you continuously answer. "Andreah was quiet for a moment trying to think of what to say until Celeste spoke it into existence and said "you know why you still answer (she giggled then said) it's quite simple actually you see you need me just as much as I need you what we got Dreah baby is sorta like a bartering love triangle with privileges.

I got what you need, and you go what I need in the size of a green colored Tic Tac that makes a body feel so relax when I soak ass naked in this 6 jet jacuzzi over a glass of Chardonnay. As Celeste giggled Andreah on the other end listened with a smirk and a mild attitude caressing back n forth her prescription slip from her doctor for the meds Celeste was badgering on about when she said she takes a sip from her glass then opens with) AHHHHHHH the best part of this Love Triangle we got babe is thanks to this elite clientele the privileges that comes with this secret society it's doors not many in life will ever get to open.

To extend my appreciation Honey tonight me, and you are attending this all white party 8 blocks in the North Gate Direction of the white house at a underground play pen called The Garden of Eden off Pennsylvania Avenue on Philadelphia Avenue on the Northwest my treat."

Andreah spat back with "ya treat huh, and what makes you so convince that I want to go." Celeste growing irritated with the back n forth dramatics closed the call with "because sweetie you would have been cut the call so I'll tell you what, meet me tonight over in the southeast at my Smoosh House around 6:30 this evening bring your appetite, and don't be late Toodles.

"The line went dead, and Andreah looked at her phone then ended the call. She shook her head, frustrated pondering, back n forth at the last minute thinking aloud "Christ what on earth am I going to where."

With in seconds her phone made the IM (Instant Message) Byrd sound signifying she was receiving a text she activated her phone, and peeped the text was from Celeste who said and don't worry about a dress I gotchu so fix ya face honey I'll see you tonight LOL EMOGI." Andreah couldn't help but smile once she finished reading the text; she had to admit as much as Celeste over the years when they met little over 3 years ago annoyed the fuck out of her with her forward way of talking. How she would not, take no for answer.

There relationship outside of that was platonic. How the memories and moments with her journeyed with the remarkable trial of some of the most epic orgasms of a life time. Which was partially the main reason why Andreah over the years continued to call, and answer her phone including being a great supportive friend.

How they met was odd a couple of years back, Andreah was on a lunch break. The most commonplace government workers frequent at was a

Diner 9 blocks away in the East direction of the White House, called the Politician everybody including court workers dined at the establishment ran by big Susie. The Politician was notorious in the White House for it's breakfast and lunch specials.

It's been in rotation for over 40 years plus, and how it made such huge clout and publicity was when President Ronald Reagan at the time of the White House back in the early 80's of his full fledged term on the War on Drugs stopped through on an Exhibition coming back from ally country France, and ordered a Steak, Egg, and Cheese Bagel. Upon citizens, and respondents employed in the government who tuned in watching the President chow down on that homemade bagel.

There sales and consumer rotation plummeted overnight with politicians, and citizens from all walks of life for their incredible bagels and dishes off the menu, but they weren't the only people that came. The District of Columbia's outlaws-ish Underground of Playas, pimps. Hustlas, gangstas, and macks also frequent daily, but there was only one polished playa Big Susie appreciated, and never grew concerned whenever she appeared with her entourage.

This particular day the Politician was packed, and Andreah feverishly darted her eyes back and forth on her Bulova Watch and the thick line in front of her. She sighed in frustration furiously tapping her foot hard into the tile floor hollering at the top of her lungs "For Goodness Sake I've been here for almost and hour Sir, waiting...how much longer before I'm late." Everybody in attendance who was privately engaging in conversations amongst their immediate congregation all paused in unison as they stopped and zoned in on the angry black women get irate.

She felt embarrassed and uncomfortable as all those eyes in attendance stared at her and talked amongst each other until a women in her defense spoke up loud enough for all to hear when she said "what's the matter y'all act like y'all never seen an angry sister before carry on there isn't nothing to see here." All the eyes in the building followed the voice to place a face to who spoke. What they saw was an elegant well-dressed and sexy light bright damn their white women. In a two-piece onesie Juicy Couture darkest purple suit with black purple dyed hair, a Fendi Manolo Hat with jewels all over her body. Making her favor one of those hot models in an Essence Magazines with a pair of Su Yung Pearlish Black Spaghetti Strapped Pump Heels complementing a flawless mani an pedicure.

All went hack to what they were all doing. As if Andreah's out burst seconds ago never happened. Most in attendance knew her well, and previously and continuously still required her services enjoying her quiet, discreet, unrushed business. Others just knew of her through word of mouth, and feared her connections so they minded there on business and spoke nothing of it ever again.

Andreah looked at the well-dressed 5 6 rocking body frame of a woman that emerged from her seat, and walked towards her. She was enthralled with the respect and beauty that oozed off of this women, who was walking towards her. She reminded Andreah of a woman she wanted to be like when she was younger when she was getting constantly abused sexually and physically by her father.

Whenever she was out of eye sight she would look at her mother's Ebony collection and get mesmerize off of all the beautiful black men & women posed in the latest fashions. Wishing one day her life would be like what she imagined, on the pages instead of the strife she faced daily. The women spoke to Andreah and said "Grilled Chicken Caesar Salad with a Diet Coke no ice right" Andreah raised her right eyebrow like the Rock, and said "Ye ye Yesssss but how did you know that."

The women signaled to the man with orders growling "YOU! White Boy Wonder get ya pretty ass over here, come on hurry up." The young man from behind the counter was there in a flash stuttering uncontrollably "Ye ye yes ma'am" the women said "listen here sweet cheeks remember this face and this order Grilled Chicken Caesar Salad with a Diet Coke no ice right ever-time this lovely young lady comes in here at..." The women, and the young man paused and looked at Andreah who said "uh uh uh Mon Monday thru Friday 12:00 p.m. noon."

The woman then said "so that means champ that shit should be done 15 minutes Carly no excuses you copy slick." The young man stuttered yes ma'am and as he tried to take off, she grabbed him than barked "Excuse me who said you we're excused, matter of fact where is Big Susie; Susie... The young man turned beet red as he begged and wined "dear god ma'am please..... please.... don't call Ms. Susie I'm on it please I need this job."

Andreah felt sorry for the young man from the trouble she stirred up, but she couldn't help but feel empowered by this anonymous woman's actions. Plus to her surprise was attracted to her aura, demeanor, and raw beauty on the surface. She motioned to say something to face Andreah and said "how much time do you have left to finish your meal, and make it back on time through this traffic to get back to work."

Andreah said it doesn't matter I'm going to be late anyway one more tardy and I will be suspended without pay. The women was forward and considered no regards for her next statement when she asked "Well what department do you work for "Andreah shot back with "Excuse me", but the women pulled her Galaxy S5 and asked again "Honey do you want to keep your job, or not come on what's it going to be."

Andreah was so taken back with her confusion it was one thing to getting her order with lunch met on demand, but now this anonymous women was talking about sustaining her governmental job in the District Court. Puzzled Andreah was only able to say "Who.... Who.... Who... are you" the women smiled and placed her phone back in her Louis Vuitton Purse and simply said "consider me just a friend for now that is trying to keep the interest of a sister valid in the Nations Capital, there's not that many us, but there's plenty of us."

The women handed her, her business card before she turned on her heels, and walked back to her entourage, the card said Sexy Men & Women making deals in Lollipopz Loafers & Heels with a website address, hot line, and direct line to speak with Madam Celeste. Andreah yelled to her back "so what you suppose to be some female Hugh Hefner or something" her entourage laughed. As one attractive woman in her company said "No Boo…. Boo…. much better sweetie" but the women closed with "I'll tell you what, why don't you find out our contact information is all there so you have a blessed day darling."

The young man from earlier came rushing out towards Andreah with her order in hand. and apologetically said "my apologies ma'am for your wait, but here is your meal. Here is your refund back and here is my number, call me personally whenever you frequent back, this is on the house enjoy." The young man nervously bowed his head before he departed and as Andreah watched him go she then qued in and looked back at the women whom matched her same confidence.

Andreah said, "what is your name miss. The women answered sarcastically "Celeste honey, but if you happen to forget it's on my card I just gave you." Andreah felt embarrassed and dumbfounded at that dire moment since she literally just seconds prior Celeste had just given her, her business card.

She hustled towards the exit, but not before first saying upon leaving "Hey Celeste" Celeste never broke her promiscuous stare at Andreah so she sexily said "hmmmmm yessss dear" Andreah said with hope "uhummmm I work for Justice John McConnelly in the U.S. District Court 1st Circuit as a Stenographer just in case you still wanted to know."

Celeste smiled as she coquettishly responded back with "hmmmmm you better get going, Ms. Phillips I wouldn't want you to be anymore late than what you already are…..URRRRRRRRRR. (Sounds of cars honking back in reality)" snatched Andreah back. Who is now behind the wheel of her Baby Blue Audi Q7 at a green light on the corner of Northwest/21" street. A couple blocks away from her psyche doctor's building holding up traffic.

"MOVE BITCH; WHAT THE FUCK; GET THE FUCK OUT OF THE WAY YOU DUMB ASS HO; ANY FUCKING DAY GRANDMA" was the comments of road rage occupants in vehicles awaiting for Andreah to go before the light turned red again. Finally adjusting and coming to, she gave her Audi some gas and shouted out "I'm sorry you guys while other occupants continued to roar as she pulled off.

Andreah spoke to ALEXA in her car, and asked "ALEXA what time is it, how much time do I got till the Pharmacy closes and where is the closest one in the vicinity." ALEXA a computer advance software program took sole control of the cars surround sound system and her computerize voice echoed off the interior when she said ".....Please Hold..... Destination confirmed your coordinates confirm that your proximity range of pharmaceutical stores are 5 total.

If you make a right on Liberty Avenue and proceed a quarter mile up the road within 50 yards of each other you'll see a Rite-Aid Pharmaceutical Store availability hours are Monday thru Saturday 8:00 AM to 11:00 P.M. at night. Proceed further and you'll encounter a CVS Pharmaceutical Store availability hours from Monday thru Saturday 8:00 A.M. to 11:00 P.M. at night with the exception of a 24 hour drive thru for medical prescriptions at this rate of speed of 30 mph you'll reach your destination within approximately 18 minutes and 26 seconds......)"

ALEXA continued to talk about the other destinations of the other pharmaceutical stores until Andreah said "Thank You ALEXA that will be all." ALEXA stopped speaking and the music by ELLA MAI's banging new single called (Boo'd Up) came popping crispfully out of her factory made system.

She bend a sharp left onto Liberty Avenue, and sung allowed to Ella Mai's lyrics. Her phone came in with a chirping bird sound as a notification popped up on her touchscreen, and showed Celeste picture that was taken 4 minutes ago. Andreah touch the screen to open the notification, and instantly in seconds her jaw dropped when she seen the flawless dress draped on the woman that ordained in her perspective the most curvaceous body in this lifetime.

Although she was unaware of the make of the breathe-taking cloth which was a number made by Victoria Beckham with the right side a thick silk strap vanilla peach gown that stopped at the mid-thigh level with these incredible white Alexander McQueen pumps to make the gown stand out, and pop. The accessory that completed it was the Sun Disc Nefertiti necklace accompanied with pink, red, and yellow gems giving the number by Victoria Beckham a more royal splash and effect.

"O my God this dress is to die for "Andreah gasped out as she read the text from Celeste that said "scoooo what do you think." Andreah was speechless, and when she responds back with a text all she could say was "ooooooommmmmmmmggggggggggg" with star struck emojis. With the reassurance of knowing she was going to look fabulous tonight she briefly dawned on the event.

Curious in wondering what tonight's festivities were going to entail. In the past she was always given, and invite from Celeste, and small associates she made relationships with over the years, but respectfully declined majority of the time since she was very much a secretive discreet type women, and loathed attention. Tonight though was different not only was Celeste not taking no for, and answer it was nevertheless that time of the month were she needed her fix and Celeste couldn't have been more perfect with timing.

She figured the least she could of done was attend some freak-nic promoted by Celeste, and her Elite Clientele in return for everlasting pleasure from one of Celeste's A-listing hung young beautiful boy studs. A smile crept across her face as she imagined a handsome young stud eat her box into ecstasy, and she creamed all over his face with her sweet juices. Her clit throbbed in pain as she envisioned the anecdote being chilling sexy lips of a fiery young man putting out her flame.

Rubbing her thighs together trying to decrease her anticipation

Another notification came in from Celeste, and it read "LMAO (with emojis) I knew you would approve honey; see you tonight Dreah bring your appetite and leave ya panties girl you won't need them. "She closed with a flirtatious smirking emoji which made Andreah bite her bottom lip, as she now waited for her prescription in the 24 hour drive-thru off Liberty Avenue.

Brainstorming she couldn't contain herself as she placed her hand down near her crotch, and began playing with her pussy she gasped lightly, and then started moaning beyond control envisioning a Hershey brown chocolate young man sucking away on her elite lapping up every single drop of juice that fell. The young man in her vision commanded her to turn on her side as he stroke his exceptional 11 inch toy soldier, and slowly buried it deep inside her tight womanhood.

Gasping and moaning louder as she powerfully releases all over her fingers and scream aloud "Oh gawd yeeeesssss." as she catches her breath a shooken up horny state of a Caucasian blonde hair blue-eyed young man in the drive-thru window intercom announced "Ahhhhh ma'am your prescription." Her eyes instantly open to the maximum length of high beams upon hearing the young man's voice catching her in the act.

She quickly shoved her hand inside the small glass that has her prescription ready in a bag once it was in her hand, and snatched it back inside her car she floored it out of there leaving the puzzled homy young man baffled as he said "you... you.... You..... have a good night ma'am." 20 yards north up the avenue on Liberty she speeds like a mad woman down the block to gain a wider distance from the creep in the drive-thru.

At the red-light she calms down a bit and rationally collects her thoughts on all that just happen as she says, "wow did I really just do that." She giggles to herself as she recalls seconds ago the shock baffled look on the young Caucasian man's face. She sexily purred to herself as she savored her taste from her fingers that seconds ago was knocking down the flood gates of heaven as she said aloud to herself in the car "hmmmmm babyboy babyboy ummmm if you were just a bit darker" she laughed aloud.

Through Celeste service she occasionally requested a young white stud here, and there an enjoyed levels of intimacy with them, but when it came to penetration the way she liked it the young white ones had the stamina, but couldn't rock the boat the way she needed it how the firm long, hung, and strong black and brown young men satisfied her.

Sucking now on her 2 fingers, and taking another look back at the notification with the breath-taking dress she pictured herself in it walking around Celeste's event being the life of the party and the main attraction. Gawking young men, and partygoers enthralled from her essence the light turned green, as she came to and gave the VA little gas but not before first saying after reading Celeste last text and said "see you soon honey, and don't you worry dear there will definitely be no need for these.. "as she took her panties, and hung them on the rearview mirror....

Chapter 2

Who Is That?

Dressed in a comfortable shoulder to calve length peacoat sustaining the cold chills of the thunderous winter cold front increased from the ocean shore of the Potomac River. Andreah with knitted gloves, hat, and scarf shivered at the doorstep of Celeste large mini mansion on the outskirts of a more quiet suburban section of D.C. that was slightly only a couple miles away from one of the most notorious neighborhoods in the nation that was called Berry Farms.

Ringing away on the doorbell Celeste found humor in watching Andreah freeze her ass off watching her on her security footage speaking out on her intercom saying "damn girl it must be cold out there the way you shaking that turkey you wanna come inside baby." Andreah looked around, and seen the camera then flicked a middle finger at it and growled "bitch stop dark playing games and come open this door before I take this party back on the road, and go home to my King Kong it's to cold to be fucking around Les."

Celeste began to laugh aloud for her to hear her in the intercom as she said "(chuckles loud) Ahhhhh Dreah, Dreah, Dreah always quick to run home with ya party pooping ass... Well I ain't going for that tonight honey." The door emerged open and when Andreah looked inside her jaw dropped from the beautiful layout of her front entrance. "Girl pick up Yo jaw and bring that ass inside your letting out my heat."

As Andreah inched her way inside and the glass wooden gold fixture front doors closed behind her the ambiance of awe soiled her eyes as she took in the front aspect of her house that had a handsome dark chocolate complexion muscled bound chiseled man in black spandex polo briefs oiled up all over the place with a silver platter holding a glass of wine as the man said in a French debonair "Bonjour Mademoiselle Madam Celeste is in the art room gallery awaiting your presence could I interest you in a glass of Vintage wine."

Andreah flirtatiously bit her bottom lip as she said to the African French courtier "Thanks, but no thanks Monsieur to many glasses of that might get me in trouble." The man nodded to her as if she was the Queen of England when he responded back with "very well Madam, Madam Celeste is down the hall to your right the door should be open can I take your coat for you." The man extended one of his muscular arms and Andreah followed it as she tried her best to stop sneak-peeking at the African Frenchmen's package when she removed her coat and handed it to him.

He smiled as he said aloud in his European accent "Hmmmmm damn I love being right remarking at her captivating body. Before Andreah could respond and say something to the man he was already walking out of the room with her coat in one arm and the silver platter with the glass of Vintage Wine in his other hand.

She animatedly fanned herself with her hand as she watched the man walk away then once he was out of eye-shot she began to walk. Celeste house was absolutely stunning in a breathtaking I would of never known type of way. The Madam with a wide variety stable of many young men & women from various cultures and flavors mini mansion size compound with a Minoan/Greek architectural style made the 12 bedroom, 8 bathrooms, 2 kitchens, a living room, a dining room, with a wine cellar, attic, basement efficiency, plus a library with a private study.

Raise her status quo at least in the eyes of Andreah to a whole other level as she traveled down the extended hallway walls adorned with a royal vanilla peach plum decor plus portraits and monuments of revolutionary heroes and revolvers sadly etched and erased out of history, Inches away from the door and Celeste's library connected next to her private study she hears the sound of ginger sweet moans escape off the voice of a gorgeous petite sexy young woman whom was black, but due to her fair skin complexion could of possibly been mix with Caucasian or his panic descent arch her back and spread her thick yellow legs wide with her eyes to the artistic painted ceiling as a dark complexion man fell to his knees, and performed to unlock the golden gates of heaven.

Andreah now at the front door of the two-door glass authentic Macedonian style looking library in favor of Ancient Greece Golden Era to peep that the man that was giving the oral sex to the curvaceous woman so out and expose was the same man from earlier that collected her purse and coat now making her pussy super moist. She frozen in astonishment and slightly embarrassed as she continued to watch and not excuse herself. Fighting to contain herself from staring so hard the young woman caught Andreah out of her peripheral vision, through extended pants and moans. Andreah hesitantly shuddered to say, "dear God I iii I'm sorr eee."

But to Andreah surprise the beautiful young woman in ecstasy instead zoned in on Andreah biting her bottom lip raw revealing all of her sexual faces of pleasure at her while she palms ferociously the back of the African Frenchmen's head burying his face deeper in her womanhood as she moans uncontrollably "Oh Gawd Yesssss...Yes... Yes.... oOOOOOouuuuu Shiiiiiiiiiiittttttt."

Andreah was completely blown as she watched this young woman get her pussy ate so thoroughly. She could not help herself as she was so Hot, and desperately trying to fight the urge to not touch herself. Biting her bottom lip she managed through a faint moan, assertively.

Clearing her throat to say "Ahh uhmm ummm I'm sorry to bother y'all but I seem to be lost uhhhhhh is Cell."

The African Frenchman emerged his face from between the young woman legs and hiked up her skirt. He instead now used his left pointer and middle finger to insert it in and out of the young woman's soaking wet opening as he used his right thumb to caress in smooth circles around her clitoris when he said in his thick French accent "Oh we... we...

27

Mademoiselle…. Philips my apologies Madam Celeste is in her study over there."

With a pearly white smile and a simple head nod in the direction towards the two glass doors closed with heavy hieroglyphic inscriptions inscribed all over both doors. The man as if after she announced her presence went back to doing what he was doing as if she wasn't even there when this time he stood behind her with 11 inches of rock hard black python and slowly eased it inside her from behind.

The young woman gasped as half of her body laid sprawled across the reception desk with wild arms moving freely across the table knocking all the items of importance off the desk within arm's reach. Andreah inched past the party of two and with dignity although it was a little to late stepped pass them trying not to look at them as she made it to Celeste Study doors. She went to knock until the African Frenchman said "ummmmm Mademoiselle Philips your better off just walking in my lady Madam Celeste won't hear you I'm certain."

Andreah looked back at him whom now was in full stride pumping away biting and licking his lips sexually in her direction undressing every piece of clothing adage on her body with his eyes as he finally said to Andreah "Mademoiselle if there is anything else you may need tonight…" he applied deeper strokes to the young Denzel in pleasurable distress when he finished with "ANYTHING PLEASE. DON'T HESITATE. TO. CALL. I'LL. BE. HAPPY. TO. OBLIGE. AU REVOIR."

Andreah's clit bumped with firing desire as she couldn't take it anymore and quickly opened the door to Celeste's study and was baffled when she caught Celeste the women of the hour in a silky nightrobe hugging her frame marvelously faced hooked into one of those new virtual reality Oculus Go gadgets that mentally make you feel your very much apart of that reality when she said "ooooooouuu shit no fair you cheated you boney ragu noodle eating bitch DO OVER COME ON."

Andreah shut the doors behind her and just stared at Celeste for a moment before she spoke. She thought to herself here I am after three years of knowing this woman thinking I got this female Don Juan Bishop figure truly figured out down to a T. I'm now slapping myself in the face for judging this book by it's cover.

Celeste was and has many titles but one thing she was not was some colorful ass simple minded madam without an agenda. Andreah at that very moment could clearly see that all them black exploitative movies back in the day in the late 60's Carly 70's plus all the way up to the modernize ideology of what the younger generation portrayed as a pimp.

That Celeste by far was the narrative to the reason why these cheesy three-star rating actors were able to have a profession and careers because of the real deals like her and others that took pimping and hoeing not as a fad but nevertheless a serious business, lifestyle, and profession. She was in awe with Celeste as the decor, activity and size of the house was something out of a espionage movie were Celeste was the infamous attractive female villain in one of her remote playpens in the states.

In all her essence she just was sitting back having a blast while gorgeous sexy young women and men from probably allover the world feast on each other in sexual gain to phatten the designer purses of Celeste from and elite clientele which now made a nervous Andreah wonder who all outside of herself frequent Celeste discreet service.

Celeste could still be heard a excited mess ranting off at her new toy the VR gadget when Andreah nervously spoke up and said "AHHHH CELESTE!" Celeste paused and snatched off the huge helmet looking gadget and upon seeing Andreah she smiled and jumped-up trotting towards her for a hug with open arms saying "DREAH Honey your here ooo0oouuu scrunch ya tall ass down here and give me some love girl."

Celeste was every bit of 5'3 but whenever she broke out in a pair of Stilettos or 4-to-6-inch pumps she could fool the best of them beside Andreah who said with a laugh "bitch if you grow a few feet a sister wouldn't have to get eye level with your toddler ass." The women hugged

29

for a few seconds laughing and embracing amongst each other until Celeste fired back with "Awwweeee Ok Ms. Law Abiding Sophisticated Black Booty from out the District got jokes tonight huh good one bitch you only get one the next I'm going to walk these toddler legs all up and down that federal property you trying to hide in that Gawdy looking dress what on earth honey is that thing..."

Celeste nitpicked at her threads throwing off the impression that it was the most terrible looking thing she'd ever seen. "Andreah usually would have a comeback but at that moment had a case of starry-itis as Celeste playful insults now peaked her worry as she insecurely said "it's my stomach isn't it Lord Jesus I knew it I knew I was gaining weight and everybody said I was tripping no wonder that delicious looking man at your front door didn't even crack a look my way..."

Andreah a frantic worried mess began uncontrollably babbling away until Celeste peeped her comment really trouble her then she said "Oh sweetie Nooo no... no.... no.... I'm sorry I thought you knew I was just toying with you, and hold up wait a minute did I hear you correctly when you insulted that work of art, body of a Goddess in my humble abode you insult that figure again we gone have a problem.

Andreah blushed and smiled as her and Celeste both did a head to toe on her lovely acrobatic frame that favored a thicker version of Monica the RNB Singer. Andreah sniffled as she began to speak again and said "your just saying that just to make me feel better Les I thought we were better than that."

Celeste embraced Andreah with a loving sisterly hug, and said "OH HONEY STOP it 3 years of my mess and your acting like you don't know me please you know Les keep it funky like feet, and hands down girl you already know I don't need a fitness guru to tell me, or the world that you got one of the hottest bodies to be a cougar now as far as your lay baby uhhhhhh." Was all Celeste said with raw honesty!

Andreah countered with "WOW Les really" Andreah spun around

then posed which made Celeste countered back with those days of attracting them horndawgs at the Politico is over darling now come on right this way I got something for you that's gonna make self-made suckas scream Fuck a prenup when we fetch you up in this..." Andreah said aloud "Lets wait before you go." Celeste open the doors to her study wide open and before Andreah could finish her sentence Celeste was walking out of her study passing her two escorts that were still fucking from earlier and said aloud over the moans "Girl come on I wanna show you the rest of the house I can't believe all these years we've known each other this is the first time you have ever come by.

Andreah frozen in place as Celeste by-passed them like they didn't exist both the male & female escort giggled as the African Frenchman said aloud "I think Mademoiselle Philips like you all the man had Valery aka Val for short now scooched up on the same receptionist desk both of them now ass naked as the man parted her legs and penetrated her missionary style. Valery looked over at Andreah whose heart-thumped loudly and fiery passion from before in her pants became ablaze as she sniffed the air, and it smelt of the pleasurable sex amongst the couple now with the strong sweet stench of her own pheromones as Valery interjected with either that Awode, or she sadly never seen a phat big black dick stretch a pretty pink young pussy before.

Valery pushed Awode a couple of steps back then went to all fours on the receptionist desk. Giving full access to Andreah of her swollen sloppy wet pussy as she cut her eyes over her shoulder seductively gazing at Andreah as she nibbled on her shoulder at Andreah and wiggled her tongue at Andreah telling her to come here. Andreah was so raw and open and could not explain why suddenly this possessive seductress name Valery made her question her sexuality.

As she was thirsty to see if that magical tongue ring could bring about ease on her throbbing deprived clit as she had fun with a mouthful gulf around Awode's length. He reached forward as he took both hands and separated Valery's ass cheeks giving Andreah a deeper view of Valery's milky cum filled pink insides.

Until Celeste hollered breaking her trance from the next room down the hall "DREAH! Girl would you come on before were late, we only got an hour for me to show you the rest of the house and get dressed so come on." Andreah upon hearing Celeste voice high-tailed it out of there quick, so quick that when Awode laughed aloud and whispered in the thickness of the lust filled air "hmmm maybe next time my lady maybe next time" his sound muffled as Andreah was already down the hall in search for Celeste.

As she now entered back in near the front door connected near the living room with a fireplace and a huge fleet of stairs to the second floor. Celeste emerged with two glasses of Chardonnay and a smile then said "there you are I was beginning to think them 2 back there were holding you hostage beyond your will ummmmm that man Awode is something special ain't he."

She giggled as she passed Andreah her glass who was all over the place in confusion as she empathically blurted out "girl special ain't the word dear God am I the only one here tripping like Kunta Kinte wasn't back there putting a foot long in that yella ass bitch back there in ya... Bitch you got a Library." Celeste laughed now even harder, and it irked Andreah a little bit when she snapped back with "Oh really Les I amuse you now you know what forget it I don't got this shit to do freaky ass young gigolos and hookers fucking all over the house, and shit carefree o00ouuu the Devil is a lie I tell you...

Andreah bolted for the door while Celeste a hysterical mess continued to laugh, and now jumped in Andreah's line of travel and said "DREAH honey wait I'm sorry sweetie that was rude of me, come on please don't leave we got one magical night in store for us darling and all jokes aside I'm happy you are my guest of honor. Please let's start over let's go have a seat in the winery and whatever questions you may have my word I'll answer them all."

Celeste extended her arm whose hand held firmly, but loose on the base of the Chardonnay towards the direction of the living room that followed along into a spacious kitchen were a long side door that lead to a cozy patio 12 feet away from the patio was the winery that was equipped with a built in handmade bar & 50 inch Big Screen TV's decorated shelfs, and storages filled and displayed with some of the most exquisite years of wine and liquor of the house built in a 9 by 5 6 jet jacuzzi in ground with heighten effects that made the water change colors of paradise that through virtual intelligence matched the mood in the present state that your feeling.

Andreah looked at Celeste and a huge part of her wanted to give in to Celeste adventurous night of glamour and pampering but a very…. Very… small portion of her that was the size of a peanut that could cause a mild tummy ache was her conscience screaming girl get low with all this wealth comes danger. Instead Andreah ignoring her gut instinct decided and said "any indication I get Les your blowing smoke up my ass I swear.." Celeste grinned and smiled she reached for Anfrah's hand and gave it a light tug when she said "Girl I gave you my word now come on I wanna show you the rest of this Big ass house it's not daily I get guests."

As they both walked through the living room as Celeste talked while she gave her the tour. Andreah couldn't help but convey a remark to Celeste's statement about loneliness when she said "Bitch miss me you are talking this loneliness crap as if 20 feet away from us now we didn't just see Idris Alba ploughing away at Zoe Saldana. "Andreah giggled but curiosity was behind her address and Celeste with no contentment respond.

"DREAH I'm gonna tell you a secret the young male and female in the other room you've seen." She giggled when she looked square in Andreah's eyes when she said "I bought them both." As Celeste flirtatiously giggled amongst them the expression of no way was plastered all over Andreah's face, and deep inside it tickled Celeste as she new exactly what was about to come out of Andreah's mouth next when she said "What! What do you mean you bought them?"

With no hesitation Celeste said "you heard me correctly Dreah I bought them for a good deal to especially since there both from France, but the wife was extradited to Amsterdam for some petty larceny charge. I almost lost out on this package deal to a wealthy vodka n Cranberry bitch named Nikkita that own all the damn clubs up and down the East called Claws thank God for vouchers I've grew acquainted with over the years through clients and their overseas connections.

I guess I should be thanking you to Honey your also a huge reason of this success. "Puzzled trying to make sense of it all she barked "Hold up did you just say that's his wife, you bought them for a good deal wait a minute who the fuck is Nikkita, and what do you mean you should be thanking me girl I swear to God you better not have me implicated up in some sex slave shit I don't got that too.." Celeste said SHOOOSHHH as she rested her finger on Andreah's full lips with a smirk she said "Dreah baby relax whether you know it believe it or not I value your request of my service, confidentiality, and friendship after all these years.

Quite frankly I some what feel offended that you even fathom such thoughts of me incriminating you in any shape of fashion. Over the years Hun I've looked to you as a little sister out here in this turf, and one of my motto's is nevertheless hold on to those that hold on to you; you never gave me no reason to think like that so why give me one now. "Andreah was all cars as she was attentive when Celeste spoke; for years her relationship with Celeste has been just strictly dickly business with her sexually deprived pussy occasionally and somedays addictively yearning for a young, hung, black dick to take her vibrant sex drive placing it back on smooth planes of steadiness.

Andreah's pussy had a mind of its own and thanks to her healthy income employed by the nation's capital government paying for Celeste's playmates to come play was peanuts to her quiet humble livelihood. It wasn't till that very moment when Andreah realized after listening to Celeste that all these years she invited her to discreet A-listing parties, cruises, overseas vacations on her expense, gifts that she always returns to Celeste with a modest Thank you, that she couldn't accept.

All the way up to free appointments when she was down and out and two young-stud pampering specials escorted and dined out to restaurants, and places she could only dream about. She now saw Celeste had no motive she genuinely wanted a sisterly bond with her, and at that moment she felt guilty after all these years from holding her guard and shield up like a Spartan and also at that very moment being a rude guest as she apologetically said "listen Les honey! don't know how to say this but..."

Celeste cut her short then said, "then don't say it because there's nothing sorry about the women, I have some time ago grown accustomed to them, plus sideways so call myself liking her funky ass just a little bit." Both shared a heart-warming laugh with a smile as Andreah looked at both their baby-sat glasses and said "well with that all out in the open let's make a toast." Celeste ecstatically said "Yeyyy let's...to new beginnings of a firm, fine, powerful, black strong sisterhood in White America.

Andreah clanged her glass with hers and had some words to say herself when she said aloud "To the Truth and may whomever be the first to dishonor that burn in hell." Celeste paused suddenly coming over a cold chill down her spine when she downed her glass not before first saying to Andreah "Hmmmmm to the Truth I like that."

She cut one eye at Andreah to make sure she drank. Then tapped the bottom of her glass up to make sure she got a nice gulp when she said "uh uh bitch drink that ass up because tonight as promise your my guest of honor, and I'm getting your ass lit so turn up." "Oooooouuu" Andreah jumped as Celeste laid a playful smack on her phat ass.

She switched her Selma Hayek juicy booty into the kitchen with the two glasses in hand and Andreah plopped a seat in her comfortable love chair and gasped in oozing pleasure off how good her furniture felt on her body. As she yelled in the direction of the kitchen "Ooooo wow this love scat feels amazing where can I get one of these at for the low low girl.

Celeste laughed as she prepared the glasses again and said Girl the only way honey I can make that happen is if I flew you over there and at this time of year the weather is unpredictable."

Letting lose a little bit Andreah responded back with "Damn Les you got it made like that shoot maybe I should reconsider my profession." Celeste grabbed the bottle of Chardonnay and filled her glass when she said "Uh uh darling don't you dare without sisters like you there wouldn't be sisters like me, and vice versa your in a beautiful position sweetie be proud of that I know your parents are."

At the sight of hearing that word her whole body cringed. As she visualizes her mother getting her ass whipped for failing to indoctrinate Islam in her. While her father was incarcerated How to raise her to utilize her left hand, to refine when using the bathroom. When she was drilled under submission to the Islamic Faith.

Trying her best to shake the vivid graphic depicted images. She responds back to Celeste with "Ye ye yeah my parents sadly are dead; have been for quite some time now "Celeste paused momentarily for a minute in the kitchen, and allowed her words to sink in. Part of her believed her which to her wasn't hard to believe because the reflection in her sheltered disposition called towards that, but her inner intuition screamed to her there was more, but she decided not to press on, and instead said "Dear Lord Dreah my God I'm so sorry honey."

Andreah unmoved with her on her comment said with fire "shit don't be, it was for the best." Celeste choked up for a second for the first time feeling pinned up against the wall not knowing how to respond. Or where to go as she reached in her bra in search for her candy jar, Andreah call it her Spidey senses tingling switched up the vibe and ask "Hey LES not to be all in your business, but I'm just curious how much did your big balling ass run on that happily married couple in there if I were to guess hmmmmm about 25 45 55 thou."

Celeste was crushing up a half a gram of Molly to a fine grind of salt when Andreah asked her comment with playful insult towards her pricing range on her new sex puppets. She swiped it with her hand into Andreah's glass and licked the remaining residue of the crystal stone and whispered under her breath "Sisssssss shit 55 though huh bitch try 200 long a piece what chu think this is seasoned floor seats at the Wizards for 6 months this is International playing at its best chile ye ain't know."

She blew the remaining residue not worth intake off the counter. Then quickly checked herself as she remembered who she was talking to. When she said jokingly "Chile you wouldn't believe me if I told you the investment, I put in on them newlywed active puppets." As she filled her glass up with the Chardonnay. Spun it around then walked into the living room where Andreah was still seated.

Celeste with the glasses, and bottle in tow walked over towards Andreah as she passed her, her glass and jokingly said "besides, it doesn't matter how much I dropped on them there mine now, and what I got you got sis. "Andreah smiled and said "really you seem so sure" then Celeste said "you make it sound so complex; it's really quite simple."

Accepting her glass and taking a sip she couldn't help but touch herself from feeling so aroused. Celeste smiled inside as her plan was coming to fruitarian, and she had Andreah right where she wanted her when asked "Honey are you ok." More alert and cautious Andreah checked herself, and said "Ye yea I'm fine as a matter of fact I feel great."

Celeste chuckled, and simply said that's great she raised to her feet grabbed Andreah and finished giving her a tour of her spacious abode. Explaining the depth, decor, paintings, and monuments exhibited all throughout her house going into explicit detail where she purchased art, furniture, monuments from her reason behind it, and also why.

Andreah felt so relaxed and free she surprised herself, and even Celeste with her forwardness, and freshness and Celeste loved every moment of it. In Celeste master bedroom inside her retail store sized closet that stores some of the most sexiest numbers that haven't even hit the market yet.

Andreah's eyes dropped as she laid eyes on the remarkable looking gown that she was going to be wearing this evening.

As she breathlessly struggled to say "haaaaahhhhhhh 00000 my God Let's look. "Celeste giggled and jokingly said "Yes Dreah honey I see it…. it's beautiful and there's only one thing its missing". Celeste clapped 3 times, loud enough for 2 fair olive oil complexion fiery carrot type red hair, and green eyed twins roughly between 5'2" and 5'4" both 115 lbs. Pilates yoga frames favoring next to kin of Lindsay Lohan models on command.

As they snapped into action appearing hip to hip next to Celeste as they said in unison "you called Madame?"…. they were dressed in silky lingerie light fabric nightgowns with nothing underneath except for their Victoria Secret panties. Andreah almost fell out when she peeped these young beauties bow before Celeste. Celeste in rare form said "ladies this dress these shoes, and whatever accessories her eyes adore needs to be on this work of art (Celeste motion towards Andreah's body) by the next hour tops.

If not less I'm a leave y'all to it take care of my girl now." With nothing else to say Celeste turned on her toes, and left them to it not before Andreah said Les Darling…" Celeste turned back on her toes then Andreah said "I've been so busy all these years, and even all this night judging and assuming the worst of you, and I haven't had the chance yet to make amends and tell you Thank you Honey thank you so much for all of this."

Andreah was flooded with emotions, and she couldn't explain her sudden rawness conveyed amongst strangers outside of Celeste who grew warningly towards Andreah's affection. She respond back to Andreah "well your quite welcome sweetie this is your night so I just want you to lay back relax, and thank me when the night is over and the lucky man, or men (she giggle) who is worthy of catching your eye tonight strike gold.

An is privilege to take that lovely gown off of you. She turned to walk away again, and overheard the twins Kayla and Kamil telling Andreah to take off her clothes so they could go to work making her look ballroom ready. Call it the Molly talking, but Andreah couldn't help herself when she asked the twins "Sooooo how much did my girl pay for you little helpers."

Before Celeste exit out the room she said aloud "They came with the package deal honey money talks, and half-stepping gets you moonwalking with Michael Jackson on the big dipper. As the girls went to work on Andreah. Celeste made it down the hallway down the main steps then back in the direction of the kitchen.

Where Awode and Valery her European male and female paid escorts sat in the kitchen. In robes with cups of coffee as Awode said in his accent "Hey sexy where's your guest." Celeste went to the refrigerator and grab a bottle of Mount Fuji water took a chug then said "she's upstairs getting taken care of by the twins for tonight how about y'all though y'all down already."

The couple giggled as Valery now took a chance, and said "For now my lady for now one thing were beginning to learn about you is there is no such thing as rest under your care; it would be foolish for me and my love to fuck like rabbits when there is much work that needs to be done for your trouble." Celeste nodded as she took another chug of her fuji water. She then said to them both" Well that's quite thoughtful of y'all I appreciate that acknowledgment, but tonight I'm only gonna need of y'all service more later into the evening possibly in the brink of the morning so y'all good fa now." The both of them Awode and Valery smiled as they prematurely side hug. and said "were only a phone call away madam any request for the attire for the special occasion.

"Celeste walked away, and thought of that for a second until it came to her, and she said "we going Will & Jada tonight, but Val, I want you to swing this time I think you got Ms. Philips curious rock the boat baby. As Celeste left the kitchen leaving Awode and Valery to their thoughts she trotted away with her own thoughts orchestrating back n forth her game plan.

39

The lengths she had to endure in the game to get to where she was at. Now amongst the elite caliber of players was far from a cakewalk in the park. Starting off herself a drip baby in the mean wicked streets of the nation's capital D.C. at such a young age she sadly became victim made victims, and players victim all to get exactly where she was.

At this point in the game right now......came with a mountain top full of more problems, and possible International turf wars, and enemies if she didn't tread carefully and cautiously. She lost count of how many pimps kidnapped her, raped her, made her work off tabs for violation of pimp conduct and through it all the one responsible for all her misfortune that ran so deep.

She peacefully rests deep at the bottom of the Potomac River surprisingly from natural causes leaving behind a daughter which is Celeste with such a personal vendetta against Life let alone a sour disposition towards love. Through all her heartache and pain and literally being a product of her environment, she capitalizes quick and master the game of Life playing chess on the playas in rotation, and shortly in time branched out beginning to do her own thing.

She caught shade, and pole guarded from playas and macks who refused to acknowledge her pimp hand and Prada heels since in their sight she was nothing more than a renegade whore going against the Format. Nevertheless, with her entourage of urban thotties, and trailer park trash hoes plus the mind frame of a Corporate Visionary.

Little Celeste overtime unbeknownst her drive introduces a New age of pimping and hoeing to the masses that left a lot of ole school polish macks written out of history, and the remainder having to switch up there pitch to remain relevant, and knotted up (money). It did not take long for young Celeste at the time to take her show on the road and blow up like the World Trade Center.

Still and all despite the once upon a time playa that used to smite her for having wandering eyes (eye to eye w/a pimp which was a no no). But who now raised the cups, and tilted their hats to her silkiness and vision? She never allowed that to get her big-headed, nor naive as she remains reserved and instilled in her the following to always perform a quiet, discreet, unrushed, back-breaking experience and service.

This motto, and profession is what scored her A-listing feeding family capital clientele, and a abundance of Top Notch Billboard perspective male and female escorts. To fulfill the instant demand of deprived sexual appetites of men and women. Who had the money to blow.... Which explain her investment on the French Couple, she was on a vacation to Prague courteous, and sincere regards to a client who for confidential purposes introduce himself as Chadwick Turner.

However, overtime and one medicated night in a herbal essence store in Denver, Colorado Jacquelyn one of Celeste's new turnouts spotted his picture on a flyer. How he was running to be Governor she flipped out as she immediately called Celeste and gave her the news.

It didn't take long for Governor Joseph Reddick his real name to get so spooked out that his levels of kindness to swear her to secrecy were above, and beyond. Which explained his full expense covered round trip to Prague. On her way there though, there was a pitstop in Paris, France to board another plane to Prague.

The layover till departure was a 2-hour hold, and instead of sitting around the airport she took a taxi into the city, deep in the heart of Paris beyond the amazing tourist attraction. Call it destiny being that her bloodline is anointed Pimp Royalty.

But along the outskirts she caught a glimpse of the nightlife in a secluded marked off section the natives referred to as there Red-Light District. A complete newbie to the International Scale of Prostitution she stumbled across a handsome dark complexion man name Awode that beyond his charm and amazing sex drive.

Had a past that was so wicked that he was on the run from 4 countries for a series of unsolved murders. That they couldn't prove he committed but had strong belief he did and a bounty out for his head for 200,000 euros if he was captured dead or alive.

But what made the narrative even more bizarre was that he wasn't alone he had, and accomplice who was a lovely young lady. Who was of fair light bright yellow complexion and belong to the Fulani Tribe. Before she made her voyage over to France through the ridged rafts of the Black Sea.

Awode and Valery back in their native homeland where first cousins from different tribes, him being from the Ebo Tribe. Both were born from royal backgrounds and prestige. Were already ordained at birth they were to marry making the tribes interlocked as a Clan and being the sole controllers of the West of Africa.

Against the wishes of their tribal families Valery took flight for a better life in Europe. Shortly after Awode departed to aid her, and also in search for the same reasons. Upon reunion in Spain, and other countries along their journey. Until it ended in France when Valery was captured by what they thought were authorities.

But turned out to be kidnappers employed by this closed wrap tight Inter-State Human Trafficking Sex Slave Business. Awode was all on his own fending to survive and trying to Devise a plan to rescue his cousin by volunteering himself to be sold. One lucky night after learning the whereabouts of his cousin Valery.

Stumbling across a tourist who was green to this elite level of the business. Celeste became their Lifeline, and overtime after thorough screening and engaging in minor business transactions in remote areas. Celeste became a pledge member in the international ring of Sex and Trust and rewarded a lamented Black Card.

That was used only for guest of honors whom where private invites to auction shows on parties all throughout the world in secure remote areas. A year later with a close to $400,000 American Currency investment in 2 cousins and twin sisters. That's equivalent in wealth next to 200.000 euros plus a vigorous roundabout task it took to get all 4 of them to the states.

Celeste now back in her study room watching the flirtatious activities of her twin Barcelonian Barbies on her high-end security footage give her girl Andreah a exclusive makeover. She qued in as she listened attentively of the party of 3'speak. She retrieved her box of Virginia Slim Long cigarettes.

Pulled out one took a deep drag and exhaled loudly. Tonight, was a big night and she had to make sure there was no room for errors. Feeling the effects of the Molly and a little bubbly from the Chardonnay. She rested her free hand between her full legs and sensitive twat and massaged it while she thought aloud saying "Relax Les Deep Breath's Honey Tonight Is Going to Be Fine No Worries" Or so she HOPED...

Chapter 3

Butterflies

8 blocks away from the all-white party at an undisclosed location D.C. nationals and upper echelons refer to as The Adam & Eve Lounge!

Andreah & Celeste in the back of an all-Black stretch Limo excursion truck. Looking absolutely fabulous in there flawless gowns for the evening. Were Blitz! As they were in the back of the stretch limo licking shots of Deuces chasing it with Moscato wine.

Enjoying each other's company as Andreah screamed "uurrrrgggghhh God that burns Jesus Les what the hell is that." Beyonce and Jay-Z song DRUNK & LOVE was pounding out of the factory made stereos, the limo and before Celeste could answer her correctly she sung Hova's! lyrics when he rapped "A Deu'ce is the Shit if I do say so myself If I do say so myself If I do say so myself."

Celeste playfully consoled Andreah by rubbing and patting her back saying "Awwweeee Darling does the Deu'ce make you wanna tap out honey ummmmm stop being such a wuss." Andreah smirked as she looked at Celeste and barked aloud "Ho fuck you and you can kiss all this ass bitch because that A Douche is strong O my GOD." Celeste giggles again and this time said "Bitch it's A Deu'ce not a Douche with cha simple ass."

Andreah added on saying "WHATEVER doesn't change the fact that I still can't breathe." Andreah rolled down the window for some fresh air and Celeste continued to laugh as she jokingly said "umm hmmm well you make sure your non-breathing ass.

Don't throw up on that $5,000 gown at least till after the party." Andreah flicked her a middle finger while her head was still out the window. But seconds later the glass that separated them from the driver rolled down the window and a deep baritone voice that packed the same volume, and size sounded off with "Madam Celeste were approximately 3 minutes away from our destination will there be anything else you and Madam Philips need this evening.

"Celeste told the personal bodyguard thank you, but that would be all. When he rolled the window up. She dived in her purse for her mirror and lipstick applied on her make-up and then got the attention of Andreah and said "Come on silly were almost there so get ready."

Andreah brought her head back inside and growled "ready; ready for what were are we I thought you said.... Celeste cut her short and said "ugh that's the problem darling you think to much now come here and lemme glam you up..." Celeste mumbled undetected words under her breath as she did Andreah's face. But Andreah couldn't help herself as she said "Les darling why is this event so big for you what's the big deal give it to me raw honey."

Celeste looked at her and took a deep breath and sighed "DREAH baby you got two kinds of people in this world and they are those that get right, and sadly those that get left behind and these kinds of people are all after one specific thing... as Celeste tried to finish her statement. Andreah cut in and said "Jesus Christ let me take a wild guess Uhhhhhh Ma..." Celeste not appreciating being cut short barked back "Power bitch, and lots of it.

Hell what the fuck is money if a jackass can't do nothing with it, better yet what the fuck does it matter if you're the most knowledgeable being in the world." Andreah was quiet as Celeste captured her full undivided attention and when Celeste witnessed that she finished off saying "you know people kill me when they part-there lips incautiously to say Money is the Root of all Evil huh; how the fuck is something that is man made out of paper and lamented and sealed with U.S. ink evil ha ha bitch that's a Trademark; no.... no..... you see money is not the root of all evil darling it's what people do with that money that make it the root of all evil, and don't you ever forget that Dreah I'm serious now."

Andreah nodded her head like a obedient toddler, as Celeste continued with "Money, Power, and Respect Al Pacino and my girl Kim ummm no one could have quoted it better champ what the fuck is this world without someone in power to make Power moves for the masses to respect it, or reject it. Tonight, honey your about to witness history in the making and rub an make acquaintances with some of the most powerful shoulders in the country whom hold the strings to the economical direction in the world. My promise to you is this sweetie you play ya cards right, and follow my lead you'll retire from office a very wealthy black women with credentials that will stain the history books for centuries on counting, however though my love if not and you wish to be complacent with were your at in life."

The limo came to a halt and one could be able to feel the driver door opened as the concierge hustled to the back to open the door for Celeste and Andreah. As Celeste finished her statement firmly when she said then by all means my dear stay here, and I'll make sure this fine gentleman escort and drive you home safely to your home for us to never speak of this again. Now if what I just said just disturbed you which I pray it did... "Celeste stuck her hand out for the fine young man in a suit & tie to accept as she carefully stepped down out of the limo."

As she adjusted herself and regained her composure, she centered her attention back on Andreah and ended with "then are chariot awaits darling". Celeste extended her hand for Andreah to grab, but it stood out there for a little while as Andreah pondered back n forth.

What to do, decisions..... decisions...... as she pondered and pondered knowing she was on borrowed time. Her conscious roared at her screaming that this was a bad idea. But the desire of wanting so much more out of life.

Then the shitty circumstantial hand she was served sounded so appealing as she nervously extended her hand and said "O My God Les I swear you better not be blowing smoke up my ass." Celeste grabbed her hand and helped her, and her marvelous looking gown out of the limo and said "come honey let mama show you better than I can tell ya slick."

Now out of the limo and fully adjusted. Both of them passing the courtyard and engaging what appeared to look like a ancient vacant looking museum building, that resembled a religious monarchy. The brisk nippy wind chill of the D.C. evening night took flight blowing strong against the party of 3 Manhattan strollers to there destination.

Once there the Concierge pressed the button and in the series of seconds a masculine voice came out through the intercom and said "NAME & PURPOSE "Celeste spoke aloud over the strong winds and said "Sale Sex Talk Less Finessing Minds one orgasm at a time Baby." Within seconds the bolted door opened and the Concierge with them centered upon them both and said "is there anything else you need me for this evening Ma'am" Celeste thanked him and said no.

That would be all but did say she would call him when they were ready to turn in for the night. As she removed a knot from her bra, and peeled off a crisp blue 100 dollar bill. The Concierge happily accepted then lightly bowed as he kissed her hand and raised it to his forehead.

He did the same with Andreah only thing different he didn't kiss her hand then he hustled off to his car leaving the girls to themselves. "Damn girl do you have that effect on all the men & women" Andreah muttered as she shivered in her gown still standing outside as Celeste responded with "Chile please don't confuse fear with love it will get you killed before you even get started you know, Celeste can control fear, but I can't control love."

Andreah allowed that to marinate deeply as she was trying to understand more about the women over the years she secretly admired plus in awe over her meticulous Lifestyle. Growing chiller by the moment Andreah said once more that makes sense, but you said get started on what." Celeste grinned as she extended her arm and said "Come in, and find out puppet after you...Ladies First!"

Chapter 4

The Forbidden Fruit

"O my God Les what is this place and why is it so dark in here" Andreah said the sound of her, and Celeste designer heels stabbed the floor as it echoed throughout the vacant building. Andreah raised her eyes to the ceiling and saw ancient text and pictures of a large variety of world cultures plastered all over the ceiling in sort of like a voyage.

The faces of the inhabitants in the painting where black faces rooted in Ancient African Cultures conveying the beginning of human life making it's way up the Nile River from the southern tip of the continent all the way up to the Northeast part of the continent were civilization began. As they both continued to walk through the large lobby of the building the paintings began to change in styles of attire, but still remain the same in melanin content of flawless dark black complexions.

Ancient Egyptian, Ethiopian, Middle Eastern, Persian, and far East Asia and even European, all the images of the paintings where of black and brown people then gradually overtime through different climatical regions throughout the planet; the body and skin-type began to adapt, and features of the original inhabitants began to take it's course. "Way back.at least as far back as the existence of humans go which is estimated to be 5.5 to 7 million years ago to this date.

Land masses, vegetation, and terrain from the thanks of water were produced and connected as one before the tectonic plates in the mass of the earth incurred through the primordial elements of the universe making it shift and split into the 7 regional continents of today. The highest or many also enjoy addressing him as the Mighty One, God, or Allah tested his Trillions of years investment of this world first with fowl, creepy crawling things, species of the sea, and beast to see if life can withstand the living conditions of this world."

Celeste paused in her steps and with a snap of her fingers the lights came on in the building. As she continued to talk when she said "as you can see (she extended her hand openly for better glimpses of the portraits all over the ceiling and walls of the building) the images were astonishing as they conveyed countless failed attempts. In the birthplace of life manifested into flesh as Celeste continued with. Technically most scientist misconstrue the facts of where humanity took flight (ha ha) quite frankly it was considered and accident.

With another snap of her fingers the lights now ceased except, one that beamed down on Andreah spotlighting her as the main attraction as Celeste babbled on about "Dreah honey how much do you appreciate your blackness Darling..." She phrased it as if she was asking her a question which puzzled her. When she responded back with what kind of questions is that Celeste said with a giggle "a honest one my dear what you think it was a coincidence you where ordained with the flawless features of a God my Queen. Come on Dreah think about it I'm pretty sure you grew up in the church.

What on earth do you think them scholars were talking about in the book of Genesis when it stated. God created the heavens and the earth from out of triple darkness to light shaped with matter and made with form and all that biblical crap huh." Andreah snapped and said leave my upcoming out of this you don't know shit of my past Les."

Celeste countered back with "Dreah sweetie don't make this personal because the secret of our divinity alone is already unbearable to continuously hold. But the beauty of our legacy that continues to resurface in the faces of the 42 evildoers. Is enough to make the most rebellious of our kind cry with hope girl.

So you better believe it, and own it because there ain't no running from reality and that reality is you my precious beautiful black queen. You my lovie are a Goddess and without a doubt are the mother of all races. The womb of all answers the elitist class of deity of a private stock."

Andreah was all ears as Celeste dropped a jewel and said "Heaven what is it the kingdom of righteousness the Land of Milk & Honey. The castle of the mighty one where life is started and life is giving. Hmmm sounds very much similar to what all us woman got between there heavenly thighs.

Triple Darkness what is that the stage of infancy dumb, deaf, and blindness. Not by choice, but by design what you think the ideology of this mystifying being. Without form was just gliding in the clouds creating shit in the time frame of 7 days oh wait my apologies 6 days my bad he rested on the day (ha ha Please).

Try 77 trillion years and that number honey is not even accurate. Since no living man, women, or child can account to the timeline of the galaxy's manifestation. Since the human family's birth record only carries back to millions plus years.

Were all life according to the bible came from. Eve come on sweetie open your mind and tune in your ears. God self-created from triple darkness hmmm sounds like the womb of a Goddess to me forming and taking shape inside heaven from a thoughtful seed.

A self-made originator deep in outer space unseen by the fretful eye due to the magnitude of how heavy and powerful the Science of the stars and cosmos are, but care, and loves us enough. So much to meet our understanding with divine beings. Clothed in his likeness for us over time to master strive, overstand fully the secret of salvation, and why through trials and tribulations.

Plus, temptation we're battle-tested for reassurance for a guaranteed seat back to once upon a time were we all were once very much in tune with before envy, trickery, corruption, and deceit weighed it's toll. The sound of Celeste Louboutin heels could be heard piercing through the marble floor as Andreah searched for her line of travel through the darkness and said "50 what's the Secret." The sound of the elevator doors could be heard opening as Andreah spotted Celeste about to enter the elevator who said, "LOVE sweetie pure unconditional love."

She extended her arm invitingly waiting for Andreah to come. Lightly holding up her gown she hustled over in the direction of the elevator and entered once the solid metal steel door closed. Celeste wasted no time when she said "Dreah honey I must fair warn you what your about to experience tonight why this remote location is so off the grid and why what I'm about to say about what you see in this place the people, events and things must not never leave this building whatsoever ca' pcash.

"Andreah searched her eyes for severity, and upon seeing she was not joking. She nodded her head and jumped as the door of the elevator behind her opened. She was staring down the gigantic braulick black Greek chiseled figures of 2 dark chocolate men oiled down from head to toe, with clean shaved heads jet black polo boxer briefs making their packages look gift wrapped as they stood at the golden door at parade rest with Trojan army sandals awaiting for the lovely occupants of the elevator to exit off. Celeste smiled admiring her delicious eye candy hold post professionally and appetizingly as she walked off and said "Come on baby stay close follow my league darling"….

Guardian Angels

The bouncer at the door with a metal wand in hand moved thoroughly up and down both Celeste and Andreah. As the other bouncer whose name was Dormeus said "Good evening ladies welcome to the Garden of Eden is this y'all's first time." Celeste did the talking as she said "Awwweeee you must be new honey I'm Madam Les, and this is my girl Andreah she is my guest tonight, and yes, it is her 1st time so be gentle boys."

The 2 men looked at each other, and the one with the wand announced in his earpiece from control over…" another masculine voice respond "CONTROL OVER" the man sounded back saying "eyes from control we need a visual there's a lady down here saying she's Mother May over."

The men from control zoomed in from there camera, and when they peeped Celeste blow a kiss to the camera the man stuttered back in the earpiece "That's A.A.A. Affirmative champ be on ya best behavior. "Upon the bouncer hearing that he snapped into action taking a knee kissing her hand pressing it close to his forehead when he tried to speak, but was cut short when Celeste said "don't you dare apologize honey you were doing your job and I respect that now keep doing it."

He raised his eyes to her from still being knelt down on one knee, and was able to peep what she meant; he raised to his feet, and repeated the same respect to Andreah kneeling down without kissing her hand then said "welcome my lady my name is Lazarus and I'll be your pass into paradise this evening, but before that I must breakdown the ground rules to you this evening #1.) What happens at the Garden of Eden stays at the Garden of Eden do you understand #2.) Personal relationships with members, staff, or employees will not be tolerated if we get wind of such activity carried on outside of the Garden your membership will be revoked an finally #3.) This is important, any unwelcoming attention warranted from your actions that becomes a target here at the Garden of Eden you shall be outcast are we clear."

Andreah giggled aloud finding humor in the demur of the young mans address. But when she peeped the much serious demeanor in both the 2 young men as well as Celeste she shyly came to a halt and said "Oooookkk yall must be serious hmmm riiiittteeee."

Celeste smirk, and with one snap of her fingers. Dormeus dispersed off towards the hollow wall near the pathway of the entrance of the golden door placed his hand up against the wall and in seconds a nano digitalizes intelligent security screening detector emerged with a touchscreen awaiting instruction. Andreah gasped she couldn't help. but feel at that moment that whatever was beyond that Golden Door safeguarded with such advanced technology that she only witnessed in the White House.

When order to run errands for the clerk was a secret society that was so specially reserved that the congregation would be willing to go to the lengths of dying over it if anyone so happen to expose its secrets. As the young man emerged back with a golden treasure box. That favored Egyptian relics with Ancient Hieroglyphs on it.

Andreah with no hesitation asked Dormeus "what is that both the young men smiled as Celeste spoke aloud, and said, "it's the Forbidden Fruit from the tree of knowledge open the box" Andreah on the defense muttered "What; Why!" Celeste with no filter flat out said, "because bitch without it you not gaining access up in my shit now can you hurry up before we're late."

Celeste downed her shot of Courvoisier and as she swallowed she lightly fanned herself enjoying the burning sensation go down. As it warmed her chest and honey brown nipples. Andreah stared at the ripe red apple in the padded black stereotyped Styrofoam, as she was hesitant to grab the apple.

With the apple now clinched in her right palm, they all looked at her in anticipation with smiles. She was a nervous wreck with butterflies and goose bumps all over as she prayed that she didn't say something stupid to embarrass Celeste. As she looked back at her, and said before she bit a huge chunk into the apple "You only live once right."

Chomping down now on the apple the party of 3 gazed in attentively at her as she munched away to the point to were it was safe enough to swallow. Upon the large gulp as she stomach the juicy apple instantly she felt a distilling chill of erotic pleasure sweeping over her body from head to toe. As she nervously attempted to cover her self believing for some odd reason she was naked.

"Ahhhhh Ooooo00ouuuuuu." she said as she bit her bottom lip, and did her best to suppress her lustful thoughts, to be birth off her lips accidentally. Dormeus already aware what was happening smiled. As he whispered in his deep baritone voice in her ear while caressing her shoulder on her strapless dress saying "Ma'am are you OK."

Upon his touch her body responded in overdrive as she came so hard, she bit her bottom lip causing a light trickle of blood to pour down her chin as she gasped loudly "UHHHHHHHHH OH GOD YESSSSSSSS." Her mind was all over the place in lustful array as she vividly drew back to the moment where she freely on her own accord allowed her body to a man; the man of her dreams which was Jeff her childhood love.

Steamy images of these magical brief encounters made her hot and moist. As the timeline of her sexual appetite continued with other young studs requested from Celeste's service. That provided Andreah with some of the most memorable spine corralling organisms in a lifetime.

Andreah ferociously shook as her eyes took snapshots of the back of her head. She finally came to, and when she did she took a deep breath regain back consciousness with the party of 3 in awe. As Lazarus the host said with joy welcome to the Garden of Eden my lady where all your desires awaits" both men bowed as the golden doors slowly emerged open as Andreah was able to mutter out "HAAAAAAAO my GOD."

Chapter 5

The Perfect Atum

Inside the Lobby of the lounge.

The atmosphere beyond the door exuded an angelic divine decor throughout the main floor. All in attendance cohorts with invitations were adorned in white while guest of more higher calibers were dressed in brighter colors. Making sure not to violate the terms of Celeste's strict dress code.

The main floor itself was breath-taking. The floor was a glossy Egyptian gold applied with a professional wax job that mirrored the reflection of the entire congregation in attendance The floor was literally clean enough to eat off of. As the monstrous size walls with ancient Egyptian texts, and symbols displaying the tradition of Black Supremacy.

All the way up to the absence of it, was stacked with text books in shelfs piled up ceiling high length covering all four corner walls of the ducked off establishment. The Alexandria style library setting made Andreah gasped as she asked in disbelief "O my God this place is absolutely beautiful Les."

At the ceiling black female employees of all shades dressed in holy Greek garments of purple, blue, gold, white, and creme silks strapped in harnesses gazed upon the audience as some look in amazement while the others paid no mind whatsoever.

At the center of the lobby was a water fountain with a statute of an elephant and the Queen of Ndonga at the time her name was Nzinga in tribal ware. Protruding out of the trunk of the elephant was crystal clear water. That poured into the fountain making the color a fluorescent teal which was absolutely remarkable completing it with expensive decors of glass chandeliers and priceless monuments, portraits, mural's, and custom art.

That all in attendance converted and drooled off of that was backed with rich history "Dear God Ms. Phillips is that you" upon hearing her name she snap out of her zone in search for the familiar voice, and as it emerge from amongst the crowd in a Tom Ford suite that was royal blue with a baby blue tie she paused as she looked at her supervisor and said "Justice McConnelly is that you."

He giggled then respectfully corrected her when he said "well actually no in this setting it's just John my dear, Justice McConnelly only exist during office hours how are you though Ms. Phillips I must say I'm somewhat surprised to see you here." Andreah paused but then shot back with really why is that Sii. mean John." Her employer John shot back with "Well let's just say......Oh John Johnny Honey."

A feminine voice also emerged which was another familiar speech that Andreah recognized and upon recognition she couldn't help it as she said with astoundment "Leslie is that you." Leslie was a bright young Caucasian women with rich Korean descent ascended from her mother side. She stood a even 5'5" with heels jet black brownish locks a lb. shy of 120 lbs. pretty and petite with a marvelous looking body from intense workouts 5 out of the week on her personal Peloton machine

She also was employed under John just like her back in the district court of the nation which made the encounter make Leslie feel a little uneasy at first. As she tried with a straight face to say "Ah what a pleasant surprise quite a shocker to see you here ha ha-ha."

She abrasively laughed trying to lighten the mood from the state of worry. Since there supervisor John was married. Both Andreah and Leslie knew that since they worked with each other and shared intimate girl talks on the job about Justice John McConnelly's infidelities.

Ideas about whom the home wrecking scandalous Thottie might be creeping around with the boss. Andreah now wide-awake to what was going down and weird "ye ye yea you don't say quite a shocker to see you both here too." The eerie silence between the party of 3 could be detected as Celeste in the nick of time stepped up and greeted Justice McConnelly and Leslie with "Oh John and Lizzy I'm so happy you could make it I see y'all met my date for this evening."

Justice McConnelly cleared his throat as he said "Ah um uhmm it's good to see you to Celeste, and yes as a matter of fact we both..." Leslie brushed him not wanting to be mentioned in clear sight. Which made Justice McConnelly redirect his whole entire statement.

When he finished his statement saying "well as a matter of fact we all just met umm ummm Madame Celeste would you please excuse me suddenly I just feel a little under the weather. In a flash Justice McConnelly came, and went with the wind in the direction of the bathroom. Leslie just smiled as the women centered there attention back on her.

When she said "Aww I should go check on him. All night he's been saying he wasn't feeling to well (she bowed to Celeste then said) wonderful party my lady and thank you kindly again for the invite. As always you look absolutely stunning.

They greeted with the rubbing of cheeks kissing loudly in the air. As Leslie said in French au revoir. Then raised her head nervously in the direction of her mentor. Who she looked to as a mother with the puppy dog eyes of please don't judge me as she said with a half-hearted smile *Ms. Phillips it was a pleasure enjoy the rest of the party excuse me." As quickly, as she finished her statement was more or less how quickly she took off in the direction of Justice McConnelly.

In her sexy Estrada gown complementing Vincent Cortez 6" black heels. Looking at the bounce in her booty and the bop in her shoulders she could not help but giggle as she turned her attention back to Andreah and said "My my aren't you quite the shocker" she mustered to say in her best impersonation of a bougie European fashionista."

Andreah smirked trying to contain her laughter of Celeste's on point impersonation she had to admit it was funny as hell. When she seriously asked "Les honey what is this place I feel like I'm at work not at no damn party, what the hell are they doing here." Celeste looked in the direction of Justice McConnelly and Leslie and said, "You mean John and his servant" Andreah's eyes almost fell out of there sockets upon hearing Celeste say that when she barked "servant girl what you mean servant I work with that scandalous ass ho only thing that Thot is servicing is a married woman's treasure."

Celeste with no thought into her next response nor hesitation said "Exactly." Dumbfounded Andreah thought about what Celeste had said, and quickly remembered hours ago the startling revelation she embarked back at Celeste house with the African French sex slave couple. Flabbergasted she looked at Celeste whom found much humor in her stockiness when Andreah stuttered to say "Yu yu you're a sex slave trafficker..."

Celeste covered her mouth, without detection muscled her way through the crowd, and whispered in her car "Easy Darling you gotta practice a better choice of words. My dear especially around this type of setting. You have some very high caliber elite kind of people from throughout the nation and all over the world. That are very powerful and have a tremendous amount to lose and they won't hesitate."

Andreah began to worry as she studied all the familiar faces in rotation Plus vivid ones she recalled on HLN (Headlines News) holding serious power. At that moment, she felt like all eyes in the room where on her, like Tupac the rapper and instantly could smell her uneasiness ooze off her nervous stricken body. Feeling like she was about to throw up.

She broke from Celeste's restraints which made everybody know key in on them as Andreah bolted for the closest door in haste. Finally, outside of the lobby near a lounge area hyper ventilating uncontrollably. Celeste on her heels consoling her willingly and able to listen said "Dreah sweetie you have to calm down honey I need you to breathe and take deep breaths baby come on."

Andreah with her right hand began to fan herself. As Celeste ordered a beautiful high yellow hazel eyed goddess to fetch her 2 glasses and a bottle of champagne. With a snap of her fingers the gorgeous young lady was off.

While Andreah through pants finally calming down a little bit asked "Ok hmmmmm wow so Lemme see if I got this right. So your not a pimp or is it Madam?? No of course not your not a pimp. There's because there are levels to this shit right that explains why a large majority of my staff that I work with and some of the most richest people in the world. Is out there in that room right now which explains why you get more respect than the President of the friggin United States of a friggin America... Dreah"!

Celeste shouted over Andreah pacing back and forth speaking aloud so freely. The women from earlier re-emerged back with the glasses and cham-pipple in hand. Celeste directed the young women to leave the glasses, bottle, and vamoose as Andreah continued to assume and pace back and forth saying.

"No on second thought you ain't no human trafficker. Christ what was I thinking with all these connections. In there this is just a hoax you're a God damn Terrorist Boom that's it, it's starting to make sense now.

All this Afrocentric Egypto Osiris shit Haha you ain't think I knew that shit did you. You ain't the only one that knows history Bitch, with your philosophical pimping ass. I knew I should of just stayed my simple minded black thirsty ass at home with my pills, batteries, and footlong instead of out here in this dress trying to look cute and fit in with all these white people..."

Celeste giggled loudly as she popped the cork on the bubbly and poured both of them a glass. As she continued to laugh saying "Dreah..." Andreah continued on now saying "I'm glad you think this is so funny Les because I'm about to show you how funny it is to me DEUCES. "Andreah made her way back to the life of the party, but before she reached the door Celeste said aloud "well wait honey before you go, don't you at least want to know what I do and what all these major political figures are here for."

Andreah didn't even bother to acknowledge her as she caresses the door knob and said aloud "fuck what you do, and fuck this place boo boo I don't got this shit to do nor could care less." Celeste now cracking up hysterically as she also made her way towards the door with the glasses in hand announcing to Andreah passing her her glass saying "Oh chile trust me your not gonna wanna miss this.

As Celeste opened the door and entered back into the lobby. Everybody in attendance upon seeing her reappear on que they all clapped. As Celeste in all her elegance treated the path that lead all the way up to the stage with a runway like her very own red carpet."

Andreah watched as she slowly followed suit behind her as Celeste greeted all as if she was Michelle Obama herself. Celeste's tight nit security detail as Celeste was escorted up the four steps to the stage by one armed gentleman; remaining detail formed a barrier prohibiting Andreah access from the stage until Celeste howled "at ease boys the ladies with me."

Instantly the men created a path and escorted her up the flight of stairs. Until she was standing on the platform absorbing in the gaze, and the thunderous claps from the audience. The audience only stopped because as Celeste reached the podium she raised both arms waved them Criss cross and announced "Thank You Thank You Thank You man you just don't know how awesome that still feels to hear y'all praise after all these years of being in business...Ahhhhh it's truly a blessing from above."

A patron from the crowd screamed out that's because you're a blessing Celeste you friggin rock man" the crowd erupted in laughter and cheers from the forward comment coming from the anonymous invite. Celeste smiled and looked over in the direction of Andreah, who appeared nervous with her babysitting glass of champagne still in hand.

She signaled with her left hand for her to come closer. As she responded back to the crowd playfully well I better friggin rock God Damn it after all the hard work I put in for all of y'all pleasure shoot..." the crowd continued to erupt in laughter until Celeste recaptured back there attention and said "(chuckles) I'm just kidding you know I love y'all. But ladies and gentlemen before we get this show on the road allow me to introduce my date for this evening.

Now a small amount of you may know this lovely Goddess of a women. But for those of you who don't. Allow me to break the ice, and introduce the gal that has been over the years a amazing friend and a sister without a mister.

Blood couldn't make us any closer ladies and gentlemen please give a warming welcome for the divine an lovely Ms. Andreah Phillips make some noise everybody. "Thunderous claps and now whistles increased loudly sounding like a encore from a amazing play orchestrated by a profound director. As Andreah who was a nervous mess inched a little closer to Celeste.

At the podium and simply just smiled on the surface. Her casual smile with a shy wave as the crowd continued to clap until Celeste spoke out saying "doesn't she look so DELISH everyone one more round of applause for her y'all give it up darlings."

The crowd clapped again for a few seconds then Celeste snatched back the show saying "it's because of wonderful women like Andreah and people like her why I'm still in business and proud to be able to do what I love to do for not just me, but for all of y'all to you know. If I may Andreah (she spoke aloud to the crowd with Andreah by her side in the microphone) I would like to share to the crowd a small taste of what we just discussed briefly in the lounge area.

It's a little silly actually my lovely baby sister believes me to be some sex-trafficking terrorist crazy right." The crowd erupted in laughter while small increments broken within the company chit chatted amongst each other.

Celeste chimed in "now…… now…… everybody let's not get judgmental we all remember how most where when it was there 1" time, and they ate from the tree of knowledge hmmm."

All in attendance silenced selectively recalling back to their own experience with the Forbidden Fruit and there guide into the garden capitalizing off the vulnerability of the masses she announced in the microphone. "Ahhhhh there we go y'all you see now that's better Andreah is no different than no man or woman in this room she is all of you on the day when y'all first was given the key to Heaven although she asked to many damn questions."

The crowd giggled as Celeste nudged Andreah playfully in a sisterly conduct. Andreah smirked masking her true intention of what she thought and felt. Celeste continued on to say "let's nevertheless try to answer them one at a time starting with her 1" one which was what were here for y'all are y'all ready for the show."

Ecstatic the crowd went nuts as Celeste then said, "good well without further or do let's get this shin-dig crackin… Lights." The lights in the lobby dim downed as the stage lit up fluorescently with a assortment of beautiful colors. She qued the music and the hit smash pop single (One Night Stand by Chris Brown featuring Keri Hilson) exploded out of the factory-made club party sized speakers.

Slowly the curtains behind Celeste and Andreah slightly opened. A beautiful French vanilla cappuccino complexion barbie doll with Amazon forest green eyes jet black Persian luscious locks of hair, standing 5'7, 130 lbs., flat 4 pack stomach with full pretty pink lips sporting a pair of Louis Vuitton heels adorned in captivating eye candy lingerie designed by Celeste famine which was called REBELLA REZ.

The young flawless beauty looked incredible as she strutted and sashayed down the runway demanding. The catwalk as Celeste spoke aloud "ladies and gentlemen big rollers and chauffeurs pull out your credit cards, and checkbooks for this delicious treat lets welcome the precious Golnesa Dravidian Sloan AKA The Black Persian Pussycat.

This beauty is 20 years of age was born in Croatia to a Russian father and Prussian mother. She stands at a amazing 5'7, 130 lbs. as you can see all in the right places. She is sporting one of my newest numbers on the scene this season a rich cranberry mahogany color the bra and panties.

The design was inspired one magical evening in Buenos Aires, Argentina on the coral reef shores near there river bank and I came in counter with a breath-taking painting of the style of dress of the village women and wa-lah here you have it REBELLA REZ latest style Malowaka, Cremes, Lotions. Perfumes, Oils, and even Conditioners and Shampoo are also involved in the package deal for Matowaka and the price range of this line is now available at $799.99 for the lingerie beauty products raking in a $299.99 making this package deal $1,000.00 plus tax.

Golnesa is a foreign exchange student from over in Paris on a student visa to attend Howard University. In our lovely nation's capital majoring in Economics and Computer Science. She speaks 6 different languages fluently with English thank God being one of them.

Giggles escaped out of the congregation as they all feasted their eyes on the Persian Beauty when Celeste closed with one more time give a round of applause for the amazing Golnesa D Sloan everybody." As Celeste spoke to her in Arabi telling her to stand off a posed to the side. The show continued as more gorgeous beauties spilled out on the stage.

As Celeste commentated and host every single one. In total it had to have been 10 plus girls all ranging between the ages of 18 and 25 years of age. With flawless natural beauty and insurmountable skill sets making them all a total package.

Andreah off to the side stared on in amazement and lust. She more or less been strictly dickly all her life and never in a lifetime imagine a woman questioning her sexuality. Looking at all those beautiful young ladies from all over the world made her nipples get hard, but they were nowhere near as hard for the fly looking divas like they were for Celeste.

Seeing her in her element and how she drew the crowd. Made her regret Celeste telling her not to where panties this evening. She knew in her soul that her pussy was so hot anyone within arm's reach of her had to smell her powerful sweet pheromones linger freely in the air.

She couldn't explain at that very moment the incredulous urge her body yeaned for a release. The more she fought it trying to contain it the more toxic the fiery desire returned back. Whenever her eyes glazed in lust as Celeste on a roll completely stole the show and coquettishly purred saying "PurrrrrrFECT my sweets can get a ou ou oooooooouuuuuu (howls like a wolve) gentleman.

The men in attendance howled as the women on stage just smiled and posed as instructed. Far off on the stage posing and pushing in REBELLE REZ lingerie with delightful heels looking like Miss American contestants. Celeste cut the music and sound off in the microphone "now that the boyz done have had their fun I most certainly can't forget my lovely ladies.. the women in attendance all went nuts cheering in pandemonium loudly Andreah braced herself as she didn't know what to expect next all she knew was whatever it was she prepared herself to be blown as Celeste cut her eyes in the direction of Andreah smiled then said in the microphone "I hope y'all didn't bring no panties girls DJ spin that shit."

Trey songs infamous cut single "This is Chapter V" came in clear and crispy as a gentleman that stood 6'6, 250 lbs. all solid cut muscle, sporting a REBELLA REZ for men dress button up a royal purplish black with a same color Fedora hat with a pink feather, midnight black complexion with flawless Ethiopian African features, with a pair of silky black Calvin dress pants, with a pair of pink mauri loafers with a golden emblem on the tongues of the designer shoes.

The man with his smooth GQ suave bop strolled down the catwalk and as he made it to the end he stared off into the crowd with a look of seriousness. Then as if his timing couldn't have been better as if he knew the beat was about to drop. The gentlemen with a full row of pearly whites gnawed down on his bottom lip and ripped of his clothing leaving him only in a pair of snow white comfort snub fit briefs made and designed by Celeste's REBELLA REZ apparel line for men.

All the women in attendance went mad as they stormed near the stage like a stampede running from danger thirsty to touch and cop a feel of the African sculpted warrior like man. Security immediately took position making sure the women don't get to out of hand as Celeste said "Breath Stretch and shake babies because this delicious work of art of a Kushite king is to dye for my darlings um um um you'll never wanna let him Go as he stands a scorching 6'6, 250 Ibs of god-like depth and muscle hailing from the cradle of humanity mother Africa honey Aaaaayooo0o (Cardi B impersonation) can I get a Bombay to that Yeeeesssss

This godly man before he jumped out the Cape name was Mustafa Alif Kirkome, 21 years of age, a native of Addis Ababa, Ethiopia. However, discovered in Naples, Italy where he tilled farms in the vineyards of Sicily and went to school for Humanitarianism and to become a Doctor ladies.

The dress shirt you kinky little animals are fighting over is or new European line for men were giving a test drive called REBELLA REZ presenting Grimaldi. We also specialize in the package deal shopping on our site the Cologne, oil, bodywash, soap, lotion, shaving creme and aftershave for men. Pricing range is starting out from $399.00 to $499.00 but if you purchase now, ladies and gentlemen you'll be in for a treat as you'll receive a pair of these comfortable snug fit briefs designed by myself for free that are so comfortable you'll think your free falling ain't that right son of man."

Mustafa smiled at Celeste and then faced the women in the crowd shook his junk and it instantly popped out hanging freely for all in attendance to see. The women were beginning to get out of hand screaming all types of freak nasty shit they wanted to do with Mustafa and his python. Playing right into Celeste spider web she bit her bottom lip and said "stall em out my Austrian king these fish are having a gill fight over that treasure!

Easy Access briefs Quickie panties on sale now ladies and gentlemen one more round of applause. Everybody for the epic Mustafa Alif Kirkome y'all." Thunderous claps sounded like a shower of bullets from a MP4 on the frontline of war erupting in Rwanda from the congregation and especially from the lustful horny women in rare form.

The show continued on as 10 plus men poured out to the stage from all beautiful walks of life. Throughout the world of originality, you name it from a Black Arab to a Black Russian or Asian. Celeste aims to please and supplying the demand was her pleasure.

As the music alternated back and forth between the hottest artist of the year. Celeste babbled on about the skillset, charm, and beauty of the young men appearing from behind the curtain. Andreah in a daze muffled out Celeste's roundabout commentating and absorbed in the eye candy of a lifetime.

She surprised herself with all of the raunchy sexual thoughts she played out in her mind. Until Celeste grabbed her attention with one more time a warm round of applause for those lovely Gentz, yes yes honey give it up to em hmmm.." everybody applauded. Whistling out sexually until Celeste said "now without further or do ladies and gentlemen the main event of the evening what you all come here for... well technically all the ladies fellas no offense."

The crowd mumbled and braced themselves for the inevitable. When Celeste then said "he is the reason why these doors remain open, the life of the party and a addictive drug that women can't get enough of ummm hold on to your skirts puppets as I welcome to you the young and restless AAAAAATTTTTUUUUMMMM."

The music intro of PRETTY RICKY'S AGE AIN'T NOTHING BUT A NUMBER came on. As a dark brown Hershey chocolate complexion man appeared in a pharaonic robe dipped in gold with masonic symbols scribed in royal blue lettering. The thickness of the crowd was so silent you could hear a pin drop. As ATUM graced the stage gliding down the catwalk as if he was floating.

Clean shaven he wore a Egyptian like crown showered in black and blue jewels a hawk mounted amongst the center of the headdress representing the son of Ausar "Heru". The hawk in Ancient Egyptian culture was of prestigious rank and hierarchy back then.

As Atum came to the end of the walk exuding all his superiority and flame. Atum smiled into the masses his perfectly pearly white teeth. Then through his peripheral he caught a glimpse of Andreah which made him feel warm inside.

Outside of Andreah looking absolutely stunning in her dress. The feeling he felt override lust he weirdly felt a sense of love and homeliness with her and it freaked him out. Because for years that yearning for love and security he needed was sadly missing and replaced with anger, hatred, emptiness, and rawness, but he wasn't alone.

Andreah who was approximately 12 to 15 feet away. Captured his gaze and met it with the feeling of warmness. But through that feeling a intense fiery chill swarmed all over her body and resonated deep in her gut causing her to have excruciating pain and cramps.

As she clenched her stomach groaning lightly. Atum felt this strange obsession upon seeing her wince in pain, to come to her aide. Once he cut his eyes in the direction of Celeste who was infuriated shooting a look at him that read "boy what the fuck are you doing snap out of it,"

Within seconds he shook the amazing feeling and connection and jump right into perform mode his body shook, pop, vibrated, and move incredibly to the beat. When the DJ cut his tables to perfection scratching at the lyrical bar sung by the R&B artist out of the Pretty Ricky group, Baby Blue when he said, "I'm a young man but my dick grown up."

When the DJ finally stop cutting Atum was already damn there half naked. With his silk robe to the stage headdress dispersed into the masses of the crowd as he performed like Channing Tatum. Who starred in Step Up covered in mummified like cloth the color of white wrapped around his privates as he moved.

The women who before was being subdued by Celeste's security detail now cheers and went nuts. As the firing desire that burned with anticipation between their legs became unbearable for them to resist and control.

While the women were throwing there thongs and panties that where scattered on the stage. Andreah now in the cut sat back in the darkness of the curtains and admired from a far. As she touched herself and visualized Atum taming the flame resonating all throughout her body.

Keeping her remote focus on Atum mesmerize off the way he was able to move his body to the beat. She grew so enthralled with his performance that as she played with herself near, and area were if one paid attention they would see. She became careless and at that very moment could care less who spotted her.

So long as she got her shit off. The performance from Atum lasted for a brief minute more. As it came to and end the crowd was screaming for an encore.

His eyes met with Andreah's as did hers as their gaze lasted for what seemed like an extremity. Until Celeste broke their trance speaking into the intercom saying "Oooo0o0owwwwweeeee damn daddy now that's what I call a show give it up for the Grown an Sexy Mr. Forever young Atum everybody wasn't he great." She stood next to him snuggling his right side allowing his massive arm to drape down her curvaceous body.

As the crowd continued to go nuts. Celeste looked over her prized shoulder and peeped Andreah out of the corner of her eye disheveled and with an appearance of gouged eyed over her prized possession. ATUM which made her smile until she kirked out and iced grilled Andreah with a stare.

That would make Lucifer's general Spawn tremble in fear into lowering his weapon Andreah taken back from the episode unfolding between the death match stares. She quickly recovered and regained control of herself.

While Celeste as if seconds before didn't just put on and intimidation factor with Andreah, said in the microphone "let the bidding begin she extended her arms invitingly to the male and female models and passed the microphone to Atum whispering something into his ear: The procedure took 4 to 5 seconds and from there Celeste switched off the stage leaving the rest of the show hosted by a half-naked ATUM. As Celeste came over to Andreah and said, "come my darling come follow me."

The smell of Celeste's Black spell by Victoria Secret's fragrance line lingered in the air. As it made Andreah turn on her toes and follow Celeste's scent. It was a tad dark beyond the stage.

In the back she extended her hand blindly guiding herself through the dark. When Celeste gently grasped her hand and pulled her into her off centered secluded room.

Ducked off inside Celeste immediately shut the door. While Andreah said "uhhhhhh why is it so dark in here were are we." Celeste sucked her teeth and said to her "Awwweeee is someone afraid of the lil bitty dark "Celeste teased in a babyish voice.

Andreah not in the mood of playing around shot back with "ha ha ha a bitch funny, but seriously lights please." before she could finish her sentence the lights in the room activated a little startled she jumped. But as her nerves settled, she was able to peep, that she was inside what appeared to be a mini movie theater.

The size of a tanning and sauna bedroom. Somewhat similar to the ones that appeared in celebrities' mansions on MTV Cribs TV show back in the days. "Wh wh what the hell is all this" Andreah said aloud Celeste respond' you really can't help it I'm starting to see hmmm this Dreah is the presentation room after every show all the male and female escorts get chosen then upon acceptance the ones requested retreat to their dressing rooms to get ready to perform?

The flare in Andreah's jaw line made Celeste smiled. As she knew Andreah was about to fire away with another damn question. Beating her to the punch Celeste barked "what I mean by perform is quite simple those males, or females requested walk through the garden bare in flesh demonstrate amongst each other they're very final world premiere before they drive off in the sunset to be..."

Andreah cut her off and screamed "S.OLD." Celeste allowed her forwardness to miss her, and flatly said "FREE to be absolutely FREE from the shit fest that once condemned their life to HELL. "Andreah being a smart ass popped back with "Oh so you are doing God's work now is that what you calling all of this."

Celeste rubbed her temples both sides with her pointer and ring fingers this was a sign that signified she was on the verge of cracking, and about to lash out she took deep breaths before she began to speak. To Andreah again a little calmer than before. She said "look Dreah check it out honey it's like this..."

She pressed the button on her remote that automatically pulled the drapes back. Once pulled back it was a thick padded slab of glass. That favored the ones in the precincts throughout the nation in their interrogation rooms where one side you can see clearly, and the other side you can't see at all.

Inside the door beyond the glass favored an amazon ambiance seaside tannish sand fresh cut rich green grass bushes, and forest like trees measured to the length of room. Temperature size, a beautiful waterfall that ended at a willow freshwater pond that was 3 feet deep with exotic fish, and a fountain. Of true desire that didn't disperse of pure fresh water.

It was showered with treats that every sinful man and women cry and die for. All the young men and women from earlier 6 from each totaling in 12 appeared naked from head to toe in the exotic atmosphere. Andreah's eyes popped out of there sockets as she qued in on all the naked men and women in full.

They all frolicked over freely to the fountain as many grabbed there substance of choice, and smoked, injected, or sniffed away into ecstasy.

Celeste activated the volume in the room as the young men and women talked fresh to each other.

Banger Brothers Porno Production had nothing on the 6 beautiful men and women in attendance inside Celeste's Garden of Eden. As the action commenced and Andreah sat back in pure hotness in moistness that soiled her $5,000.00 dress. As she witnessed girl on girl action boy on girl and so on.

Celeste took place behind Andreah caressing her shoulders then said "you may not approve of my line of work" HELL quite frankly from Bi-partisan standards. You and a small company the size of a Salem village maybe the only appraising ballot in the whole entire world. Hmmm so what should that tell you well let's see ummm out of 7 plus billion people throughout the world.

You and that so called high and modest following sadly don't even equate to the size of a wishing bone. To even be considered a voice ha ha ha such a shame what religion and politics has revert to disapproving of the public practice of Tantric Yoga better known as divine sex in the secret temples. Every man and woman you've witnessed today darling are here freely upon there on will ha ha my my my dear you watch entirely to many movies what kind of monster do you take me to be.

Atum without knocking came into the mini theater, and peeped his mother Celeste without company. Already knew what was going down when he seen the 12 he auctioned off earlier in the Garden. He immediately fell before her on his knees, and pleaded "dear mother forgive me I was unaware you where with guest."

She smiled as she lightly bowed, and kissed him on his head. As he gently grabbed her right hand like the rest kissed her hand then pressed it against his forehead. She shivered in delight as she looked at her babyboy then cut her eyes in the noisy direction of Andreah, and said aloud "A rise my prince where are my manners forgive me sweetie... Dreah honey I would like for you to meet my precious son Atum; Atum this is Andreah Phillips."

Atum looked in the direction of Andreah. Who arise to her feet from her seat, but never broke eye contact with the fine young man she was lusting over a minute or so ago. Every step she took towards him she could hear the heavy thumps of her heartbeat.

She couldn't help but keep staring at him as the young man resembled someone of her dark past. She hasn't thought of since that heinous day. Lost in the young man's eyes that reminded her of the childhood love Jeff.

As she invited his hand for a handshake. The faint sounds of a Life Support machine flatlining bled loudly in her ears until a deep voice snatched her out of her trance and said "it's a pleasure to meet you Madam Phillips." Back on land she stared at him then Celeste and flatly flashed a smile.

Then walked off focusing her attention back on the sex puppets performing the most epic orgy. She'd ever seen well the only orgy she'd ever seen Celeste whispered something in Atum's car and, within seconds he was gone.

She edged over closer to Andreah whose head at that moment was all over the place. Then whispered to her upon planting a kiss on her cheek "Just imagine darling everything in life you ever want literally at your disposal MONEY, POWER, RESPECT..." Celeste snatched her closer as she ran her fingers up Andreah's gown and grazed her hot moist lips of her phat pussy with 2 of her fingers.

As Andreah gasped and moaned when Celeste finished saying "and let us not forget SEX yessss my dear SEX beyond your most wildest dreams hmmm (she sucked and kissed her neck from behind her) what would you do" continuously playing skillfully in Andreah's pussy. Andreah panted uncontrollably as she vibrated still watching the orgy of young men and women in ecstasy Celeste removed her hand and savored the taste of Andreah's juices for herself.

When between licks and sucks she said "ummmmm join me my sweet join me in the ranks of making this nation great again darling, and under are ruling class that matters the most" she caressed her hips and fondled her ass. As Awode and Valery the African French couple from Celeste's humble abode appeared from out of nowhere and took over from there. Andreah felt the delicate manicured hands of Valery caress her boobs, and with ease was able to unzip her gown and watch it fall before her as the lovely looking Valery whispered "don't be afraid Madam Phillips please allow me.

"Before Andreah could protest it was too late as the high yellow beauty took one of her nipples in her mouth and licked and sucked with the power of a vacuum cleaner. As she stepped fully out of her gown now completely nude only covered in the accessories and jewels plus Louis Vuitton heels that complemented the gown. Awode kissed Celeste on the cheek and said "go ahead Madam Moselle we got this she is in good hands now."

Celeste smiled as she turned on her heels then made it for the door, but she didn't depart until she blew a kiss into the air and heard her servant say, "I knew you couldn't resist Madam Phillips." Celeste shut the door behind her and through the darkness navigated herself to the security room where tonight's earnings awaited with her man of the hour.

A knock at the door alerted Atum that Celeste was outside awaiting entry. As he rosed to his feet to open the door with a mild attitude. With his attention still on the security camera zoomed in on intense action between Andreah, Awode and Valery.

He opened the door looked at Celeste and with a smirk upon seeing her smuggest smile he said aloud "Uh hello Mah-ther" giving her his back as he walked away, she giggled aloud off his irritation and said "ewww… what bit you in that sexy chocolate ass of yours" back at the desk he cleared his throat and said "nothing here."

He tossed the mini duffel bag in the air and Celeste caught it as Atum said "that's tonight's earnings from the door care to count it." Purring like a sexy kitten Celeste announced "ooooooouuu should I big daddy" Atum cringed in disgust then focused his attention back on the surveillance camera as he watched Awode and Valery have there way with Andreah.

Which made Atum grow "who is this women." Celeste sucked her teeth then barked damn does it matter" Atum then fired back with "it does if you want to remain to keep these doors open Jesus sometimes I wonder." She cut him off and barked sometimes you wonder what exactly my son.

Atum looked at her and bit his tongue as he said "forget about it just forget about it." She cut him off again and growled "forget about it I shall, and shall should you if you value your tongue." Perturbed he sulked in an angered silence then jumped to his feet and yelled "the overseas deposits of the ladies & gentlemen that made purchases for this evening our uploaded in our accounts if you will excuse me...."

Celeste blocked his line of travel and pleaded saying "HONEY WAIT JUST WAIT PLEASE" she caressed his muscular forearm and he said "what ma what is it she nuzzled her face in his muscular pecs wining "babiche please I'm sorry you know I love you more than anything in the world please tell me you know that." Her wines and cries always got the best of him

When he was a kid and even now as a young man she was able to still woo him. Watching him attentively as he got tangled in her invisible web. He shuddered like he used to when he was little and she pounced on the opportunity of his gullible rawness and playfully pushed him to the FUTONE.

Where they both collapsed and Celeste in rare form said "Daddy without you, and your amazing brain and... with ease she dismembered his robe and whipped out his dick and said and this life saver right here (she lightly nibbled on the head then spit on the tip stroking him with both hands). We wouldn't be here right now at this level in the game. You hear me daddy that's because of you."

She ran her slimy wet tongue down his girth pass his balls then tickled his gooch (better known as the perineum or taint) with her tongue and sucked it. Making him hiss and jump in excitement as she sucked on his balls. While stroking him to perfection as he pre-came then upon feeling his jizz she traced her tongue back up to his length then relaxed her throat and deep-throated him sucking him away as if his dick was the last firm organ in the world.

Atum lost it as he always been a sucker over Celeste sex games. Especially her dick sucking skills. She'd been playing these mind games on him and many others for years.

But especially him since she adopted him many moons ago. Atum could never stare at her for too long. Because if he did he would immediately come he focused his attention back on the camera of the women he just met.

Now getting penetrated by Awode from behind with a face full of Valery's pussy. As did Valery who was now on her back with a face full of Andreah's pussy sucking and nibbling away on her clit. As Andreah went wild screaming "AHHHHHHHH SHIT YESSSSSSSS YESS YESS YESS AH AH OOOOOO OOOUUU GOD This feels incredible "Smack".

A firm smack on Andreah's ass cuts the air as Awode firmly spanks away and strokes Andreah faster burying a thumb in her ass saying aloud that's it baby cream on this dick ummm release that sweet milk all over this dick uhhhhhh you love this dick huh you love this dick say you love this dick." She panted struggling to escape out a moan as Valery did a special trick on her clit which made Andreah color his dick with all her juices.

Her body relaxed as his dick slipped out of her sloppy wet hole and completely body planted over Valery's tiny high yellow petite frame. Valery able to slip from under Andreah. Smiled as she directed Awode over to her and began sucking the juices off of Awode dripping dick.

Andreah saw the appetizing sight and joined in as they both took turns changing faces, Between the two Atum and Awode it was a competition as the ladies in pure lust and ecstasy sucked away in profession. It didn't take long for the two men to pop a load seconds apart from each other and all sit in sexual bliss.

With saturated pheromones lingering richly in the air. Deep breaths escapes all as there approximately 25 yards in length away from each other north in different rooms. Lost in there uncomplexity of thoughts.

Outside of one seconds of silence boiled down as Celeste the odd ball out of the pack. Weaved together a infamous plan of action to attack on her new project Andreah. She was fully aware Andreah was not going to be a easy conquer.

One night of sexual bliss was not going to cut it hell she tried for 3 years and to no avail failed. Andreah was a tough cookie, but Celeste in her mind was tougher. She centered her attention back on her limped dick half naked prince and smirked off the thought admiring how she was so fortunate to have him.

Sadly she was robbed of the pleasure of birthing kids so when she came across him he was a baby literally. Not proud of highlights in her life on how she brought him up now. That he has grown he began proving to be a major asset to her after all.

She lived in fear everyday that one day she would wake-up and lose that. She couldn't bare the thought nor idea of losing him and she already had it made up in her mind that if that day were to ever come it would be over her dead body.

Erasing that out of her head space and focusing in on Atum with his dick still in her hand. She rubbed it across her cheek then kissed it and said "Daddy I just want you to know I love you and you mean the world to me..(deep sighs with watery eyes). I just don't know what I would do without you."

He looked at her then witnessed her sincerity. Then pulled her into his lap aligned his the tip of his dick & buried in her pussy. Once he hiked her dress up to waste level and said, "how much you say you love daddy again."

Flirtatiously she cooed like a giddy little four year old. That said "ummm dis much dah dee." Atum now inside her they both gasped as Celeste now able to gain momentum rode Atum to his pace into heaven.

There session this time lasted for a few minutes until they grew tired and fell asleep. Preparing for a big day tomorrow, as she rested in Atum's muscular arms. She pondered back between thoughts until her eyes got heavy and the final words that fell off her lips were "LET THE GAMES BEGIN."

Chapter 6

The Corporate Skirt

The rise of the early morning sun came beaming through the closed drapes and blinds of Andreah's master bedroom windows. The shinning rays of the sun danced on her beautiful coffee brown face, and hugged her eyes as she squinted restlessly to keep them closed. She yawns deeply feeling her energy release out of her sore body.

As she stretches in her bed to maximum capacity. Listening to the sounds of her bones crack. Made her purr and groan with a giggle in pleasure.

Upon opening her eyes peeping she was back in her comfortable room she closed her eyes. With a huge grin on her face until it hit her. "Haaaaahhhhhhh..." she snapped the top part of her body fully erect. Then search around her room trying to fathom how on earth did she wine up back in her room. Safe and sound she grabbed her girls (breast) and peep she had a white t-shirt on. From there she snatched her thick fluffy comforter off her body and allowed it to fall to the floor. Then looked down at her legs and peeped she had her favorite royal blue night-tower pajama bottoms on.

"What the fuck." was all she could say. As she looked at her pretty little pedicured feet wondering in disillusion if last night really even happened. Curious as she bit her bottom lip she stuck her hand in her pajama bottoms and rubbed across her kitty.

A light gasp escaped her lips as she removed her hand and it was super wet with sticky cum dangling on her fingers like a snot rocket. In a flash she jumped out of her bed and stormed into her connected bathroom slamming the door. Her mind was racing with a thousand thoughts per minute.

How did I get here? Who put these clothes on me? Where is my 5 thousand dollar gown? How do they know where I live? O my God I can't believe this nigga came in me?

Were some of the most key ones. She wasn't necessarily concerned about Awode coming inside her. She been on the pill now for a minute just in case of any close calls. What trouble her was how Awode ran up in her unprotected and had no regards of treating her with respect to pull out.

In all her sexcapades she was careful and cautious she worried if he had something. But then that thought immediately pushed it out of her mind. As she replayed that magical night back in her head and at that moment felt like a low down whore.

But surprisingly instead of shame she felt a rush. Continuously playing back the magical night she was able to recall now. How they all ended back up drunk and super saucy at her house. From the bathroom she stormed back into her bedroom and peeped the $5,000 dollar gown, it had a note on that said

"Last night Madam Phillips was wonderful and we both want to thank you for such a amazing evening. We pray that you find it in your heart to forgive are intrusion We thought of it to be of the utmost disrespect to just leave you bare in the premiere room and not escort you back to your quarters safely. We all were a little over intoxication levels. So instead of leaving you unattended and exposed we clothed you in your night garments and awaited until you returned to bed then quietly let ourselves out. Madam Phillips me and Val want to thank you thrice. From the warmest parts of our souls. Lately me and Val sexually have been declining from each other. Then you came along and.. well let's just say in the nick of time your a blessing from above. If I could speak freely on behalf of me and Val we would hope our encounters don't end here, however if so we fully understand and wish you safe travels my lady."

Ovah Awode and Valery

Andreah covered her mouth as she read the end of the letter. Still in Awe over the whole ordeal. Her pussy queaf thinking about the both of them. Which made her jokingly slap her thigh and yell "uh uh bad girl that's why were in this mess right now."

She couldn't help herself as she flashed a heartwarming flirtatious smile. Then cut her eyes in the direction of her alarm clock and peeped she was late for her psyche appointment. "SHIIITTTT" she yelled snapping to her feet again.

She darted back into her bedroom and turned on her shower head. Activating the steamy hot water that made the mirrors and the whole entire room foggy. She wiggled out of her pajama bottoms as they fell to the fluffy carpeted floor when she pulled her t-shirt over her head as the shirt fell to the floor the image of her father Stretch.

Popped off the glass making her scream in a high pitch harmony "AHHHHHHHH Ha Ha Huhhhh" her heart thumped loudly in her eardrums as she regained her composure as she rocked back and forth Indian style on the floor chanting "quiet place Quiet place its all in your head Quiet Place Quiet Place Stretch is dead breath breath breath" she continued this for a little while longer until her beating heart stopped pounding. To the point where she thought it might burst out of her chest.

She slowly eased to her feet to look in the mirror and sighed deeply. When it was riddled in fog from the steam of the water. Bare ass naked she eased her body into the shower under the water, and allowed the water to seep into her pores and relax her mind and body.

She truly didn't have much planned for today. It was Sunday and her usual was church, grocery shopping, cleaning up the house and lounging until she had to wake up bright and early in the morning for work. Church and religion for obvious reasons was never her thing.

But through the course of time Celeste and let her tell you with her sanctified ass. Would drag her over to the house of God to listen and receive the word. Today though she would have to make a rain check on Jesus, and hustle on over to the clinic, and then her psyche doctor.

She hated the fact that she had to compensate her double for appointments scheduled over the weekend. But urgent matters such as these she wasted no time pleasuring herself. Like she usually does in the shower, and jumped out shooting over quickly to her room. While meanwhile at the planet fitness across town on the Northeast side of DC.:

Atum was repping on the incline bench 2 45 lb. plates on each side. Which weighed out to be 225 lb. without the metal clamps to keep the plates in place so they didn't slip off the bar. He wore a all white armor Air Jordan workout visor that made him look like a broody super hero.

He also had a pair of black basketball shorts, with shin high black athletic socks with a pair of white workout powerlifting sneakers sized 12, that were identical to wrestling sneakers players use to compete.

Strapped to his right bicep was a compartment that his iPod and phone was in that played his favorite workout playlist. As the song that played in his Dre-beat Super sonic headphones. Was a joint that had the streets in a frenzy which was called All About It by Frenchie, Jadakiss, and Fab.

"Ride around the city with a loaded gun LOADED. If them people grab you then you know you done FINISH get indicted call your lawyer give all ya ones now you gotta fight it or go on the run." As the beat dropped he pumped away still rapping along to the music of kiss lyrics he screwed and chopped as he blocked out all sounds and surroundings around him.

On lookers looked on from there treadmills and attended machines at Atum as the star struck the masses with his vigorous circuit training. As he finished his set at the incline bench. He jumped up from there then started curling the 50 lb. dumbbells. Once down there he strapped around his waist a deadlifting belt looped a Steel chain through the belt loop then connected 2 45 lbs plates dangling from the chain as he made his way over to the dip bar, and repped out 25 for 3 clips.

Pumped up and full of energy. He made his way over to the cross cable cord machine, and engaged in his cool off phase. As he began working out his gigantic traps that look like hangers on steroids.

Looking in the supersize mirrors growling with workout faces two women from a far gazed on in lust. He smiled to himself as he thought about an additional workout with the both of them in the shower room. All along while admiring them he did in what they called in the player world as a heat check which consist of analyzing a sucka from head to toe where the only concern is about 2 things and 2 things only value and worth.

It took a sharper eye for one to be able to estimate profit from a vic. With their guard down and since these ladies weren't dressed for the occasion and out an expose in workout gear. It didn't take long for Atum to peep that these middle-aged Caucasian Ukrainian cougars.

With Payless Sketchers Gabriel Brother t-shirts and spandex and Tiffany jeweler watches. Not only cared more about zeroes in their account. Then their appearance, however also had a hidden burning desire for dark chocolate men.

As they continued to stare from a far like little hyenas in heat. As Atum phone rung in his headphones screaming incoming call with the ringtone Run by Jay-Z and Beyonce notifying him it was Celeste. Who was saved under his phone as mother from hell.

He cringed off of the sound of her ringtone. As he looked at his smart watch and grew disgusted at her priceless provocative photo. He allowed it to ring out until he thought wise of that, and decided to answer knowing that if he didn't she would harass him.

On the 4" attempt he answered on the line and said "Yes Celeste what do you want" picking up on his attitude she barked back with "Nigga don't get lippy with me where you at…" He took a seat near a open bench and then took a deep breath and said "where else would I be at; at 1:00 in the afternoon on a Sunday.

I'm at the gym is there something you want. Testing the waters Celeste shot back with "You know what Atum you been acting like a little bitch lately why don't you tell me what's really good lil daddy." Atum bit his tongue making it bleed.

As she continued to babble on until Atum grew tired, and barked "bitch ain't nobody trying to hear that shit, now I'm asking you again is there something you want or what." Celeste paused from the other side of the phone as she was taken back from Atum forwardness. Atum was stunned as well to as he began to grow nervous every second that flew by, and she remained quiet over the phone."

He he Hel HELLOOOO" he managed to blurt out, but it was to late as Celeste hung up the phone leaving him dumbfounded in confusion ALEXA notified him in his ear that the other party disconnected the call. In his headphones upon hearing that he activated his watch to check the time and peeped it was a little after 2. He usually goes for 2 hours, but today he would have to make a rain check and hurry back to the house and clear the air between him and Celeste his mother. As he put his weights back. He was getting ready to leave when the middle-aged Ukrainian cougars from earlier pulled up on him. Catching him off guard as the brave one out of the bunch tapped his bicep and said "Hey hello excuse me Sir." Atum pulled off his headphones looked at the women and gave them both a head to toe smile and said "Hey ladies I'm not in your way am 1." The party of two giggled flirtatiously as the bold one of the pack said "Dear God heavens no you are absolutely fine isn't he Meghan."

She tapped her who was lustfully occupied until she came to and said "uh uh Oh yes yes fine indeed I mean..." embarrassment swarmed over the women and Atum picked up on it immediately it warmed him the effect. He had on these women and now up close able to see their beauty they looked pretty good plus appetizing. Although he wasn't in the right head space.

At the moment being a perfect gentlemen of the art. He softened the mood and said "it's quite alright madams I know what you mean and thank you I really needed to hear that... "The bolder women from earlier peeped her window and slid in then said "Oh sweetie please call me Chesa and you've meet my girl Meghan's shy self (pssssshhhh) she act like she never seen a hunk like yourself before."

As Chesa continued to giggle. Atum felt a weird feeling shadow over his nerves he quizzed the cheesy acting temptress, and called this little fling officially over as he said "hmmm very well Chesa and Meghan I hate to be a party pooper ladies, but I need to get going enjoy yawl's workout and the rest of yawl's afternoon if you'll excuse me." When he made a move to step the nervous one from before stepped in his line of path batting her eyes sexually at him.

Until her partner in crime Chesa spoke aloud, and said "Aww Atum baby leaving so soon that sucks I really was just getting loosen up me, and my girl to work out are legs, and core we figured maybe you can give us some pointers in all since your profile exudes how much of a phenomenal trainer you are; you are a trainer aren't you." Chesa who was now in a sports bra instead of her t-shirt from earlier revealing her FBI badge that swung freely from her neck.

While she continued to stretch in sexual positions her partner Meghan joined in on the charade, and added "yea Atum a little birdie told me you sure do know how to make a body feel good." Now with his attention centered back on Meghan who was stretching her legs slowly twisting her hips around that revealed her FBI badge as she groped her own ass in excitement. As the 2 of them now stood next to each other Atum with a smirk, and suave demeanor stated **famm my apologies ladies where are my manners I'm not in some kind of trouble am I."

Chesa the more polished agent announced "for now no, but if you want to keep it like that. Atum laughed cut them off and had them on alert when he said "ha ha sorry sweetheart not a fan of mild threats, and with all do respect if I'm not in any trouble or under arrest here than

I think I should go not really a big fan of protecting and serving your kind no offense." He had Chesa's badge in his hand, and her soul in his eyes as he didn't break his piercing stare through her being.

He kissed her badge, and let it fall as the heavy metal smacked her stomach and by then turned on his heels, and shouted out "you officers enjoy the rest of your workout, and afternoon excuse me precious." He extended his muscular forearm, and lightly with respect moved her partner Meghan out of his line of travel and kept stepping.

Meghan attempted to pursue him but the flagging of her partner halted her in her tracks. As Chesa spoke out to him saying "Oh Atummm....." He stopped, and turned around for her to say "just curious what gave us away you know off the record." Atum sighed as he had to admit he dig shorta's wits in plagiarism she almost had em, but the key word was simple ALMOST with confidence he said "well wouldn't you like to know.to bad you still remain wanting to know take care officer."

As he finished his sentence, he was already in the locker room skipping his usual jumping in the shower. Instead, he just hustled over to his locker got dressed, and pondered back and forth on the heated dispute over the phone with him, and Celeste. He checked his smart watch for texts, emails, missed calls, and notifications.

Besides incoming calls from regulars, and new clients responding to his newsfeed. No calls no nothing where from Celeste which worried him as that was odd to him. Half-way dressed he was rushing to get out of the door until he heard the Twitter bird sound notifying him somebody respond to his newsfeed.

He pulled out his phone, and checked it and when he seen who it was. He now officially was noid as it was the 2 feds from earlier that said "we got our eyes on you Atum stick around will be in touch." He struggled trying to figure out how in the world did they get his number, and who was the rotten apple in their company.

He couldn't pinpoint nobody to save the life of him, and it troubled him dearly. The last scare him, and Celeste had was years back when they were still hustling to get the elite clientele, they got now from out of the landmark diner the Politico. While transporting keys of Afghan pure grade A dope through a diplomatic route operated by US Customs that was extended through the state representative of D.C.

At the time who now was campaigning running to be governor. On the expense of his granddaughter who secretly had a fling with Atum. Allowing Celeste to seize in on the reward of political protection, and immunity to freely run her enterprise while her sex slave/son fuck the brains out of the granddaughter of the future governor of the nation's capital state.

To her as to him it was money well spent, since it serves tremendous privilege, and exclusive protection and free reign amongst authorities to do them. Now revisited with the same unnecessary attention. The hairs on the back of his neck stood up as he shot out of the locker room with gym bag in hand towards the exit. All looked at him whom which he paid no mind to, ignoring the employee calling after him since he was not in the mood. While meanwhile 25 yards away:

Andreah inside her baby blue Audi Q7. Was in such a rush as she parked her car near a small restaurant next to the planet fitness gym in the jam packed parking lot. That when she jumped out of her car, and slammed the door behind her; her jacket got caught and when she took quick strides in the direction to the nearby gas station her jacket ripped, and completely torn the whole bottom half of the design.

"Aggghhhh Nooo." she screamed; onlookers in the parking lot going about their day. Witness Andreah's dilemma minding her business. While others who found it amusing, and where very rude laughed, and taunted her while she tried to pull herself together screaming "kiss my ass all of you find something better to do with y'all miserable lives."

She growled at all who had ear's: instead of patiently opening her driver side door to remove her bottom half of her trench coat she ripped the remaining part of her coat leaving her appearance atrocious at best. In such a hurry completely oblivious to her surroundings.\ So caught up in her phone texting back and forth with her psychiatrist informing her she was there, and would be at her door in the next two minutes.

The thought didn't register in her head that her line of travel to the gas station was next to the exit ramp of highway 443, and tractor trailers, trucks, cars you name it came flying down the highway with no regard for slowing down for pedestrian life. Coming off the ramp entering the main road with 3 lanes at an average speed of 45 miles per hour easily completely zoned out from the real world hearing pedestrians scream "Lady O my God look out" It didn't dawn on her until the loud honks escaped out of the oncoming traffic, and by the time she picked up her head it was to late "Brrrmm Brrrmm Brrrmm Brrrmmmm."

In the nick of time literally a foot and a half from total impact, Atum like a mutant with super human strength ran up to Andreah snatched her up and pulled her out of the way. Just before she would of became road kill. She took a deep breath, and her instant reaction was to grab tight upon the security that came to her aid.

With her face buried in the muscular pees of this anonymous man. As he held her like a groom with his bride caring his prize to the honeymoon sweet. The sound of his deep voice captured her attention when he said "WHEW that was a close call are you ok ma'am you almost got yourself killed."

She raised her face out of his braulic pecs to identify the face of the voice that spoke with genuine concern. Eyes locked on her knight in shining armor. She almost melted as she stared into the brown pools of Atum that took her back for a second ride reminding her of her love Jeff as she whispered "Oh my God baby is it really you."

Atum was taken back by this women, and for the first time was at a lost for words, but he enjoyed the cause of it. When he stormed out of the gym littering through the parking lot searching for his car. He overheard the commotion from the on lookers clowning her while others were trying to fore warn her of the danger ahead that she dismissed carelessly.

Upon the time she exited her vehicle up to the matter at hand. He recognized her instantly from the other night were they both shared a moment of clarity and uniqueness. As Atum gazed at the gorgeous cocoa brown chocolate goddess cradled in his arms like a newborn.

He couldn't help but smile trying his best to disguise the instant fuzziness and chills inside every moment he spent staring at her when he uttered out "uh uh I'm sorry Miss I'm afraid that's not me my name is Atum I believe we met." She shook her head, and came to as she looked around analyzing all gather around coming to their aid making sure all was well.

Some out of the growing entourage pulled out their phones recording away. Something that grew to be very common nature to citizens and millennials in the thriving 21st century. Andreah not enjoying being in the spotlight of everybody's gossip.

Glanced out towards the bizzy street, and peeped her phone was completely finished. She wailed like a wounded wild animal and spazzed out as she said "Ahhhhh no no noo 000000 not my phone Nooo boy put me down no no no." Jumping out of his arms storming back into the bizzy street with no regard for the speedy traffic.

The thick crowd gasped as oncoming traffic car horns erupting simultaneously. Atum before he could even fathom what he was doing his body reacted, and snatched up Andreah again back to safety. As the cars missed her by a foot, but took out the damage on the remaining parts of her phone that was intended for her.

Atum snapped as he barked "God damn it woman what the hell is the matter with you what you got a death wish or something huh..." Andreah usually had all the lip in the world when it came to someone popping off at the mouth. She shocked herself with the humbling disposition from when Atum.

Came at her with some sense when she finally blurted out "wh wh what's it to you anyway boy ain't nobody tell you to play captain Save-a-Ho." Atum looked at her liked she had lost her damn mind. But instead waved up his hand to signify to oncoming traffic to halt when they did he shot out to the street, and picked up what was left of her phone.

Returning back to her with her phone in hand. He planted the phone into her chest and barked "next time you want to dive off the deep end make sure you do it when nobodies watching, and actually gives a fuck." He shoulder bumped her hard knocking her off her feet which caused her to trot back a few steps.

As Atum walked back in the direction of his car. Everybody else looked at her in awe. With some who still had there phones recording.

A lot of people gave her the stare of she was a snobby nosed bitch. But when she looked in Atum's direction whom now gained some distance from where she was. Call it a moment of gratitude, but she stormed off in his direction shouting "Hold up wait wait STOP" a few feet away ATUM stopped in his tracks, and halfway turned his body to the voice that was out of breath but said "(catching her breath) forgive me I'm not that good at this, but... Thank You Thank You for you know."

Atum playing the role of a hard ass shot buck with "Nah miss I don't know you thanking me for what." Andreah a little startled from his reapproach curtailed around his forwardness then pleaded saying "Ok I had that coming your right what want to Thank You for is saving this snobby ole gals life from being road kill it's not everyday a women of my stature gets a guardian angel of a fine young man like yourself."

Atum searched her eyes for sincerity. To make sure she wasn't blowing smoke up his ass. Locked in a stare-off with her again that warming all to familiar fuzzy feeling came back again, and no matter how much he tried to shake it, it was unbreakable.

Trying to remain a float on the surface he said "snobby without question I agree... however old hmmm your only as old as you feel my lady but overall your welcome, and I'm glad your okay." Atum turned to leave until Andreah stopped him in his tracks again, and said "how do you know how I feel mister where our my manners my apologies Andreah Phillips you are."

As she extended her hand, he accepted it, and said "Atum Smith at your service, and your right I do not know how you feel, but I know one way to find out." Andreah's eyebrow raised out of curiosity when she said "Oh really how is that Mr. Smith" jumping into true Mack status he flat out said "by allowing a gentlemen to repay you for your troubles of replacing your damaged phone with a better plan.

I have a buddy across town that is a wiz-kid with gadgets like these." She smiled off of his invite to help fix her phone. It's not that she couldn't cover the damage herself, but she had to admit the attention she was getting from him had her feelings in a bunch and she couldn't fathom the thought of telling him no.

Flirtatiously playing hard to crack she said "Awwweeee Atum that's really sweet Thank You let me find out that's the new way now how millennial's push up on us Cougars." Atum marveled off her flirtatious approach shot back smoothly with "Well with all do respect Ms. Phillips I like to think of you as the most beautiful feline of the Amazon my precious black panther. But it's really no trouble at all what do you say."

Andreah giggled at his reference of her being a precious black panther. She felt Atum making her weak for attention, and she didn't enjoy being portrayed as a weakling modestly she replied "Thank you Atum I appreciate that, but I'll past I actually have somewhere I need to be." Disappointed but refusing to show it he smiled then said before leaving "Ok ok Ms. Phillips sorry that I held you up, and enjoy the rest of your afternoon."

Turning on his heels walking back to the direction of his car. She watched him smoothly walk away. He couldn't resist to ask she bit her bottom lip saying "Atum...I'm sorry wait one more time."

Stopping again he turned around to face her, and this time she blurted out "Ahhhhh you know I. Ummm (clearing her throat) I know this nice spot across town with awesome lunch specials uh yu you care to join me." Atum smiled and said "Ah yea sure I got room in the tank" while 40 yards away ducked off in a jet black Impala with authentic lens for a camera.

Chesa snapped away as she heard her partner bark "Chessss we've been here for almost a half an hour, snapping pictures of this guy I'll give you that he's sexy, but come on we have a job to do can we go." Chesa continued to snap away with a smirk, as she dryly answered her partner saying, "And what exactly do you think we're doing Meg huh taking pictures of Mother Nature or something."

Her partner Meghan frowned in confusion until she heard her partner "AH HA Meg look check this out." Meghan grabbed her binoculars and seen Atum escorting Andreah back to her car closing the door behind her. He hustles back to his car starting his engine pulling out of his parking space, signaling for Andreah to follow him.

When she said aloud "were are they going* Chesa responded that's a very good question because I have not the slightest idea, but that's irrelevant check this out." Chesa skimmed through her photo gallery and showed all the clippings from the time he exited the gym up to the incident ending with Andreah and him pulling off separately in their own cars following each other.

Meghan studied the pictures thoroughly, which made her ask what you think Chess that somehow these two are connected or something." Chesa stared at her partner with irritation, and then said, "it kind of looks like that don't you think Meg...I mean damn did you look at the pictures rescuing a damsel in distress, or not; how many good Samaritans do you know engage victims like that without knowing them."

Agent Meghan reviewed over the clippings again and saw that Agent Chesa had a video recording. Although the only sounds were the pandemonium of the event at hand. She was unable to hear Andreah and Atum. She was able to witness the intimate attraction between the two.

So much that she asked "Ok Chess you make a valuable point. But what does she got to do with him, and his perverted whatever you wanna call her sick partner Celeste, and there operation."? Chesa pondered in thought before she answered Meghan trying to put it all together.

When she said "that I don't know yet, but what I do know Meg is that that man Atum I've been studying and watching along with Celeste for years now. When they were nothing more than credit card swiping street drug peddling parking lot pimping scrubs with not a pot to piss in, or a handle to hold it."

She gave a moment for herself to speak again then said "we had'em Meg me and my partner before God bless the dead, he died on duty we were literally closing the case ready to have the judge signed off on the warrant, and hand the indictments down to the grand jury the following morning so we could of buried Celeste's whole operation behind federal walls til the next century.

That night...I'll never forget that bitch robbed the life of a good man. Who had a beautiful wife (sobbing of cries) ki ki kids family everything 10 years later she still is free, and on top of the world while Agent Troy McIntosh rests at the bottom of the ocean of the Potomac River. Completely forgotten and swept under the rug like old news while her reign continues uh uh hell no not this time Meg that bitch dies and her son, partner, lover whoever the fuck he is to her rots in jail for the rest of his life.

My gut is screaming to me how that's going to happen, is that women in those clippings. Agent Meghan feeling for her partners trials and tribulations with concern asked, "what makes you so sure Chess." Chesa smiled as she faced her partner and said "because Meg the line of work he's in emotions and feelings don't exist and any indication of it amongst his company can get him or whoever killed; out of all the years I've been tracking this man I've never once seen him light up with affection for anyone not even Celeste."

I don't know who, or what this woman maybe to him. Nevertheless whoever she is I want a full report about this chick. On my desk by yesterday you hear me.

I want you to dig so deep that I want to know if this bitch came into the world through a C-section, or out of the coochie." She slammed on the gas pedal and mashed out of the parking lot merging into traffic quickly and smoothly throwing on there police sirens to make away through the thick afternoon traffic. They weren't in a hurry to apprehend no one just in a hurry to get to there next destination. After hearing Chesa talk and which she gave specific orders for her to dig up information on Andreah.

She was curious and wanted to know as she asked "Chesa honey what ever did happen to your old partner, I never knew he died on duty." Agent Chesa at the wheel like a mad-women reflected back to the night when her and her partner argued how they had enough evidence to bury Celeste. Her national base sex-ring operation, but Troy her partner was adamant and wanted to see her get the chair or chamber.

Troy not trying to hear it went against his partner Chesa's better judgement and dismissed her views. Went back in undercover. That night turned out to be his last night to see Agent Chesa alive, and his last on earth alive as his grim reaper called after his soul laced in a pair of high heel Stilettos and Victoria Secret Lingerie.

Celeste's measures of security back then to spot cops was nowhere near advanced as it is now. So the minute she found out Troy was a cop and his cover was blown. All hell broke lose as Celeste played possum reeling in Agent Troy with ease alerting no red flags.

All the way up to when she pounced into action and performed a murderous act. So heinous that whenever discussed it's an echo that packs volume loudly back to the headquarters of the FBI based in Virginia. A stream of tears flows freely down the face of Agent Chesa.

Back on the surface from when she went down memory lane reliving the most horrific looking crime scene. She ever step foot on out of her 15 years employed at the Bureau. Quickly shaking it off and killing the police siren as she slowed down the vehicle she qued in again what her partner Agent Meghan said which this time was "Chesa honey did you hear what I just said."

Chesa played dumb, and added "I'm sorry what did you say." Now at the red light on Northeast and 27th streets she looked around absorbing in the streets as Meghan asked again "I was asking you how did your partner pass, you never informed me he died on duty."

Chesa answered with fire when she shot back with "Quite frankly Agent Meghan that's because that information is none of your damn business for the record." Meghan looked at her with the damn seriously what face, but instead thought wise of her partners forwardness and chose to say nothing. Chesa peeping her partner change of mood tried to capitalize off of her impulsiveness as she countered back with don't take it personal Meg there's just a time and place for everything and now is not..."

Meghan cut her short and shot back with "Agent Chesa you don't have to explain yourself to me trust me I get it." Meghan stared out the window and remained silent for the rest of the ride. While Chesa fell back in her own thoughts stuck in the matters at hand,

For the first time in the entire 10 plus years investigation she finally after all the leads. She pursued felt strong about this one and it literally fell into her lap at such the perfect timing. She drifted back earlier roughly now and 11/2 hour ago when her and her partner pressed Atum.

Catching him completely off guard thinking to herself if that was a smart move to reveal there hand to him like that so soon. She was surprised he didn't recognize her since the night of her partner being brutally murdered. Weeks later when the investigation was launched she was one of the officers present that questioned Celeste with him present.

Now that she thought about it he had to have been no older than 14 or 15 at the time. So it made so much sense to her being that ever since that day this was the first time she ever approached and spoke to him personally. Thinking a million miles per minute she tried to play out how that conversation between Atum and Celeste.

What was it going to consist of, and prayed it wasn't going to expose there source that got her and her partner so far. She looked over at her perturbed partner Agent Meghan, and smiled; her concerns for her and her ex-partner which warmed her.

But there was something that was just above peoples paygrade. Plus it wasn't there concern and only needed to be informed on a need to know basis. With a full understanding of that and now a new lead to work with.

She consoled her partner Meghan's hand, and said aloud "one day you'll understand, but until then let's get to work shall we." Meghan looked at her hand then Chesa and was able to see the willingness to reason. That touched Meghan and all that was left to say was when she said "I'm with you girl let's throw the book at these Thugz..."

Chapter 7

Lose Lips

Celeste in a sexy number by her favorite American stylist Michael Kor's. With the Nittany Lion Blue Flannel jacket and pants golden emblem of the MK symbol styled around her acrobatic hips. A fresh white pair of Zanott heels complimenting a flawless mani & Pedi with her hair style in a bobby exuding off her natural beauty and features.

As she sat in the same back office her and Atum the other day where fucking each other's brains out. She inhaled deeply on a long Virginia Slim cigarette babysitting a glass of rich cognac on the rocks. She was steaming mad after she had just cut the line with Atum and his disrespectful tongue with attitude.

Smoking wasn't her thing she absolutely despise it. She would only chase some nicotine to knock off the edge, or calm her nerves from frustration or aggravation. As she plucked the ash on the Virginia Slim with her right hand.

That adorned a stylist white glove from Michael Kor's the same colors as her heels. Deep in thought completely while in her zone. She barely heard the light knock on the door from the masculine voice that kept calling out her name.

"Celeste. Celeste. Are you in there" shaking her head she recognized the voice then said "Yeaaa come in I'm in here. "As she ended her sentence the door popped open and she squinted for facial recognition and light smirked as she said "Mr. Tadrian Meltray um ummm to what do I owe the pleasure of this surprise visit." Tadrian Meltray better known as Raw was a partner in crime for her back in her glory days.

He wasn't the tallest, standing only 5'4 165lbs, however what he lacked in height he made up in size as his 165 lbs. frame made him look like a lightweight boxing champion. Hershey chocolate complexion with a dark Caesar and a debonair style and grace. He flashed a long time no hear from smile and said "Well well well if isn't play pimping to big pimping Celeste, or should I say…"

Celeste already knew what he was about to say an cut him off quickly and barked "No no second thought you shouldn't Raw please why don't you have a seat we have a lot to discuss." Raw seeing the instant switch of demeanor made him regret leaving his pistol out in his car. As he shot back with "Nah I think I'll stand so wassup you called me here I know it's not because you missed me."

Celeste disregarded his statement and didn't even bother to answer him back. As she jumped on her office phone speed-dialed her touch up detail as she barked on the phone "Bring her in." Seconds seem like hours as Celeste and Raw sat in silence until Celeste office door burst open with Awode and his goons in tow with a once gorgeous looking Leslie.

But now beauty was robbed with a beat down so severe her mother would struggle trying to recognize her. As Leslie cried pleaded and begged for her life to Celeste when she said "let me go let me go let me go you bastards I didn't do anything I swear" Leslie didn't realize that she was in front of Celeste, and her face and hair was so disheveled. She wreaked and smelled of vomit and urine.

As if she literally just got done bathing in it making every body in the room stomachs and nose turn. As Celeste barked "ill what the fuck y'all; y'all couldn't give this Ho a shower or something what the fuck; then Leslie pleaded "Les honey whatever these motherfucka's told you is a bull face lie.

Until Awode from left field cold cocked and blasted Leslie across her face. Almost knocking her out cold which made Raw fidget upon hearing her bones crack when he growled "A yo what the fuck man what the fuck y'all niggas got going on up in here Moe." Celeste chuckled as she looked at her scared-straight ole school wing man and barked "nigga stop bitching and acting like you foreign to taming a hoe as a matter of fact if my track record serves me correctly back in the day you used to get off on this right chere right."

Raw looked at her and knew exactly what she meant by that. As he briefly reflected back to when they where much younger starting in the game green as all hell. On the Ho-stroll mimicking ole school playa's trying to apply the pimp and ho conduct off visual.

That specific incident young Raw at the time allowed this ole school guerrilla mack borrow his car molding him on how to tame his Ho, and poor Celeste this specific night learned a valuable lesson. Of what talking back got you in the pimp world when the ole school mack flew off the lip, and said to his upcoming protege "well bless the pimp God from above Slim looks like you got yourself a bitch with no house-training you better tighten the muscle on that ho bo."

Raw looked at Skins the ole school mack than at Celeste. His whore who was up on game and braced herself for a smackdown she thought was coming. When Raw fired and sent Celeste from her shoulders to the floor.

Celeste faking a lightweight cry trying to make her daddy Raw look favored in front of his mentor Skins. Skins chuckles loudly as he howls aloud "Awwweeee youngblood check you out with your fly self you put tips on this yella ho hmmmmm. Nice not a blemish nor bruise can be traced impressive slick very impressive.

However it's only but so many times you can spank a ho until she finds pleasure in it. "Confused; Raw with Celeste who was still in her T-shirt and panties. Distress looking on the floor. Skins in rare form growled "front line, and center Ho."

Celeste dumbfounded looked at her Daddy Raw for re-assurance. But was caught off guard when Skins growled back with "bitch don't look at him class is in session girl baby boy know what's going on, now make me repeat myself again now." Skins whipped out his dick and stepped towards her upon seeing his dick Celeste assumed Skins wanted to sample her goodies.

So in her demoralize state she got on all fours hiked up her t-shirt giving up a lovely view for Skins to have his way with her. In utter surprise she was shocked when he kicked her in the uses and growled "Ho I said front line and center what the hell is wrong with you ya snatch don't belong to me what the fuck am I gonna do with that on ya knees girl come on now."

She wanted to cry from the power in Skins kick. But thinking wise of that she did as told, and raised up to her knees and prepared to suck him off as she stroke his length he growled "Whores that got loose lips like you better learn quick in this game how to either humble themselves or back that shit up. Welcome to practice baby class is now in session work dem jaws girl."

She cut her eyes at Raw again exuding the facial expression of help. Until Skins grew tired and slammed her head down on his length. Almost making Celeste gagg until she caught her breath and braced herself for the violent ride as Skins skull fucked the shit out of her.

Coaching her to relax her glands and take the dick. Raw sat back and watched as Skins worked out Celeste's mouth to maximum potential. As she groaned and moaned as Skins word play jump back and forth from Thuggish actions to soothing verbs of encouragement.

Celeste's mind was completely blown and fucked. As one minute she went from feeling violated to now feeling sexually desired and inspired. Her state of mind was undesirable back than at 19 years of age.

However now 29 years later a grown women with the mind state to be able to comprehend now. That she was being prep for turn out purposes. From the luxury of her office chair behind her pine oak tree desk.

She cut the air with "lift that chopstick eating bitch to her feet cuz" Awode and his goons did as they were told. While Celeste emerged from her chair walking out now in the front of her desk. Giving all a great view of her body laced in her Michael Kohrs lay.

As she barked at a battered Leslie saying, "now what was you saying earlier sweetie my men here are bull face liars really you don't say well how so puddin." Sniffles escape out of Leslie little petite nose. As she wines and plead searching for the words to say. As she cries out "Ce ce Celeste whatever those idiots said it's a lie and I can explain please let me ex..."

Celeste growing tired of her wining cut her short and growled "explain what honey that's what we're all trying to figure out you call my men liars, liars about what." A worried mess she searched for the words to say, but Celeste grew irritated and placed a finger on her lips saying "Shooooossssshhhhh lee lee baby all that wining and crying for what if I wanted to talk to a child I would of had one.

Now I'm asking you one more time, what our my men liars about..." Leslie cut her short and said "there liars about saying that they spotted me with the feds I'm not stupid I would never do that after all you've done for me Celeste I love you with all my heart I just needed a break from John and his madness please you have to believe me I swear."

Celeste looked at her thoroughly analyzing her body language and wordplay. Comparing the two and it wasn't matching up which made her ask further "you swear what, and you needed a break from John and his madness how so I'm lost lee lee make this make sense to me." Leslie now speaking clearly said "The other day at the party me and John were on non-speaking terms because his wife had caught us in his office off the clock doing more than just over time like he always informs her.

To his surprise she wasn't even livid she actually looked relieved. Which was odd because instead of being down in the dumps. He decided at the last minute he wanted to attend the party, so we went.

While there he grew spooked about seeing your date Andreah. They're faking his sickness immediately wanting to leave and while driving home that's' where the idle threats came of replacing me with another and sending me back to you to deport me back to my country.

That's why I ran Celeste I swear to you I wasn't going against us, and all what you did for us you have to believe me." Celeste now leaning towards her desk all ears raised to her toes in her heels and said "hmmmmm sounds convincing, but you know what is troubling me. She paused as she circled around her like a predator on wounded prey.

Then went off saying "what makes a women like yourself worry about being replaced with another by Justice McConnelly why would you have to fear about being replaced when you will be coming back to the abode of the same women you've just protested right now that you love unconditionally it just doesn't make sense." Celeste spoked aloud referring to herself in 3rd person.

As her heels clicked like horseshoes around her granite tile floor. As she continued to circle around Leslie who was a nervous wreck. Leslie tried to speak, but was interrupted when Celeste spoke over her, and said "correct me if I wrong puddin, but did you say something about the feds honey hmmmmm that's funny my men whom you convicted as liars never mention nothing to me about you interacting with the suit's until just now."

All in the room where quiet Leslie searched in Celeste eyes for sympathy. But when she delivered facts with assertiveness once innocent Leslie broke contact whimpering in fear. Knowing that she fucked up when Celeste bark with a mild chuckle "hmmm you know what I think girl..."

She allowed her words to drag enveloping the whole atmosphere of the room. When she continued with "I think your full of shit and my men caught you in the nick of time before you could cause serious damage as a matter-of-fact ummm Raw how does this sound to you cuz this ho gets rescued from customs a passport away from deporting that ass back to the hump-house in South Korea. But gets fortunate and rescued by our company.

We take this ho in clothe her bathe her, give her shelter, education, and a profession the full package The American Dream. Little Leslie though wants more and for years did a damn good job concealing it. Up until now when good ole Justice McConnelly was no longer entertained by this Korean treat.

No more and decides to attend our showcase for something new. Lee Lee gets paranoid fearing the worst believing she was going to be replaced and erased. So, she thinks fast and launches a plan Hmmm now what could that plan be festering around in that adorable little rebellious mind of yours." She caressed the chin of Leslie who continued to cry and pout as she snatched away from Celeste's caressive hand while Celeste continued on to say "Ah Ha (snapping her fingers). Ms. McConnelly Bingo slick, but not slick enough bitch.

It makes sense you somehow staged Ms. McConnelly to swing by the office and catch you and Mr. McConnelly getting it on. But your crushed when Ms. McConnelly instead of being pissed and ready to sign them papers. She was unmoved and relieved; fearing the worst that John would find out about your staging of his infidelity causing an alimony suit.

You seduce John to come to the showcasing making all in attendance presume all was fine. Until you specially spike his drink. Causing him to be under the weather.

So, you can access his phone to reach your federal buddy requesting immunity for exchange of American citizenship throughout the country. So long as you bring down the most discreet sex-trafficking international service since John Conforte. Placing the blame on John due to their judicial connection "ooooooouuu God Damn y'all help me Jesus ain't I something like a pimp damn that bitch good umm umm."

Overtly animated but on point like a number 2 pencil. All the hard legs in the room sat back in awe how Celeste was so sharp and precise with her accusations. What made it so believable was when the once hysterical mess of Leslie switch her wining approach and barked "(sniffles of cries) yu yu you got it all wrong Mami. 11 I wasn't rescued by your pretty boy goons.

They tricked me into this nightmare you Americans call the American dream. So, there you happy now there you have it the cats out of the bag. Yeal talked to the Feds, and it's only a matter of time Celeste. Cherish your days while you can you low-life child molesting dawg…"

Awode and his goons went to work on her. As she screamed at the top of her lungs, Atrocious remarks while she curled up in a ball and screamed.

Raw could be heard through the pandemonium telling them to stop. The goons only stopped because they heard their boss Celeste say aloud "ite that's enough, this bitch is bleeding on my floor" Raw looked at the poor girl who was bloodied and beaten bad. As her lifeline was dangling bitch smacking the strand of death. He felt so bad for her. As he looked at his partner Celeste searching for the meaning of all this.

His wish being granted Celeste sinisterly said "just like ole times cuz you feel me" Raw snapped, but spoke with reason when he said "Yo Les baby check it out I dig where you coming from with all of this, but catch game slick I can't change the past I can only fix the future you feel me I'm." Celeste cut him short and growled "nah nigga I don't… I don't feel you not even a teeny bit cuz" them days is over slim which is why I'm glad you came Raw because I got a surprise for the both of you bitches.

She pointed at both Raw and Leslie. Who looked at each other in confusion? Until Awode and his goons snapped into action bringing Leslie to her knees and Raw attempting to snatch his pants down.

Raw put up a decent tussle. But was no match for the 3-muscle bound hittas. That easily overpowered the ole skool vet. Whom sent him sailing to the floor scuffed up pretty nice. They dragged him over to the love couch. Where Celeste and Atum were at the other night.

They threw him there as Celeste centered herself between the two of them. As she said "take off his pants", the goons as instructed ripped off Raws pants. Leaving him in Tommy Hilfiger briefs.

Shook as he screamed in fear wh wh what the hell is this are y'all niggas crazy." Leslie yelped as Celeste dragged the bitch by her long jet back Korean hair and tossed her in the direction of Raw's feet. As she flared up

and said "like I said I got a treat for you bitches I like to call a life for a life...
follow me because here are the terms and I'm only gonna say this once."

The attentiveness in the room was all ears. As if the whole country
was reliving 9/11 all over again. When Celeste puffed up and said, "whose
life is more precious don't know don't care, but Lee Lee it's like this I'll be
willing to spare your life set you free and arrange for you to be married to
a American man today making you a full-fledge citizen free to live your
life as you please on this soil."

Leslie interjected and said "But" Celeste smirked and said "Ahhhhh
you know me all too well honey Awwweeeee. But since your mouth works
faster than ya diamond (referring to her pussy). Let's put it to the test
shall we."

On Celeste que the goons snatched down Raw's Hilfiger briefs.
Pushing him to the couch as he barked "Yo yo chill man what the fuck
is this... Celeste laughed and then growled "Nigga man up stop bitching
play ya cards right you can come out of this victorious to with a possible
job mother fucka hold em down."

The goons held him down. As Celeste continued as she looked at
her bronze face blue Kor's watch and announced "90 seconds...you got
approximately 90 seconds. Lee Lee to make this nigga come.

With that loose lip of yours no exceptions nor a second late. Failure to
do so then I'm going to allow these lovely men to finish the job now. As
for you champ your job opportunity is simple tighten them nuts baby and
you want lose ya dick or this job opportunity can you dig it."

Raw and Leslie looked at each other. Then at Celeste and they said
in unison and if we don't entertain your sick game." Celeste smirked then
said, "Oh darling y'all already are, and if y'all were smart with only 70
seconds remaining I would get crackin if I was y'all."

Fear flushed over both of their bodies. Upon hearing the time, they
had left. Leslie not wasting no more time.

Went right to work until Celeste yelled aloud "Ummm bitch your hands didn't get you here ya mouth did honey dock 30 seconds from this Ho..." Leslie cried in disbelief. But suppressed her tears and went to work.

The sound of moaning, groaning, breathing, slurping, and sucking escaped the nostrils and mouthful of Leslie. As Raw remained stationed on the couch fighting the urge of ejaculation. He focused his attention on a painting of Mozart on the wall by Celeste's desk.

Trying his best to tune out the sexual noises of Leslie. As through every sucking of his dick sliding deeper down her throat. He felt his dick get harder and harder. Hissing through tears he stared at Celeste. Who appeared to receive such humor and gratitude in her sick little game. She was playing as she said, "she got that sloppy toppy don't she daddy umm hmm just like you like it huh."

Leslie with tear-stained cheeks locked her eyes in on Raw. Knowing she didn't have much time left. So, improvising she raised her head up off his dick and nibbled at his nuts and gouch.

Fully aware that those areas were the most sensitive for most men." Raw howled sounding like a warrior in the heat of a bloodied battle. That was not in his favor.

As the pleasure he was receiving from Leslie. Sparked from his toes igniting all the way up shooting pass his calf muscles and thighs. Burying a sensational fire in his nuts fighting the self-resistance of himself to erupt.

Sweat of perspiration trickled from Raw's forehead. As he continued to fight the urge while enjoying the pleasure of it all. As Leslie graduated Alexis's porn star status style.

As she completely got into it not caring at the moment of the outcome. Awode and his goons were disgusted with the acts Devised by Celeste sick and twisted mind. But when they witnessed Leslie performed on Raw and how her pleasure caused him to sweat.

In there on hushed perverted thoughts they selectively grew aroused. As some took deep sighs, and breaths while others grabbed their manhood. Celeste looked at her watch the whole entire time playing a commentator talking shit, and barked "Oooooouuu 10 seconds y'all how bad do y'all want it come on baby 9,8,7.6.5."

The suspense in the room was thick. The face off was heighten between the 2 growls, moans, hissing, and gagging of Leslie. Increased as Celeste counted down the idle seconds left of life or death. Breathing and panting escaped Raw's pitch as he howled and couldn't hold it anymore.

With a leap of faith left Leslie popped her tongued now able to locked on Raw's tip of his dick and powerfully sucked away. His last words were "no fair no fair Ahhhhh No Fui..time" Celeste screamed and as soon as Leslie let go.

Raw uncontrollably let loose. Coming his hot warm sticky load all over Leslie's face. As Leslie smiled while his dick continued to jerk. Shooting and painting her whole face until Celeste purred coquettish "Hmmmmm good job honey damn good job Boom." The echo of the close impact and loud sound from her Baby Blue Chrome 9.

Made everybody in the room jump for unwarranted cover. Frozen in fear and unable to hear due to her ears ringing loudly from the discharge of Celeste's gun. Her mind finally registering to what occurred.

As she looked at her blood stained shirt and hands. From touching her face mixed in with the semen that once was ejaculated by the dick of Raw. Until it was blown off now shooting profusely streams of blood by Celeste acts.

Leslie screamed loudly as Raw remained stationery in the seat in utter shock. As Celeste venomously barked "welcome to womanhood motherfucka." With one swift motion Celeste emerged behind a traumatize mess of Leslie.

Who didn't peep it coming, As Celeste in one swift motion snapped Leslie neck in two Killing her instantly as she sinisterly whispered to her corpse "Sorry puddin ain't no such thing as tiebreakers."

She kicked the corpse of Leslie. While stepping over her limp body. Making her goons tremble in fear. All except Awode her Captain of her security detail. Outside of her sex puppet and slave. With her smoking gun in hand.

Straddling on top of her dickless partner from back in the days. She zeroed in on him and playfully shivered. As if she were cold taunting an mimicking him.

When she said "Burrrrrrhhh dear god Daddy you're so cold Aww she wrapped her arms around Raw in battered consoling. He remained stationery in utter shock bleeding out profusely struggling to say "Fu fu fu fuck you bi bi bi Bitch there there there's places fa fa fa for tra tra tra urrrrrgggghhh Fuck..."

A giggling Celeste still straddled on top of him. Completely destroying forever from wearing again her $900.00 Michael Kor's cat suit. Erected to her knees she threw her bosom in his face.

That smelled of the sweet fume of Burberry. As she whispered in his ear "ummmm take your last good whiff of top notch pussy ever again in this life because where you're going the army of evil is gonna get medieval on ya dickless ass..." She kissed him on the cheek.

As she raised to her feet smiling at him for the last time. When she said "the pimp God don't like ugly cuz in the next life daddy." She raised her gun pointed it directly at Raw's head who screamed "Fu Fu Fu Fuck you Bitch yu yu you gon gonna get yur...Boom (shell casing clinging on the tile floor).

As Celeste with her cherry red Revlon lipstick lips lightly blew on the barrel of her Baby 9. Then looked in the direction of her goons. All three of them excluding Awode looked at her with this eerie petrified disposition.

They glanced over at the two dead bodies. Then looked at Celeste with her smoking gun and the bravest one out of the party of three said aloud "WELL NOW, cuz who got dem ends you, or ya boy Awode or what's ya name again homie." Boom Boom Boom "Celeste with precise aim planted 3 headshots into the men.

Killing them instantly upon impact. Watching them drop like

dominoes. Slapping the floor so hard it sounded like the Big Show choke slamming an opponent through a WWF ring.

Awode smirked with a light giggle. As he shook his head in an East and West directions. Already knowing what was in store when Celeste growled "Sloppy Wow absolutely fucking sloppy where da fuck did you find these fools huh didn't I say outsiders boy."

Awode looked at her with slight irritation and said "man these niggas said they was from Cali what the fuck you want me to do Les." She snapped then shot back with "what I want you to do is tighten the fuck up champ. God damn a blind man can tell these fools ain't from Cali please. How many gangbanging home boys you know from Cali fidget and bitch up at the sight of gun play. I told you to hire me some outta town hittas. With a serious murder game not these weak ass locals bruh."

Awode couldn't help but laugh when he said "well madam it's not everyday a man witnesses someone blowing a niggas dick off. So up close and personal I wouldn't expect you to understand." Before Awode could respond it was to late.

Celeste in her Zanotti heels snapped into action so fast that when she pistol whipped Awode. The gun accidentally went off. Sending Awode with a gaping gash sailing toward the floor.

In shock believing Celeste had shot him unable to hear, eyes bugged out like headlights he screamed "you crazy bitch you shot me I can't believe you shot uhhhhhh..." Celeste pressed the burning barrel entry of her pistol onto Awode's neck. Making him scream like a little bitch.

When she growled "fool shut the fuck up this cap barely grazed you slick..." She snatched him up and shoved her gun down his mouth and shouted "now what where you saying lil daddy huh Mami wouldn't understand: hmm that's odd; who got who's dick in there mouth right now."

She pulled the firing pin back on her pistol and stared down on Awode venomously.

For the first time in a while. When Celeste first grabbed them him and his cousin. When they were much younger tears streamed down his face in fear.

Like when he was much younger, and Celeste beat him for stealing out of her purse. When she witnessed him frail up in fear. It kicked her spirit with joy.

As she recalled back to when he was younger, and she instilled the fear of God in him. In acceptance towards the transition of power reverse. At hand she smashed Awode to the floor pointing her gun at him yelling "clean this mess up now before you become a part of it HURRY UP."

She walked back in the direction of her desk. While Awode ice-grilled her with hate. As he arose to his feet and did as he was told.

Starting off first getting rid of Leslie's body. Picking her up until Celeste bark "nah nigga leave that ho right there I got something special for that one." She searched in her phone for her contacts then smiled when she seen Andreah's name and pressed dial and said aloud "I wonder what your little kinky ass is doing."

She smiled then listened to the end of her receiver where the feminine voice said "please enjoy the music while your party is reached." The ringtone of Beyonce dope track called Such a Bigego. While meanwhile across town from the Verizon Wireless Store to lunch at Sylvia's Ole fashion joint.

"Now lie and say that doesn't taste like a slice of heaven girl." Atum had a full bite on a fork of Sylvia's notorious cinnamon crumble peach cobbler pie. That's been ranked #1 an native's request every time people frequent the establishment.

Andreah practically orgasmed as she took a bit of the fork full of the cobbler. That Atum held flirtatiously feeding her like a baby. Savoring every taste of the cobbler allowing it's flavor to swim around her mouth igniting taste senses she never imagined she had.

Lightly opening her eyes observing Atum receive pleasure from pampering and feeding her. The immediate attention she was getting from Atum made her feel absolutely warm inside Imagining thoughts that was rated to grown, sexy and mature for most audiences.

Atum smiled a row of pearly whites. That made one presume his amazing looking teeth was his million-dollar signature trademark. Instead of judging what her body was saying to him assuming her mind was the same.

He decided instead to just ask when he leaned in and said "Ms. Phillips can I ask you a personal question without you taking offense." His question took her back a little bit because it harbored no filter. Although the mood and setting was right and it wasn't like the afternoon wasn't magical.

With such indescribable chemistry. Her guard slightly went up. When she said, "it depends on what you want to ask me Mr. Smith."

Atum took her right hand into his hands and smoothly said "you come of to me as a woman that faced trial and error, but by the grace of God overcame and made a wonderful timeline of your mishap...I mean with a amazing career, great taste, class, and elegance. With a comfortable living such as yourself. Is there a reason why there is not a Mr. Phillips."

She takes a moderate sip of her juice before she answers him. When she said, "well what makes you think there isn't a Mr. Phillips Mr. Smith." Atum looked at her for a moment to try to get a good read when he said "quite frankly I believe you and me can agree that if there was a Mr. Phillips me and you would of never met my lady."

Andreah was stumped as she pondered back and forth what to respond back with. She knew he was right so in a dismissive polite manner she said "Hmmmmm Mr. Smith I never took you as the perfect young gentleman to judge a book by it's cover." Atum seeing the change of attitude that killed his curiosity.

Smirked and ended off with saying "well Ms. Phillips it's not everyday millennials like myself come across breath-taking covers that our page-turners like yourself please forgive me if I was to forward." He with his fork; filled it with more of the peach cobbler from earlier and seductively took a bite.

In front of her he licked his ips and hummed in delight making her super moist. Watching him eat was to much of a turn on to her. So collecting and pulling herself together. She flew out from left field and asked "Soooo Atum what's it like having a pimp as a mother."

As she finished her sentence he mildly choked. Reaching for the nearest napkin on the table to cover his mouth." Andreah a little nervous came to his aid.

To help reaching for a glass of water to pass to him. When she nervously said "Dear Lord Atum are you ok I'm so sorry that was to forward of me." Atum finally regaining his composure gulped down some ice cold water. An took a deep breath with energy saying "WHOA no that went down the wrong pipe sweetheart no apologizes your fine trust me rrrr ummmmm (clearing his throat)."

Silence lingered in the air around them for a few seconds. Until Atum said "Madam Celeste is not my mother she is... Andreah was all cars as she wanted to hear every word Atum was about to say. When she edged on anxiously saying "she is ya what."

He searched in her eyes with adolescent pools yearning for security. Being around Andreah was so mesmerizing to him. He couldn't explain for the life of him why this women he barely knew in front of him. He had such a raw connection with her.

Outside of finding her to be absolutely stunning from the time he first seen her. Up to now there first intimate conversation. Andreah strikingly reminded him of the mother he always wished he could of confided in growing up.

In the foster care before he was adopted by Celeste. When he attempted to answer Andreah her ringtone cut him off with the single "It ain't Tricking If You Got It" notifying Andreah that Celeste was calling. Which made her say aloud after looking around "ooooooouuu speaking of the Devil."

Andreah answered her phone and said aloud jokingly "hmmmmm guess who still got years left on there lifeline girl." She smirked at Atum who flashed a fake smile. While Celeste on the other end said "well let's hope honey because the hate is real girl what you doing."

Andreah did a light hearted laugh and said "oh you know me out and about mingling how about you." Celeste looked over at Leslie and the two goons lifeless corpse and said into the receiver "Ahh killing time I wanna meet up tonight you free. Andreah said back into the receiver "sorry girl some of us have work tomorrow and not the leisure and luxury of some."

Celeste chuckled then growled "ummm the working middle class God I love you people without y'all there wouldn't be a me baby ha he. Very well darling what time you gotta be in tomorrow." Andrea said "8 o'clock sharp why what you got planned with your mysterious secret surprising ass." Celeste on the other end smirked and said into the receiver "for me to know and for you to find out honey ha ha enjoy ya brunch sweetie and do me a favor when your done tell my son Atum to come straight home we need to talk bye bye..."

"WAIT A MINUTE HOW DO YOU KNOW I'M WITH" Andreah barked. But to no avail was talking to the dial tone. As she suspiciously looked at her phone. Then over to Atum who said "Ms. Phillips are you ok you look like you just seen a ghost."

Andreah began to look around wondering if she was being watched. She groped her bosom for no apparent reason. As her mind wondered until Atum said "what did she say to you."

His firmness is what triggered her question when she barked "Atum what is your relationship with Celeste sweetie." Atum looked at her and began putting 2 and 2 together. He rose from his seat and gave his back to Andreah. Attempting to leave Andreah spazzed screaming "Ah excuse me little boy I'm talking to you."

When she seen he wasn't stopping. She stormed after him screaming creating a big scene. Outside of the establishment she continued to scream at him barking "Atummm really nigga don't make me show my ass out here boy because I will now I asked you a question and..."

Atum turned around and pinned her up against the wall. Taking her by surprise when he growled "the answer to that question can fuck around and place ya face on a milk carton woman you have no idea how privileged you are to be this close to this bitch God you just don't have a clue." Andreah at that very moment was scared shitless from Atum's conviction and choice of words.

As she continued to listen to him when he said "look Ms. Phillips take heed to my warning because I'm only gonna say this once if you enjoy life stay away from that bitch if you know what's good for you people that's close to her is only around to serve a purpose and once that purpose is no longer of use Pow...(she jumped) it's over." His eyes flared up and they reminded her to much of the identical ones that made her despise her childhood.

Atum released his hold on her and she adjusted herself. As Atum stepped off in the direction of his car. Every bit of her screamed let him go and get low but her curiosity drove her mad.

As she shouted out "but what about you Atum what about your purpose to her how long will that last until your no longer of use to her." Frozen in his footsteps he allowed her words to marinate deep. For it was the first time in a while someone was concern of his safety.

Turning to face her emotionally fixated he stared at her for a while. Before he spoke, he seen she was sincere. But he couldn't be sure he could trust her just yet.

He shook the connection he felt for her at the moment and shot back with "minding mines will get you flatlined my lady you've been warned." He hopped into his car activated the engine and sped out of the parking lot. Leaving Andreah confused, shook, and in her thoughts.

She watched his Vehicle until it was beyond visual to still see. She looked around and caught the stares of passing pedestrians and patrons in the diner. Feeling uncomfortable she went back in the diner to grab her remaining belongings and to cover the bill.

With the stares of all in attendance. As she goes to the counter to pay with her Visa. The host there smiled and said "Oh ma'am thank you but that won't be necessary your bill has already been covered for this afternoon."

Andreah puzzled and said "what by who." The host looked at the bill and said "well Ms. Phillips the bill was charged to the account of Celeste Ann Ezter Smith the owner of this franchise establishment you seem surprised." Andreahs jaw dropped as she stormed out of the diner into the parking lot searching dearly for her car.

Hyper-ventilating pressing the alarm on her Audi Q7 key, as soon as she spotted her car she shot immediately over to her car and jumped in. Her hands uncontrollably shook at the steering wheel from anxiety overload.

But she willed herself to relax and she opened her center console and looked for her script. She popped a Oxy 80 and 2 perks and sat back waiting for it to work it's magic. She focusses on Atum's warnings and replayed the magical evening the other day with Awode and Valery.

As her curiosity and Danger Alerts played tug a war with the idea of still continuing to see Celeste or not. Minutes blew by and the effects of the drugs began to creep up her spine creating a sly smirk on her face. To unwind she turned on her car and allowed the engine to pur for a while.

She commanded ALEXA to play another hit by Ellai Mae called Shot back. Ellai Mae filled her whole exterior of her Audi with her lyrics. As she zoned out and begun to think about all that occurred.

As the drugs took it's course. Andreah drifted off to her happy special place. Were in this fantasy world she was the women she adored and envied the most D.C.'s poster child Madam Celeste. Despite the aura of danger and warning that oozed vividly off the bones of Celeste

She refused to bring her conscious to the terms that Celeste would inflict harm upon her. As she said aloud "were sisters, beautiful black sisters. She wouldn't dare... would she." She caressed her thigh while still vividly and momentarily in her zone envisioning, she was Celeste decked out in the latest fashion at a congregation like the event from the night before.

Surrounded around some of the most gorgeous young male and female staff at her beckoning call. Propped back in her seat enjoying the ride of the strong effects of the over-the counter prescription. Her phone does the Tweedy bird whistle indicating she had a text.

Brought back on the surface she fumbles her phone on to the floor. Carelessly as she wills her sedated body to grab it. With her phone now in hand she punches in her pass code to access her phone.

Once it open, she peeped it was a text from Celeste with emojis that read "do you still go on break at the same time." Andreah scratched her head and respond back with "yea why" with curious face looking emojis. Celeste within seconds fired back with "oh nothing just being noisy girl let's have lunch tomorrow."

Andreah paused as her inner gut screamed bitch. No what are you crazy she looked at her phone. Then chewed on her manicured thumbnail out of nervous habit.

Before she could respond Celeste had fired back with another series of text that said "if your unable to I understand it's just...I really enjoy your company in my line of work honey it's not common you come across genuine, loving, and thorough companionship. In this profession it's all an act with our feelings to the side until were all alone and have to put those emotions back on and sulk in them mother fuckas fo do lo...but you... believe it or not Dreah baby you remind me so much of what I've dreamed to be and not chosen to be by force (sadden face emoji) I know nothing of your upbringing, but the bond over the years I've grew for you might call me crazy, but always had this sense from above that I was supposed to protect you like a big sister... Overall what I'm trying to get at is I'm here by choice because I want to be here for you and if you give me a chance darling. I'll introduce you to a class of love that you only read about in fairy tales and mythology what do you say."

Andreah phone Ching out of control with Tweedy bird songs from Celeste firing text after text after text it made Andreah water up a little bit. Because what she read, she believed and yearned for, for so long that it angered her slightly. That it appeared to her 20 plus years later.

Where she believed the support was now to late. She struggled now more than ever to respond back. Battling with the disturbing news heard by Atum.

The joy she received from Celeste miraculous service. To now the emotional abused childhood strands Celeste played on Creating a fine tune of belief out of Andreah.

Staring at her screen as her conscience commenced battle with her irrational way of thinking. She thought to herself what if she really means it girl. Thinking aloud tapping her foot with anticipation.

Seconds flew by as she came to and said "Fuck it you only live once." At the speed of lightening light she punched the typo's and emoji saying to herself. If it get to real girl you know to do as she typed into her phone "Your on, I'll see you tomorrow babe."

Chapter 8

Paygrade

10:00 AM at the courthouse walking up the steps in an even pace Andreah is corporate down in Donna Karen wear from head to toe...

Her designer heels clicked loudly up the massive stretched Roman steps. As she came within 5 to 10 yards from the entrance doors. Upon entry call it a case of the Mondays, but vertical lines crammed pack with Paralegals, Esquires, Jurist, Analyst, and Respondents for the courts.

Looked agitated as they waited in line removing all the electronics and property. To be received through the cat-scans and examined through the metal detectors. While some created small chit chat with the Sheriffs.

While others were getting wand by the security detail. Andreah with a pure leaf tea drink in her hand. Waiting to get checked until a co-worker from behind came up tapping her shoulder saying "Hey girl how was your weekend."

Andreah looked over her shoulder and saw it was Patricia. Who everybody called Patty around the office for short with a smile she replied back with "Hey Patty it was good how you doing this morning." Patty was a older Caucasian women with dirty brown hair, and green eyes for her age.

She would fool one into believing she was in her mid-thirties due to the 3-times a week Zumba classes she attends in the next county over. Nevertheless, this preserve fox was a Jaw dropping 52 years of stocked beauty. Whose been employed down at that very courthouse for 32 years with perfect attendance only missing 14 days out of her entire career there.

Her and Andreah didn't conversate much outside of the cordial greetings, and HI's and bye's it never went any further. Andreah never harbored ill will towards Patty. They were just employed in different departments throughout the courthouse. But not for long as Patty warningly said with a sigh "Ahhhhh well dear after 32 years of all this the only thing good about the morning is one day your retirement will come, and God willing you'll be blessed to enjoy it until the Lord calls us home."

Both of them now surpassed the metal detectors, and where now being wand down by the Sheriffs. As Andreah said "Amen to that, but wait a minute clearly I didn't hear you right: Patty did you just say 32 years girl." Patty grabbed her belongings coming through the Cat Scan, and said "guilty as charged Hun you heard right, and it ain't nothing to be proud of believe me."

Andreah didn't know whether to say congrats, or feel sorry until Patty jokingly said "I'm kidding Ms. Phillips oh God I'm sorry you should of seen your face." She giggled as she tugged playfully on Andreah's trench coat who exalted a fake laugh for humorous regards. The both of them walked in the same direction towards the elevator conversing back and forth until the elevator doors open

Once aboard Patty asked concerningly "So how is Justice McConnelly treating you you've been in his chambers now for how long two and half years." Andreah said "a little over 3 years now, and I can't complain he's fair... "But" Patty had cut in sensing there was something else.

Andreah not wanting to be labeled around the courthouse as a gossip gal. Made her response short with "Ummm I don't know honestly I don't think it's my place Patty you know." Patty smiled as she went in her breast pocket and removed her card.

That smelled like rich perfume she had on by Katy Perry. When she said aloud with a laugh "relax sweetie your not on trial everybody and there mother in this courthouse knows good ole Justice John McConnelly doesn't know how to keep it in his pants which explains why your still a intern and that other little hussies is about to be partner it's just a breath of fresh air to finally speak to a lady with class around here after all these years."

As the elevator doors open for Patty's designated floor. Before she left, she passed Andreah her card and said "enjoy the rest of your day Ms. Phillips hopefully I'll be hearing from you soon." Andreah saw what it said on the card and then said, "what's this Patty" Andreah stuck her arm out to stop the door closing and when she saw Patty didn't stop and blended in with the bizzy floor packed with men and women in suits and skirts.

She looked around in bewilderment not believing for one second that she disappeared that quickly. As men and women boarded the elevator the door began to close, and she quickly hopped back on pressing the button to her designated floor. Now stepping off the elevator strutting through the lobby she's met by co-workers greeting her in good mornings and hellos.

Although she responded back friendly inside she felt concern and leery. Wondering if some in attendance were present at Celeste's event that passing weekend, now on the main floor 15 yards away from her office she is greeted by her boss Justice John McConnelly.

Whose more friendly than usual when he says aloud "there goes my number one gal of the hour how was your weekend Andreah...you mind if I call you Andreah." Hesitant she didn't want to voice her true thoughts. So deciding to remain professional she said "Ahh no your fine Mr. McConnelly and my weekend ummm well let's just say it was an experience how about you."

He walked over to her and gave her an unexpected hug. Which caught her by surprise. When Justice McConnelly chuckled releasing her from his embrace. When he said "Oh please Andreah call me John, or better yet call me Johnny. My friends and family call me Johnny."

Andreah now face to face with him studied him inquisitively. Then simply said "ah really you don't say well Jus. Johnny good chat, but if you would excuse me I should be..." He blocked her line of travel and said "wait a minute Andreah were you going in such a rush this morning."

She raised her eyes back up to him, and instead of showing her irritation she innocently said "well duty calls Johnny I should be going now..." He blocked her line of travel, again and then with humor said "understood...

but duty no longer calls in that direction oh no no no not my number one gal and partner, partner" he flashed a snobbish smile at her.

While draping his arm over her shoulder's. Then finished saying "your chariot awaits my lady right this way." All the paralegals and researchers in attendance gazed along as they watched Justice McConnelly escort Andreah down the hall.

To her new office which used to be her office daughter Leslie. She found it absolutely silly her boss covering her eyes escorting her across. Over to the office that used to be Leslie's.

Playing along not wanting to reveal her true intentions. When Justice McConnelly said "tah da what do you think." She opened her eyes and although she didn't want to gasp. Once she laid eyes on the new accessories and decor she couldn't help.

But to blurt out "Oh wow John it's it's II don't know what to say." Justice McConnelly emerged from behind her, and said it for her when he said "how about my God John I love it you're the best thank you."

Feeling like that was a bit much. She played on his ego and said, "damn so this is what making a partner's salary looks like huh, but what about Leslie." The office was spacious and beyond an employee's comfort.

As her new office window had a skyline view of the nation's capital D.C. The interior design of the office gave off a rich Persian aura and flavor laced in pink lemonade colors, purple and gold. With the most elite artificial intelligence gadgets a bailor for a stenographer would need for capital and property claim cases.

Artifacts and Accessories of prize vases, paintings and portraits of legal scholars blessed a signature ambiance to the clerical atmosphere. Justice McConnelly allowed himself to get to comfortable. As his hand fell from her shoulders to the center small half of her lower back.

Where his palm now was literally inches from her apple bottom. When he answered her saying "Ms. Daniels is no longer under our employment here I guess you can call it a conflict of interest sadly, but I'm pretty sure you understand and will be able to manage I know you two were very close but sometimes those who are the closest to you hurt you the most."

As his last words lingered in the air. His hand that before was cupped on the small center of her lower back fingertips now roamed freely around her firm, soft, voluptuous booty. Held in place with a burgundy thong.

Andreah upon the perverted groping and touching of Justice McConnelly had a instant flashback back to the day that scarred her for life:

"Allah uh Akbar (woosh woosh woosh) Ahhhhhh please daddy I beg of you stop pleaaausssseece." Andreah in a agonizing roar screams to no avail of a savior in sight. While her father continues reciting the Dun-ya while she hears her mother in a bellowing manner in defeat behind the bedroom door pleading, clawing, and crying for STRETCH her father to stop

"Mamaaaaa please help me he's trying to kill me HEEEELLLLPPPP... PAP." STRETCH bitched smacked her so hard it left her slumped and borderline unconscious. As she hung ass naked in her innocent youth bound in restraints on her knees.

As STRETCH growled aloud "Laad puppet no one can save you from the wrath of Allah not even myself. He then sickly leaned in towards her dazed state of mind and kissed her forehead. From there he traced a line with his tongue from her forehead passing her tear-stained cheeks ending at her lips passionately trying to kiss her.

Groaning in pleasure until all of a sudden "Arrrrgh Arrrrgggghhh Let go Let go Let go Arrrrgggghhh." Andreah with every bit of energy she could muster at that dire moment chowed down on her Daddies tongue. With the Devotion of a red nose pit refusing to let go.

The draw of the loss amount of blood trickling out of STRETCH'S inflicted wounds. Sent her in life or death frenzy, and him into immediate panic. As he threw a wild blow that connected to her rib cage.

Sending her sinking hard to the floor snapping her right wrist restraint yelping like a wild animal in pain. That struggled for air crying "Haaaa

Haaah Wh wh whyyyyyyyyy wh wh wh whyyyy me Ga Ga Ga Ga Gawd..." STRETCH now covering his mouth as his blood now continued to run freely oozing out the crevices of his fingers.

As he barked "You stupid crazy little bitch look what you made me do." He reached in her direction, and clawed at her cappuccino coffee brown acrobatic hips, and stationed her in the doggystyle position.

He spat at her womanhood and smacked her ferociously on her teenage ripe ass. Which made her hiss in pain and worry. Through a crack speech due to fractured ribs.

She thought for sure where broken her pleading fell to a teary-eyed whisper. As she wined in stricken fear "please dah daddy please you don't have to do this please I II I'm sor..." He mounted behind her mushing the back of her head face down into the floor.

As he whipped out his ruler size dick, that was soft. Smacking the back of her opening with it. Threw sick excitement grinning and saying "The Hellfire has special little places for whores like you."

As his last word cut the suspense of the air. With no regard of her sacred fortress of Heaven. He thrusted deep, and hard inside her.

Sending her body in a violent convulsion of unbearable pain. Fighting and attempting to gain freedom from these uncomfortable sexual restraints. But to no avail was suppress due to STRETCH'S massive strength.

As he thrusted away panting deeply out of breath. "Ahhhhhh that's it puppet don't fight it; just let go, and let ALLAH sissssss shit ummmm you so tight." The atrocious act carried on for several minutes.

As STRETCH befouled her in the most heinous way. Living up to each standard to why the chicks back in his native of Jersey approved of his street name. Andreah screamed and cried as nothing else seemed to work.

As she sat there defeated and defenseless wishing she were dead. She thought of the life she envisioned to have with her love Jeff. Now being short lived because she truly felt at that point once her father was finished there was no way in hell she was coming out of this alive.

It was either him or her. At that very moment she was praying God wouldn't forsake her for wanting to take her own life. Her groans, moans, and cries increased louder.

As she felt her perverted Father come inside her. When his dick jerked and pumped his seed deep in her womb. He howled in pleasurable delight until 2 bullets snatched the moment screaming "Andreeeeaaaaahhhhh Boom Boom..."

Back to reality in her spacious office with the perverted harassing hands of her boss. Still freely groping her body. He felt so entitled that he freshly whispered in her ear "So tell me Annie. hmmm Annie that's a cute name for me and you around the office how close can me and your relationship get."

He slide his hand now in the front. Trying to fondle his hands on her love canal. Which was his worst mistake.

Because before he could even blink and recant what he had said. Andreah with no hesitation slammed her back heel so hard into his nuts. That when he hunched over groaning in pain holding his crotch. She then turned around to face him and with no thought more into it wined her right leg back and kneed him square in his nose that upon impact she broke it.

As he slinked hard to his side on the office floor. As blood squirted profusely out of the elderly patriotic hands of Justice McConnelly. As he wept like a crying pig. "Ahh my nose oh God think it's broken ooo00ouuu you crazy black bitch I can't believe you, I swear before God when I'm done with you your gon wish..."

She grew annoyed with his badgering and felt a urge of empowerment. When she stepped her designer heel on his windpipe, causing him to choke. He appeared bug-eyed and mortified staring into the soulless eyes of Andreah. That in that moment she wasn't herself when she growled "Go on say it I'm gonna wish what huh WHAT."

Justice McConnelly feverishly tapped away at her stocking laced calf pleading for her to release him. Her captivity she imposed with her foot on his windpipe. As she flirted with vengeance saying "Ah da da da da Ah da da da da Awweee Johnny baby now you know I can't hear you when you pleading and bleeding all over my shit."

Beyond being able to comprehend her vengeful activity that took it's course she had every intention of killing her boss. Until a colleague of her's yelled out to her "Andreah dear God stop before you kill em." She came to and looked at her co-worker Jenna.

Then Justice McConnelly and hissed with a venomous smile saying "well well I suppose even scum like you has guardian angels to the rescue." She released her foot off of her bosses throat, and turned to leave after grabbing certain belongings, But not before first growling "Bet that will teach you the next time you go, and inappropriately invite ya cracka hands all over a ladies merchandise you'd better pray depending on how that women is feeling all you walk away with is bruised nuts and a broken nose."

She stepped over his bruised ego. Making her way to her colleague who caught the mid end of the ordeal. Blowing past her colleague she stopped and thought aloud saying "Here girl congratulations no one better than you deserve this position after the loyalty you just showed to this piece of shit just remember when Johnny Boy here grows tired honey of waxing that sweet lil ass of yours don't come crying to me when he dismisses you like a domestic suit."

Now stepping off she popped her in her fast juicy lil loose booty. Which made her jump with surprise? As she caught the keys to the office.

Andreah tossed in the air as in mid stride she said aloud "Good luck Bitch you'll need it Aanayoooo." Mimicking the young and upcoming rapper CARDI B. On the main floor as she surpassed the floor where she was employed on.

Awaiting to board the elevator all in attendance looked at her like a dear with headlights. As she paid them no mind texting away on her phone. To Celeste asking "Big Sis you bizzy."

As she raised her head and saw all where still looking at her pointing. The streets of Baltimore came out of her when she said "if y'all take a fucking picture it will last the fuck longer yo damn." As the elevator door open everybody preceded back to there own business

As did she when she board the elevator and pressed the button for the lobby courthouse floor. Inside she grows agitated as she can't receive good reception inside the elevator. As she curses aloud out of frustration.

Everybody inside tried their best to ignore her. Not wanting to be at the end of her malicious tongue lashing. The elevator door open and the remaining occupants hustled off the elevator. Leaving Andreah to her agitated self and lack of service phone.

As the doors were closing the tweedy bird song erupted notifying her that she had a message. She smiled as she saw the star struck emojis that she was able to see. Where coming from Celeste who said "Please tell me your still at work right now Dreah bear."

She practically lit up like a Christmas Tree. When she read the message. But then immediately grew irate all over again.

As her signal faded due to poor reception when the doors closed." Arrggghhhh this stupid ass phone uhhhhh what the fuck." As the elevator finally came to a halt and the doors emerged open.

She stormed out into the lobby, Thrusting her phone in the air praying for reception. When she said "Come on come on come on...Ayyyyyyeeeee Oh my God it's Miguel Ayyyyyycetece Mecceegale."

People screamed as Andreah zoned in on all the pandemonium carrying on 30 yards down the steps. Near the entrance where the Sheriffs and metal detectors are station. The crowd look like a unorganized ant colony.

Spread out trying to retrieve access through Miguel Security Detail, and Sheriffs on duty to reach Miguel. As Andreah hustled over to be noisy. Trying to figure out what was going on.

As she gained access to the crowd. She muscled her way through trying to figure out what all the fuss was about. While also trying to leave out until she heard a masculine voice holler over the chaos.

Thank you everybody I really appreciate the love and support. "But can anybody direct me to a Ms. Andreah Phillips office please." When Andreah heard her name being called she paused with curiosity and shot nerves with heighten anxiety as she uttered out "Ahhh ye ye ye yesssss that that's me."

The crowd parted like the Red Sea. As if Andreah's voice was Moses himself 8 yards away with a clear visual. She was able to see that the voice that called out her name was without a doubt Miguel. As him, and his bodyguards walked up to her and said.

"Hey Ms. Phillips it's a pleasure to meet you I was advised by Madam Celeste to commandeer you this afternoon. To have brunch at the most elegant place in the nations capital would you care to join me and my team." Miguel stuck his hand out for the invitation for her.

To accept and the whole world to Andreah. At that dire moment felt like it was moving in slow motion. Not wanting to reveal her obvious sterilities and nervousness.

The R & B Singer Miguel was having on her. She looked around absorbing in all the facial expressions of all the people there. While some were ecstatic for her, but majority where envious and jealous questioning why her.

What she was able to easily determine was everybody all had their phones out recording the whole entire thing. Not wanting to be the talk about women on social media that blew her chance and got cold feet she muttered out "uhhh ye yea ummm sure lead the way baby I mean uhm Miguel."

She blushed as Miguel the perfect gentleman went down to one knee and pressed her hand to his forehead. Like many of the young men before him did to her out of honor and respect. Her knees almost gave out seeing this mid-level star status icon bow before her.

As if she were a Goddess descended from Heaven. As they walked out of the courthouse lobby. Exiting the entrance doors the pandemonium increased 10 times in volume outside.

Walking down the steps of the courthouse in a security pyramid barrier. Where the bodyguards with the help of the Sheriffs. Did there best to forbade off the sporadic crowd as Miguel and Andreah in hand. Hustled there way over quickly to Miguel's stretched Excursion Limo Truck.

As the door open to the spacious limo deck. With the latest and greatest interior fixtures. Andreah was flabbergasted, as she uttered allowed "Oh my God this can't be happening am I really in the back of a Limo with you."

Miguel just smiled and instead of responding. He turned on the main TV screen with Celeste. Decked out in all white crowned in a stylish Fedora and Stiletto spaghetti strap pumps and said.

"Believe it Bitch now smack yo self-darling because you are in a limo with one of the most gorgeous looking up an coming men in the game right now. That's under paid advisement to pamper you, and escort you safely to one of my remote locations where will be having brunch on this brisk afternoon. So Mr. Miguel take care of my girl honey and don't have to much fun preserved all that energy for later this evening ok."

Miguel with a smile responded back with "Ma'am yes ma'am Madam you have my word Celeste." Celeste crossed her right leg over her left on the screen. Where she was at, and blew a kiss to Andreah and said "O wvah honey I'll see you soon."

The picture of the screen went black and when Andreah sat back and weighed everything. In she couldn't help but smile as Miguel reached for two glasses and a bottle of Champagne. Pouring for both himself and her passing her a glass saying "shall we make a toast Ms. Phillips."

She open her eyes, but still kept the same smile on her face from earlier. Accepting the glass of Chardonnay and said "Yes; Lets." Miguel then said "to a wonderful evening and insurmountable success may it shower all with joy"

Andreah smiled and thought of one better and said "and to new beginnings and women empowerment may the power of the pussy rank supreme." She clenched her glass with his and took a sip. While kicking off her heels in the Limo stretching out to relax.

Miguel took a moderate sip from his glass and said aloud "Salute to that." Then proceeded to play one of his songs. In the surround sound system of the Limo 'How many Drinks' featuring Kendrick Lamar.

He did in the previous beginning years of his career. While he looked at her in her relax state and asked aloud "may I my lady." She opened her eyes and seen he was inches away from her.

Which made her get moist downstairs. Curious and wondering what he had meant. Until he sealed all confusion and gently took her right foot laced in her stocking and caressed it.

Therapeutically rubbing her bottom foot and heel in pleasurable circles. She suppressed her gasping moan with clenched teeth. And a hum that made her whisper aloud "sisssssss ummmmm that feels good haaaaaahhhh o0000000ouuuuu boy you flirting with trouble now you better."

Her sentence was muted as Miguel kissed on two toes sending erotic chills up her spine. When he said aloud "relax sweetheart your in good hands right now all I want you to do is sit back relax, and enjoy the pampering and pleasure you deserve for the beautiful Queen you are." Closing her eyes not wanting for him to stop she laid back completely letting her body go vibing to the music.

While receiving a foot rub. From the man that sung the song that set her in a state of peace and serenity. At the very moment she finally knew what people meant when they figuratively say they felt like they were on top of the world.

The high of it all was to die for and she no longer struggled to understand why people of power why they would kill to keep it. While in that state of serenity she looked at her life from all the strife, trial, and error. Where she was at now and shed a tear of joy.

From all the failed attempts of suicide and encouragement of trying to force her father to kill her. She marvels in wonderment curious if God finally answered her prayers from so long ago When she constantly used to cry and ask to be Free of the Life she knew.

She lost faith in God of course over obvious reasons, But now as she sat in the back of that stretch limo. Receiving a remarkable foot rub from one of the finest entertainers up an coming in the game.

She began leaning towards God again as she gasped out loud over the music "Ahhhhhhhh now I definitely can get used to this right chere." As she downed the rest of her glass and swallowed the remaining champagne snapping her fingers to the melody,

Chapter 9

Wet Work

Back at the headquarters in the nation's capital of Maryland. The FBI Department. Agent Franchesa Liverro and her partner Agent Meghan Liverpool.

We're wearing vinyl blazer, dress pants, and black heels laced down with their service pistols and department jackets. Fired up speaking with the Captain as Agent Chesa barked: "Captain Bonzer If I may I'm asking the Bureau to strongly consider..." before she could finish her sentence the Captain cut her short, and announced over her. "Agent Liverro with all do respect we at the bureau have been considering your leads for the past 10 years now and everyone we invested energy and time in got us nowhere now all of a sudden you have a theory on a new lead because of a level of intimacy you believe maybe there between one of are prime suspects because of a video and photo gallery your showing me."

Agent Meghan her partner coming to her defense said "Cap I know your probably thinking this lead is." Captain Bonzer cut her short and growled "clean plus a waste of time; hell the women works for the district court for Christ sake, and never had not even one parking ticket y'all are wasting valuable time with this..."

Agent Chesa barked over him saying "Eddie please...listen to the girl please" The Captain sighed deeply in frustration as he gave his undivided attention to Agent Meghan who said "Throwing Andreah's file on his desk. Andreah Phillips bom March 23, 1977 in Washington DC,. on the southeast side in the Berry Farms neighborhood, no siblings, father died when she was a child, filed for emancipation a year shy of her 18th birthday, no prior education until the years she was 20 to 21 years old, and she attend Howard on a full scholarship on the financial..."

The captain grew impatient as he barked "and your point is Agent Liverpool." She fumbled a little in her speech. But quickly regained herself and said "Si si si my point is looking at the paperwork no prior education, any traces of governmental assistance, Medicare, nor birth record listed in any hospital back then that was operable.

There's not even a signature on her birth certificate under the alias Andreah Phillips:" It's been roughly 2 1/2 weeks since the incident in the parking lot had occurred when Andreah almost became roadkill. Agent Chesa called in a favor from Human Affairs and private investigations to get the best man on the job.

What they found was incredulous as Captain Bonzer chimed in to say "so now you're trying to tell me this women y'all getting all fired up about is a alias still doesn't show me rel. "Agent Chesa now stepped in, and said while tossing another file on the desk "it shows imperative relevance cap because Andreah Phillips is exactly what Agent Meg just said, and alias..."

Captain Bonzer picked up the file. While Agent Chesa went off saying "her real name is Andreah Smith-Bey it took 40,000 hits throughout the nation. However, we narrowed it down to just Maryland the number shrank by a quarter.

Making the work less extensive. She was born in Laurel, Maryland on May 25, 1977 to a mother by the name of Clarissa Stevens. Who changed her name 2 years after her daughter's birth to Khadeejah Smith-Bey. Accepting the faith of a organized Black Intelligent Extremist group called The Moorish American Science Temple.

Were pin pointing the interest to join these black militants was inspired when she was employed as a U.S.P. correctional officer at F.C.I. Marion. When we did the research on her employment history at the U.S.P. We came across investigative encounter reports from the F.C.I. administration speculating C.O. Stevens was transporting drugs and phones into the facility

She must have caught on to the heighten suspicion because months later she filed for her transfer papers off the compound. Up to visiting room, and transport detail then all of a sudden she just up and disappears." Captain Bonzer fingering through Andreah's file out of pure curiosity now says allowed "So who on earth is Paris Jones supposed to be."

Agent Meghan now spoke and said "Sir Mr. Jones is federal convict A3724567 his Moorish attribute is Malik Kubar Bey. He was the man the administration at F.C.I. Marion. Believed who Corrections Officer Stevens was bringing in drugs and contraband for while having an affair.

Captain Bonzer face frowned as he said aloud "Affair she was married..." Then Agent Chesa spoke up and said "engaged, but that's not even the creepy part check this out.... The Captain accepted another document from Agent Chesa and read on growing more confused by the moment.

As he growled "Jesus what type of sick shit is this who the hell is Jeffrey Thompson Jr." Agent Chesa said "Mr. Thompson Sir is the childhood boyfriend of Andreah. Ms. Clara Thompson son back in the summer of 1995.

There was a double homicide back in the city of Baltimore. On it's Eastside of the 2300 block of Greenwich Street. Were a standoff between Jeff and Paris ended brutally leaving only 2 battered women to be able to live and talk about it.

While Andreah's mother was diagnosed unstable and shipped off to a mental asylum Andreah under intensive care at the hospital was psyche warded and after a thorough examination of a rape kit. The test came back positive on the sperm analysis belonging to Paris her father and Jeffrey her."

The room enveloped in silence awaiting the finishing of her sentence. When Agent Meghan cut in and said "her younger brother Cap..." The Captain had to take a seat and collect his thoughts on all that was said.

When he said "Hold up hold up wait a minute rewind that and run that by me again. Because clearly I think I just heard you say Father and son just completely defiled daughter or sister or what was that again." Agent Chesa in a frustrating demur sighed taking a deep breath.

As she carefully explained "Captain follow me because this part is imperative that you listen; that day Andreah was raped we strongly believed after looking over the facts. That night going into that fatal morning around the comer from the double homicide. Jeff Thompson Jr's mother Ms. Clara Thompson house was burnt down.

She was lifeline transported to the nearest hospital. Residents within that vicinity back then that's still there recalled Jeffrey running up the block screaming Andreah's name. Which explains how Jeff ends up stiff in Andreah's bedroom."

Agent Meghan chimes in with "So what your saying is Andreah was with Jeff that following night into the morning which explains the semen, and secretions inside Andreah discharged from Jeff." Then the Captain said "making it consent and enough motivation for a perverted son of bitch like Paris to go off the deep end. Attempting to kill Ms. Thompson by burning her house down.

While he tend to his malicious acts with his daughter." Before they fell to a moment of silence Agent Chesa tapped in and said "which corroborates with both testimonies of Andreah and Ms. Thompson Jeffrey's mother." While that thought lingered in the air between the three of them. Curiosity ruffled the feathers of the Captain. As he relived his previous question and asked "Correct me if I'm wrong rookie, but you said this Jeff guy is supposed to be her younger brother do you care to explain…" Agent Meghan parted her lips to speak.

But was overruled when Agent Chesa said "They were half brother and sister Andreah didn't know nor did her mother tell Paris's two timing ass who was more than likely in the dark.

You see Andreah's mother wasn't the only CO employed at FCI Marion Jeff's mother Clara was also employed there too."

Captain Bonzer said aloud "talk about a love triangle who is this guy and why on earth are we delayed on his major influence on society." Agent Chesa finished as she said "well not necessary triangle sir try a square or better yet a rectangle because there was another party amongst the trio..." Captain Bonzer growing impatient with the anticipation growled "which is..."

Agent Meghan fumbled through the documents on the desk. When she found what she was looking for. She retrieved it placed it on top of the file.

Allowing Agent Chesa to say with assertion "Sir meet Jeffrey Thompson Sr. Deputy Warden of FCI Marion he once was employed. As the Superintendent in the Baltimore City County Jail. Until rumor had spread about his possible affiliation with The La Jaama Boys better known as The Black Guerrilla Family."

Secretive dealings of drugs and contraband transported in the jail by the county jails administration. Whom were affiliated under the leadership and guidance of high ranking general of BGF Mr. Taye White."

"Now when indictments came down hard on everyone. Leaving practically everyone involved in utter shock when they found out. That the iceberg that sunk the ship was the very one top advisor Mr. Taye White."

"The Superintendent Thompson whom now is the Deputy Warden at FCI Marion. Counts his blessing as he received the promotional transfer in the Feds. Working his way stealth fully up the chain of command."

"To become Deputy Warden walking off scotch free. Completely cleansed of his past. But although Mr. White may not have cooperated against him..." The Captain now all the way aware and fully in tune

As she finished her factual diabolical dialogue with him "he protects his interest knowing it was only a matter of time for his county operation to crumble. Since word was traveling quick throughout the city. Of his dealings in the county jail especially traveling to the wrong ears. So instead of allowing the administration he employed to tell on him he beats them to the punch."

Agent Chesa interjected and said "cooperating on all except for Mr. Thompson Sr. Since he was awaiting for employment in the Feds. Working his way up manipulating that chain of command.

So while his young leadership is on trial continually postponing the court dates..." Then Agent Meghan interjected and said "Mr. Thompson Sr. can have room to maneuver on Federal Compounds. In search for a new accomplice with similar interests. As his own allegiance to carry out the same financial agenda. As it was in the Baltimore City County Jail..."

Agent Chesa smiled then respond "while as soon as Mr. White is sentenced upon receiving his PSI report awaiting transfer..." Then Captain Bonzer concluded "Deputy Warden Jeffrey Thompson Sr. Will have so much clout and authority that he could authorize a recommendation for Mr. White. To be safeguarded in a camp due to his cooperation and Green Light. On his head throughout the whole entire Federal Penial system."

Agent Meghan followed up and said "making it business as usual as Deputy Warden Thompson employs Malik Kubar Bey Aka Paris Jones and the Moors to do the dirty dealing for the BGE..." ALL FOR A PIECE OF THE PROFIT leaving the Moors in the blind. Completely oblivious to knowing there working for a rat."

Agent Chesa said. All 3 were looking at each other in amazement. Agent Meghan couldn't help, but to say "Wow! So I take it business must of deceased since homewrecker Paris couldn't keep it in his pants.

He had the hots for Ms. Stevens. Mr. Thompson St, fiancée I'm assuming." Agent Chesa smirked then added "So getting even I guess he decided if you have sex with my wife to be. I'm a bone yours, and get a junior out of the deal."

Agent Meghan snickered in a scandalous tone and said "To bad he is only the father on the Birth Certificate..." Captain Bonzer had heard enough as he grew disgusted with the timeline.

And barked at their humor from it all as he said "Well quite the story ladies we've just killed about a good 1/2 and hour. With this nefarious perverted tale. That again holds no purpose to the matter at hand so..."

Agent Chesa snapped firing back with "God Damn it Eddie are you that blind. Into not seeing how Andreah is the cherry on the sundae. To blow open and expose that murderous child molesting son of a bitch Celeste and her whole entire operation. Can't you see that..."

FBI Director Tatiana Sanchez emerged in the nick of time into Captain Eddie Bonzer's office. Speaking into the thickness of the room and said "well I guess he can't agent so allow me; Captain we have a meeting in 5."

Captain Bonzer hustled to his feet. But not before first speaking to the ladies saying "Agent Liverro and Liverpool we've wasted enough time with this roundabout assumption until you bring me something concrete on Andreah that connects her somehow to Celeste and her Notorious Sex Operation permission to pursue is..."

Agent Chesa spoke over him and said "Sir what if I can prove that Aturn is the biological son of Andreah and if we get to her before they do. We could possibly slam dunk this case sooner than later." Director Sanchez and Captain Bonzer stopped dead in their tracks.

Turned back around looking at her attentively as the Director said "Well agent, you have my attention you got 2 minutes." Irritated from her forwardness she shrugged it off and said.

"Ma'am back around the fall of 95 months after the incident of her father and Jeff Jr's death. Throughout the course of that time the doctor that was bedside. By her nurturing her back to health. Had made reports of her having troubling nightmares."***

One Life-Threating afternoon she emerged from her sleep screaming for help. That someone was trying to kill her. Managing to break free from ICU to commandeering an employee's vehicle she went on a high speed chase." "Until and accident ended crucial winding back up in ICU for a longer stay than before. This time informed after vital tests she was with child. After attempts of trying to abort her child fearing the worst."

"To no avail each attempt failed. She had the baby on June 16, 1996. The same birthday of our prime suspect adopted son Celeste!"

Her partner Agent Meghan spoke up then said "who also was born in the same hospital. As her until he was immediately submitted into Foster-Care. Without a name or a mother. That wanted nothing to do with the child."

The Director in and irate manner barked "your own personal assumption correct. Both Agents looked at each other in a allure of confusion. As they both looked at Director Sanchez.

Agent Chesa said aloud "I beg your pardon Ma'am then Director responded with firmness as she cut the air with "No need to beg agent you heard me loud and clear these assumptions are your very own personal account on the facts of this investigation. Very good work Francesa I see why the Captain here remained to keep you on from the extensive work over the years you and your husband did on this investigation up til that tragic day of judgement."

Agent Meghan's face scrunched up in confusion. Making the Director Sanchez smile in bewilderment. As she spoke aloud saying "Hmmmm by the look on your partner's face Francesa I take it as she either A.) didn't know your partner was your husband or his cause of death off duty was finalize by his very own emotional wife's misanthropic view whom didn't seem to know how to balance out work between pleasure and this is the person who expects me to grant permission to go out back in my field please...

The look in Agent Franchesa Liverro said it all. As she looked at Director Sanchez with the most foulest face of hate. Her expression could muster while her partner and her Captain sulked quietly in there own thought.

Wishing they could come to her aid. As Director Sanchez continued on shoulder bumping Agent Franchesa hard. Walking through her as she growled "Your 2 minutes are up agent. But leave on a good note. Be fair warned if you so happen to bat a follicle of hair off your eyelash anywhere near this investigation."

"I'll have you and Lil miss Bebe Rexa here. Booked up on obstruction charges and removed effectively from duty. Do I make myself clear." Not a word was uttered as the Director and the Captain left his office.

Leaving the ladies outside of his office in the hallway. As the women watched them grow in distance then disappear down the other end of the hallway. Agent Chesa refusing to cry. Not wanting to portray any weakness. Mumbled angrily under her breath "it's Franchesa Bitch."

Stomping off furiously down the hallway. Her partner followed suit not uttering a word. At least not until there heels clacked loudly in the lobby tile floor. Oblivious on knowing their next move until she asked aloud "so what's the plan Chess."

Agent Chesa looked at her partner with the look. As to say bitch what are you deaf case closed. Not unless you want to go to jail behind this deep shit.

Outside of the building now in the parking lot. Looking for their car Agent Chesa said "there is no plan Meg case close signed and sealed don't collect no pass go on to the next. Sorry." Agent Meghan looked at her and couldn't help it as she barked "yea you sure is Sorry A Sorry piece of..."

Before she could finish her sentence. Agent Chesa already cocking back let loose smacking Agent Meghan across the face. So hard that when the thought in her head registered that her partner really slapped her.

The tingling fiery pain followed behind it. Making her instant reddish mark cheek swell up. As she winced in pain as Agent Chesa barked "Bitch don't you dare fix yo lips with disrespect when you speak to..."

She was unable to finish her sentence. As her partner by surprise caught her in the mouth and screamed "how dare you. Smack me like some fucking whore, and then demand some respect you sorry lying old backstabbing piece of shit."

The cat-fight between the women lasted for a little while. Until the crowd increased in numbers and a random agent broke it up growling aloud "Ite NOW... That's enough ladies pull ya'll selves together. What are y'all friggin kids what kind of example are y'all trying to set like this."

Both ladies catching their composure while checking their surroundings. When they saw the crowd in attendance was more than just co-workers and field agents. But also students from a field trip on tour around the department.

Agent Meghan snatched away out of the random agents grasped and barked "screw this, and screw you; you want to let this case go and allow that murderous sex trafficking whore walk cool fine by me you got to live with it not me you'd just get in my way anyway..."

On that note Agent Meghan stepped off. As her partner, and everyone else watched her dust herself off strutting up the parking lot. Seconds went by until Agent Chesa was overwhelmed with clarity.

Stormed off in the direction of her partner and screamed "Hold up Meg wait." Annoyed off the sound of her voice. She kept it pushing with no regards of stopping.

Agent Chesa realizing she was going to have to work harder than usual. Hustled up and blocked her line of travel. Where she was greeted with nasty words from her partner.

Who barked "Excuse you don't you got somewhere to be or does the Director got her heels so far up ya ass she literally moonwalking on your judgement." As much as that comment stung, she wasn't lying.

As she blurted out with "You have no idea Meg so don't try to act like you do." Agent Meghan growing impatient shot back with "No Chess you see I do get it as a matter of fact it's quite clear to me pay-grades is like a status factor around here. The higher your rank the more clout and authority you hold."

"To toss shade on the over-worked agents in the field. Who still abide by justice for all Outside of their bigot counterparts and superiors whom are guided by greed through malicious tactics caring less who they hurt. Once upon a time Chess you used to care about that."

Agent Meghan flared her face up at her in disgust. As she continued walking in no determine direction until Agent Chesa respond back with "So that's it huh; you got me and the whole bureau figured out now. But there is just one thing your missing which is one false move the repercussions is not just a minor suspension and your pension."

"Wake the fuck up Meg. Where talking about hardcore federal time in the name of equality and justice. All for what because two Federal Agents believe in what's right please. Come off ya high horse girl doing what's right is motivators that get people killed in this arena...hell why you think my husband's not here and I am..."

Agent Meghan looked at her attentively in shock. As Agent Chesa continued on and said "you have no idea how long I've waited to bury that conniving rice and bean tortilla eating bitch. With hard-core concrete evidence of her malpractice from her high and mighty seat in the bureau. So there you have it go ahead you want a persecute me for trying to be a worried wife."

"Trying to tell my husband not to go back in undercover on Celeste. Following my instinct and warm gut feeling. So be it I'll wear that final call all year round."

"Had it been my way my kids would still have a father. But since it wasn't I got to live with that. I got to carry that weight I got to explain to my kids."

"While whisking them off to college how much their father would have been proud of them. Through odious countless hours over the years working strenuously. To bring justice to my husband /partners killer. Plus the pompous bastards in the bureau that conspired against it."

Out of breath and a teary-eyed mess. As she continued to rant off on her much younger partner. Agent Meghan all ears now became swarmed with emotions.

Over the painless feat of her partner's dilemma. It took serious Devotion she thought to herself to keep a poker face. Amongst the same cohorts in the bureau whom conspired against the murder of her husband.

So many years ago. While on the surface executing pure calculation into her own private investigation. On the one solely responsible for the destruction of your happiness and family.

All those sleepless emptiness nights. Without a warm body of unconditional LOVE to cuddle with and reassure your affection Can weigh a serious toll on one's psyche.

Agent Meghan step closer to her to give her partner a warming hug. But Agent Chesa protested and growled "Noo...your sympathy is appreciated Meg. But it's unnecessary especially now if you truly are serious about aiding me. In cleaning up the house in the bureau."

Agent Meghan looked at her with a puzzling smile. She shot back with "Really.me and you cleaning up house! Just a second ago we was at each other's necks and you was promoting retreat now all of a sudden my girl Chesa is back why now huh..."

Agent Chesa smiled as she simply said "let's just say that I had to make sure that you understand fully the penalties of going rogue on the bureau it's not a game Meg. One false move the same government you believe in and love will disappoint you every time. I know this from personal experience honey. So if your with me now's the time to back off if you have second thoughts."

Agent Meghan looked at her partner with convinced eyes and said "There wasn't no turning around then when I picked up this gun and badge. There for damn sure ain't no turning around now what's the plan Chess." Agent Chesa smirked as she looked around in various directions

Before she reached in her pocket for her phone and turned up the volume on the transmitter she planted on the Director Sanchez Back in the office when the Director shoulder bumped her unprofessionally. Then said "Learn thy enemy as well as one know they self."

Agent Meg was confused. Until she identified the familiar voices over the transmitter. The captain and Commissioner. She gasped as she put two and two together than simply said "Hmmm smooth Chess real smooth..."

Commissioner Sanchez sounded off on Captain Bonzer. As she said "This investigation on Celeste Ann Ezter Smith has gone on now for to long and were getting nowhere Eddie. The Board, AG and Governor has their hands so far up my ass right now. That I could smuggle in Illegal immigrants through the freeway. My asshole has been stretched to with these noisy ass bl partisans in power."

Captain Eddie Bonzer twiddle his fingers back and forth. As he blurted out "Commissioner I get it trust me I do. But I think you should strongly consider the work Agents Liverro and Liverpool has done on Celeste and her whole oper..."

Commissioner Sanchez smacked her thigh and placed her hand on her hip and growled "You can't be serious Eddie. God you Know I always did knew you had a soft side for that kleptomaniac. It blows my mind how after all these years. She still is a suit in the field after all that has happened. Or did you forget that quick why she was suspended without pay..."

Captain Bonzer knew exactly what she meant. Was referring to out of all that was present that tragic day. He out of many didn't agree with the outcome nor how the negligence was plague of Agent Franchesa Liverro.

Which was why when he made Captain he immediately reinstated her back. As he protested and said "She's a good agent Tatiana come on... regardless the indifference between you two clearly. You can see that did you even look at the paperwork huh...come on did you."

The Commissioner in a dismissive manner flagged him off and said "Them days in the Academy was a long time ago Eddie. Many died, many got indicted, and those good ole memories got buried when mother fuckas couldn't by-pass ones achievements. In the bureau due to their own work ethic that was lacking."

Captain Bonzer shook his head and was able to utter out "what's wrong with being the bigger person Tati hub. Come on just look at the report. Just what if this gal happens to be the mother the biological mother of Celeste's adopted son Atum. Do you know what that can actually mean.

"Commissioner Sanchez looked at the report and the file on Andreah thoroughly. Suddenly her insides felt fluttery. But on the surface, she remained calm as she continued to flip through Andreah's file."

The agents report when she said "Tell you what Eddie you seem eager to support so how about this; put your career where your mouth is. If this information on this Andreah women is accurate. We'll pursue if it's a fluke like what my gut is telling me. Turn in your badge and resign so a more stealth and more qualified individual can take on the job what do you say."

Baffled and tongue-twisted he was faced with a ultimatum that he wasn't determined to gamble with, Despite the fact his conscious screamed at him adamantly to pursue and consider the lead. He wasn't that brazen enough to sacrifice his pension, career, and kids future.

So he cowardly twisted his skirt and spoke no more of it. Which made Commissioner Sanchez smirk, and smile at his unanimous defeat. As she teased with "Glad to see Captain Eddie Bonzer is back with us now if were done with the back and forth about these God Damn Agents and this madness."

She charged through the conference room doors. Were the seats were occupied with some of the most powerful suits and skirts. In attendance accompanied also with some of the most elitist and finest agents top of there class in the Nations Capital.

Some within the mesh of the attendees were responsible for the most notorious takedown operations in the mean streets of D.C. Such as the bust on Rayful Edmonds, and Alberto "Alpo" Martinez. All stand to the military style of Position of Attention out of respect to the rank of Commissioner Sanchez.

Whom respectfully acknowledge their courtesy and said aloud "Ladies and Gentlemen my sincerest apologies for my tardiness I'm starting to finally now accept how important the role of Commissioner really is..." She yawned then said "Oooouuuu not even ones dreams is off limits."

Everybody in attendance gave a lighthearted chuckle while remaining professional. Then without warning she activated the Power point presentation on the screen. That showed a picture of Big Susie, and other possible suspects involved in the lucrative prostitution ring up and down the East from Maryland to Florida.

Employing adolescent male and female children through a International Human Trafficking Agency. Seeking foreign traffickers fueled in the interest of money for service in the malicious discreet sex business. As Commissioner Sanchez said aloud "Let's get down to business shall we..."

In the parking lot of the Fed building. Now staked out in Agent Chesa's Impala. As she was station in the driver seat with Agent Meghan next to her in the passenger seat. They were all ears as they listened attentively to Commissioner Sanchez ramble off about the small sting operations.

Up and down the coast in local neighborhood massage parlors. Predominately orchestrated through Asians and Russians. From the club scene aspect campaigning her strong assumption of Big Susie and Nikkita.

To the junk-filled mind-set she sound so convincing. As she persuaded the masses in attendance that brought into how she merged the connection of the NFL Patriots Owner Robert Kraft being implicated in the prostitution ring sting in a Florida massage parlor owned by Big Susie.

The most recent suicide accomplishment of multi-millionaire Epstein in MCC Federal Detention Center in New York City. For his accusation in the Sex Slave Trafficking of young women to himself, and elite cohorts.

Which made Agent Meghan in suspicion ask "Big Susie No Way there not talking about that sweet elderly Caucasian women that owns The Notorious Politico restaurant are they." Agent Chesa continued to listen to the Commissioner. Not wanting to miss a word. But she also didn't want to be rude to her partner.

When she answered back with "AHHH YEA and NO you see that

elderly women is the poster child of the company for THE POLITICO. But as far as on the books she's not the real Big Susie." Able to detect the confusion all over her partner's face.

She continued on to say "The real Big Susie is a Asian women by the name of Su Ho Ming (the grandmother of Su Yun Ming). Who came to America around the time of President Reagan's term." "Where she was able to make amends. To establish for herself and extensive family buck in China. To get a taste of the American Dream."

"By participating in criminal elements for exchange of political protection and exposure in the nation's capital. Su Ho Ming found out quick as an Asian American what tickled the fancy of the corrupt pockets of the bigot suits and skirts of America. So seizing on that opportunity."

"She provided sex slaves, entertainment, food and cultural goods of trade, In exchange for liberty, commercial gain, and prosperity. From the same conniving suits and skirts in power allowing her to play."

Agent Meghan whose interest was now piqued asked "But if she is the real Big Susie what role does..." Already knowing her question she answered "Well Meg if you think outside the box, and review carefully back then how Su Ho Ming got established it was the term of the Reagan Era."

"Now although you more than likely was a kid back then. It's common knowledge to all citizens what Nixon and Reagans Administration where responsible for. One of the greatest conspiracies in American History."

Agent Meghan thought and then it hit her. When she barked "Ooouu The War on Drugs." Agent Chesa responded with a smile.

"Exactly. But don't' be fooled this plot was always a part of the plan. Them crooks up in office always knew the contractual agreements with international parties. With there resources in the Criminal Enterprise of guns and drugs."

"Was only entertained for two promising reasons and goals to be met." Agent Meghan all cars asked "Which are.." Agent Chesa with no hesitation said." The full fledge genocide on Black and Brown litigants, and organized parties armed with the same vision, and ambition to dismantle government and number 2.) Through the cries of the citizens whose families, children, and livelihoods were destroyed by the guns and drugs.

Arming the governments legislators to criminalize the underworlds passion. In lengthy sentences for commercial gain for the government. Leaving criminals lucky enough not to have been killed in the drug game.

Then leaving the agents in the field who seize the guns, drugs, and money. Healthy paydays, and promotions leaving prosperous gains unnoticed on the books in the departments evidence room. Yea sweetie consider Su Yung Ming's investment in the elderly women Big Susie. A needed complexion for the connection."

Agent Meghan sat back and allowed everything her partner Agent Chesa said to sink in. Everything exposed upon her made her head spin. As she said "so I guess Nanny Ming kept it in the family and appointed her granddaughter the Throne."

Agent Chesa announced "affirmative, but little Su is smart, but not no polish criminal like her grandmother and Big Su knew that which is why she molded her cautiously and thoroughly." "You see Asian customs are next to the most advance civilization of the times. The Europeans knew it, and most definitely the Americans.**

"This dates back as far as history travels with the whole folklore myth of the Marco Polo voyage. Who travel East to return back home to his country with richest." "The Royals of Europe and there rebellious kin of sailors, voyagers, and explorers in the New World. America realize the economic gain, but so did there counterparts. To which were the Asians preferably the Chinese and Japanese."

"Outside of the little history lesson though; Grandma Su Ho Ming was the pioneer of the vibrant Chinese American population. In the Nations Capital from the late 60's ending in the early 90's. Who passed it down to her daughter."

"Who sadly got indicted on 10 counts of piracy, 12 counts of human trafficking the list goes on. So while little Su gets hammered by the Feds tarnishing the family name back in China..." Agent Meghan counters in and says "The third generation of Ming's steps in and works vigorously to unblemished the family brand and nume."

Then Agent Chesa completed her sentence saying "making it impossible for her to be a primary suspect. She's nowhere near that level of organized crime plus at that time of exposure. When that fashion of business took it's course little ole Su Ho Ming was just a child if that."

The car was enveloped in silence outside of the transmitter. That recorded the whole meeting that took place inside the bureau's building. As both of them marveled in there own thoughts listening along to Commissioner Sanchez.

It just dawned on Agent Meghan's curiosity when she asked "Hey Chesa what's the deal with you, and the Commissioner y'all got history." Agent Chesa started the car engine and said "You can say that we both came out of the academy together me, her, and the Cap why do you ask."

Agent Meghan said "well outside of the obvious it just seems like a real competitive vibe, and a splash of jealously. Between y'all uhh I don't know did y'all once upon a time have chemistry. Agent Chesa reflected back on her memory.

When the bond between her and Commissioner Sanchez was cordial. Before she could respond she heard her partner say aloud "She reminds me so much of a girlfriend I grew up with that had to be tough due to the vicious hand that life served her." Agent Chesa snapped her neck in her partner's direction and said "say that again Meg."

Her partner looked at her and said aloud "Oh I'm just thinking aloud Chess that's all don't mind me." Agent Chsea barked "Too late I am minding yours now what did you just say."

Nervous a little bit Agent Meg said "WHAT about my childhood friend it's not a big deal CHESS she just reminds me of the Commissioner's attitude a little bit WHY!" Allowing that to simmer deeply she smacked her car in reverse and slammed her foot on the gas.

Giving her partner instant whiplash when she shouted aloud "hold on Meggie." The screeching of tires echoed loudly in the federal reserve parking lot. As she burned rubber smacking the car in drive speeding out of there like a mad women with a death wish.

Off to somewhere were the only person who had a clue was her. As her partner screamed "Christ what are you trying to do get us killed where are we going." Agent Chesa said nothing as she blitz down Independence Avenue.

With the sole purpose and mission in mind to fulfill. Throughout the heighten pandemonium she managed to utter out. "We gotta get to Andreah before they do she is our only hope to crack this case wide open."

Agent Meghan barked "how are we going to do that and who is they." Agent Chesa short sentence her remark and said "all you need to know Meggie is they for now..." "We are on borrowed time.

Every second counts call in a favor and ask one of our rogue operatives to run a check on Commissioner Sanchez." "I want a report so thorough on her that our people. Should be able to tell me her first kiss with what boy and if she liked it or loved it follow me."

Agent Meghan with no hesitation hopped right to it. With no questions ask as Agent Chesa cruised around the streets, Collecting her thoughts thinking of her next move.

As she said to herself "Hmmmm what's the chance of you Commissioner or possibly knowing exactly who are girl might be Baltimore city is but so Big." As her mind race trying to connect the pieces in the missing puzzle.

She then centered her attention back on the man of the hour Atum. She jumped back to the fatal day when her husband/partner was murdered in cold blood. When weeks after that she round up a much younger Atum for questions.

She almost made a break through in the interrogation room. Until

Celeste and her retained paid counsel busted up in the room disturbing the peace practically scaring Atum shitless. Back into silence when Celeste emerged into the room with a smile.

Agent Chesa saw the sudden change in young Atum's disposition. She had mixed emotions one side of her was disappointed. Her chance on a closed case was gone and the other side felt sorry for young Atum and his upbringing raised by Celeste,

Her partner's voice snatched her back from her thoughts. As she announced "he told me to give him at the most roughly 72 hours, But he'll do his best to make it sooner."

At the wheel she forward her partner's direction. In acknowledgement focusing back on her next move. Until Agent Meghan said "so what's the plan CHESS."

Chesa was still in her thoughts. As her partner asked her that. She couldn't understand for the life of her were Andreah and Celeste companionship stemmed from, or if they even knew cache other.

Her being a mother herself she couldn't imagine. Regardless the circumstance how a mother could be so quick to abandon and abort their child. It just didn't sit right with her.

Agent Chesa wondering now aloud "Does she even know..." Her partner then said "Does she know what Chess...Chess." Chesa she has to know Agent Chesa thought or maybe she doesn't she almost threw up as she imagined Atum and Andreah being intimate.

Erasing that thought quickly from her head. She brainstorm thoroughly on her detective work and came to the conclusion. When she said aloud to Agent Meghan "Call Atum and get a ETA on his whereabouts."

Agent Meghan got to it through the car's automated Al system. But was hindered when the line said through the interior of the car. "The phone number you are trying to reach has been disconnected or is no longer in service."

Agent Meghan in frustration growled "SHIT I knew it now what

CHESS." Agent Meghan looked at her partner. Who had a mischievous smirk on her face upon hearing her partner say that allowed.

She mumbled under her breath "hmmm...I got to give it to you kid your smart, but not smart enough." Already 20 steps ahead of young Atum. She knew from there last encounter in the gym. When she called him it would spook him out, and make him switch numbers. Days leading up to there gym session with Atum. She was able to obtain his number off one of his extensive social media sites and contact his smartphone carrier.

Putting on a dirty white lie on how she was court-order to track the whereabouts of his updated plan. Laughing she said aloud "it pays to be down with the most dopiest gang of America... Meggie get on the line with Sprint's Carrier and ask to speak with Tommy Tran. She commanded the Al system in the car to call Sprint's Carrier Company.

As the smart voice Siri orchestrated the command on the second dial-tone. A female receptionist came blaring through the surround sound when she professionally said "Thank you for calling Sprints Telecommunication Service this is Jane speaking." Agent Meghan then said "Yes; forward me please to Tommy Tran."

The polite receptionist said one moment as Agent Meghan acknowledge saying Thank You. The time lapse took about 2 and half minutes. Until a gentlemen emerged on the line and said "Sprint Telecommunications this is Tommy Tran how may I assist you."

Agent Chesa protruded in and said "Mr. Tran this is Agent Franchesa Liverro we've spoke in the past momentarily. I'm calling because of the clearance and authorization order I have from the Magistrate to obtain the new carrier of a Mr. Atum Smith. I'm on borrowed time so let's make this quick shall we..."

Chapter 10

The Other Cheek

Sitting ducked off in a occupied parking lot behind the wheel of his SUV. Staring out the window piercing through his tinted window in the afternoon sun. Thick in the business district of the Nation's Capital.

Atum said aloud to his passenger "say man why you got niggas up in the hottest section in the city moe what we doing here anyway." Awode who was the passenger paid no mind to Atum's wining ass and continued to scope the building that Celeste gave him specific orders to case out. In her leverage plan she had brewing. It's been weeks since the past incident that jumped off in the back office between him and Celeste and although a huge part of him still felt some type of way.

Celeste had a hunch for detecting such pint up animosity in her following and since she knew them better than they knew themselves. She took advantage of that and exploited it always in her favor already knowing outside of a serious sex-drive; Awode also had a flirtatious urge with murder and getting medieval on corpses.

After she ordered him to dispose of the three bodies. Back in the heat of the sick little game Celeste orchestrated, but preserving Leslie body for a special purpose. She then continued to feed Awode's inner dark demon by allowing him to unleash on petty dealers and competition on the Northeast side of the city that she knew all to well the police department could careless about the body-count in that specific section.

Awode already aware of the sick little mind games Celeste practice on him, Valerie, Atum, and many others when they were just kids, but she took him by surprise when she allowed. Awode to discipline Atum in front of her for reasons he was unaware of at the time until he put two and two together when Celeste stood over his befouled battered body from Awode's hand and growled "next time Lil daddy you ever come out your tongue sideways again like how you performed on that phone.

I'm going to cut that motherfucka out, and put damn good used to it in my notorious toy collection...she stepped over his beaten body tickling the hairs on his neck with her black spell scent from Vicke trotting away she just remembered as she paused with a snicker and said "hmmmm before I forget..." She turned around and faced him demanding that he looked at her giving his full attention.

Through racoon eyes with very little strength left from the beating he fixed his attention on Celeste who made a chill creep up his pine when she venomously barked "take this as your last warning boy the cougar booty you got the hots for...please don't play stupid with mami you know what I'm talking about...is off limits you dig that little daddy that goes for both of you little mother fuckas now I don't want to have this conversation again."

Back on the surface with Atum annoyingly keep calling for Awode's attention which made him snap saying "Nigga what... Damn I heard you the first-time champ, shit don't you know how to take a hint, and shut the fuck up." Atum never known for cowering up, nor backing down from no one shot back with.

"Homeboy that first one is for Free, but don't get comfortable thinking you can pull that disrespectful shit off a second time moe you got the right one." Awode broke from his concentration from scoping the building and sized Atum up with aggression, but quickly caught himself when he realized who the fly shit was coming from then barked back with "Lil bruh please save all that noise for one of these jokers out here that don't know you, or know any better. I got the right one he says this nigga tripping."

Awode mocked him, and went back to scoping the building leaving Atum salty deep in his feelings. It was and understatement to say Atum despised and hated Awode, he loathed him with a passion every since the day Celeste came back home with him, and practically his whole entire village from her vacation in Paris.

To everyone surprise as well as young Atum at the time Awode was only 5 years his senior, the day Celeste brought him and what Atum assumed was his kids who were much younger Valerie, and the twins, at the time. Forced to grow up fast and get served with the Devils Touch sadly at birth from his motherland to the infamous red light districts of the territories of Europe.

His 18 years of age back then easily made him look like the 28 years of age he was now. As Atum continued to allow his emotions to fester clutching tightly back on his burner. Awode shouted aloud "Hot Damn! we got movement baby..."

Atum was lost as he looked to see what Awode was shouting about when he ask "WE...what you mean we..we got what." Across the street from the parking lot was the courthouse that Andreah was employed at, as they watched along catching everyone spilling out of the front entrances eager to attend there 45 minute lunch break.

The man of the hour dressed in a casual navy blue suit, teal dress shirt and tie with and ole school Bulgari watch the most vintage piece on his body. He appeared to be in a rush still looking very much disheveled, but much more reserved from what had transpired early between him and Andreah.

Wasting no more idol time Awode barked aloud "tail that cracka in the navy blue, and broken nose..." Atum looked out to see what had him so pre-hype until he caught a glimpse of who it was, and said "I i is that Justice John McConnelly why you wanna tail this fool... Awode growing tired of Atum's back and forth questioning and antics in agitation stormed out the vehicle growling "urrrgggghhh fuck it when you want something done right you gotta do it yourself."

Slamming the door in pursuit of Justice John McConnelly, Atum's words had faded to the back who said "well nigga how you plan on doing that." Realizing his words never escaped the car he sighed in frustration as he said aloud in third person "hmmm your reasons why you decided to tag along with this remedial as son of a bitch is beyond me yo." Looking Awode direction who within seconds disappeared in the lunch hour rush making Atum slam his fist into his car horn as he brought his truck to life shouting "Lemme go get this nigga before he gets both of us cased up."

While 20 yards away. Awode's attire was casual European darked colored dress slacks that made him blend in perfectly in the Chocolate city lunch hour rush. He continued a even 15 yard pace and distance away from Justice John McConnelly not wanting to alert him, or any one in close proximity that may know of Justice John McConnelly or himself.

Which was practically the reason why Awode made Atum tag along with him because he knew his over thinking paranoid ass would keep him on his P's and Q's plus inform him of extra curricular activity that was out of place. Although his presence warranted a Bonafede headache at will over the years he began to view it as positive irritation to achieve a job well done with no errors in his murder game for hire under Celeste.

He smiled as he thought of Atum's fidgeting ass having and over whelming episode inside the car unknown about the deeds he had planned for Justice McConnelly. It was literally a matter of seconds he anticipated that he would see Atum, and his truck bend the comer looking for him which was all a part of his plan to get back at Celeste.

What she didn't know was; was that instead of recruiting a fall guy to ride with Awode. Awode instead nominated her prize possession Atum to get a taste of this gangstas shit, and to be his coverage plan in case the job went sour. Whether the job went sour, or not his mind was already made up that Atum wasn't to get out of this alive.

Right on schedule as if Atum couldn't have been a second late Awode smiled as he saw Atum out of his peripheral. He then proceeded to look at Justice McConnelly who now was making his way into the garage of the courthouse. He retrieved his phone out of his pocket and said in a text to Celeste voice activated "I got my eyes on the prize Madam I'll call you when the gift is wrapped."

On the rooftop of a vacant building decked out with a eccentric Macedonian atmosphere with busboys, waiters, cooks, a buffet with a stage were Miguel, and his crew performed some of his latest hits. Celeste and Andreah at a elegant prepared candlelit brunch table in a neighborhood all to familiar, and common to her upbringing in the notorious section of Southeast D.C.

Was a joyous, laughable Monday afternoon as Celeste swayed her hips in her chair singing along to Miguel's rich lyrics the song SHE BAD as she said "cuz she bad she bad she bad Aaayyooo sing it baby." Andreah couldn't help but smile as she watched Celeste, and took in the mesmerizing atmosphere.

Checking her surroundings she couldn't help but be captivated by the rooftop set-up and professional looking staff at their beckon call. She shook her head in amazement in humble appreciation and gratitude for experiencing a lifestyle that she only thought exist in the moves.

Celeste's phone began to chirp with the humming bird notification, which made her reach for her phone and check the incoming message. Still singing along and swaying to the beat when she saw where the message was coming from. With the same energy from before not giving off any indication of her true feeling she respond back with her message then placed her phone on the table and said with a smile "Uhuh Honey we don't do know babysitting around here ya dig drank up bitch..."

Andreah looked at her glass that was still filled with champagne and said "some of us citizens have to punch the clock and unfortunately don't have the leisure and luxury of some." Celeste smirked as she took a moderate sip from her glass then barked back "Ho...please who you fooling if you think ya domestic dispute ass still has a job with fresh ass Johnny after what you did to his nose and little pebbles...which if I may add girl was PRICE...LESS...Haaahhhh."

She did her best impersonation of Frenchie then finished off saying "then maybe you haven't been babysitting ya glass after all." Andreah with a grin flashed a playful middle finger at Celeste than barked "man fuck Johnny's creep ass he should be grateful that his nose and his nuts are the only things that walked away scathed uggghhh that fucking pervert I still can't shake his free-spirited ass hands that hours ago violated me."

Andreah was steaming reminiscing that vile moment for her and it was written all over her face. As Celeste sat back and absorbed in all her pain. Andreah's strife was all to familiar to her and for the first time in a while felt a inkling of emotion for her.

As she felt at that moment she was staring at herself when she reacted out, and said "Dreah baby trust me when I say if there is anyone who knows how you feel honey it's without u doubt me girl. From here on out you have my word anybody. And yes quote me I do me anybody take it upon themselves to believe it to be a bright idea to blink a eyelash your direction in the vilest of ways.

Mark my words they're gonna regret it with a passion in their next life whenever that maybe you can bank on that." Andreah stared into Celeste eyes and grew warm off what she said, had she seen into her soul, she possibly would of seen how sincere and convicted in every word she said instead Andreah asked a very heart to heart type of question when she said "Les...what makes a gal like you with all your riches, and clearly stardom so fond of a average problematic sex craze women from outta Baltimore like myself."

She bit down on her tongue super hard almost drawing blood as she realized how she slipped up and gave away her stomping grounds of where she was originally from. Praying Celeste didn't catch that as she anticipated what she thought she was thinking, and might say. Celeste with a grin extended her arms and said "Dreah babe; before you measure my success and paint this illusion in your head on how people of my caliber and yours are like oil and milk that don't mix.

Please remember and never forget I was never self-paid like the siblings of Trump, Rothschilds, Rockefellas, and Kochs. Honey I am the definition of self-made through and through an before that I was a batter child no different than you except the cities." Hearing Celeste's last words Andreah was able to see Celeste was all ears, but instead of showing her worry she masked her emotions and continued to listen on as Celeste carried on saying "Darling do you know why I brought you here." She waited for Andreah to respond who just nodded her head

No which made Celeste carry on and say "I brought you here not only just to wine and dine you of course but to open up to you about me, and nevertheless my stomping grounds and where it all began for ya young and up and coming DIVA." Extending her arms again Celeste; Andreah was able to see that Celeste was referring to her native hometown of Southeast D.C. which she wasn't oblivious to she was well aware were Celeste was from, however she remained quiet as Celeste continued on to say "You see Dreah your curious in wanting to know why I vibe with you so tough not considering the facts that we're no different from each other by far... Now granted you may have not been a drip baby like myself nevertheless, but it don't take a rocket scientist to see. That your upbringing of the pain your holding on to was not by choice, what had happen to you."

Andreah fidgeted in her seat, as she sat across from Celeste. She was completely paranoid and wondering how much did Celeste truly know leaving her skeptical on wanting to speak any futher. She relaxed a little bit, as Celeste picked back up in her conversation, however this time reflecting everything on her.

Celeste shared with her every intricate detail about her upbringing. Not leaving out one explicit detail except for one that was to personal and vowed to take to her grave. She shared with her about how her mother went in labor.

While working on the blade 8 blocks away from the Whitehouse. Gave birth to her in a shabby back alley next to a dumpster. By a local bar playas in the game of flesh frequent.

She skipped into a couple of years of physical, mental, and sexual abuse. Sharing with Andreah her first introduction to the power of the pussy. Instructed by the women she establish over the years a Love & Hate relationship for that being her mother.

From there she went on to share about how her mother abandoned her. Sold her off to some scandalous finesse pimp from out of Detroit, Michigan. But made D.C. homebased for living, business, and his sick pleasure.

Never forgetting to leave out even the brownie moments. When she believed she was in love with a man by the name of Raw. Until the luxury from the Pimp Game enticed the mind state of her love.

In the matter of time he made Celeste his first turn-out prepped, ripe, and seasoned for the plucking As Andreah continued to listen to Celeste spill her guts of the timeline of events in her life. While she even shared how her rebellious ass broke out of control under Raw's wrist. She ventured off into the lucrative international arena. Were she is in now due to faith and chance. Andreah's heartbeat through bad nerves increased a extra notch than normal.

As Celeste was finally coming to an end. In her spilling her guts when she said "well there you have it Hun. Through abuse, heartbreak, and bloodshed, this diamond in the rough, raised above all the BS plagued against me and made into a lucrative lifestyle such as this with more connections than the Black President. She giggled loudly not breaking her stare for one second, purposefully so she could study Andreah's body language towards her long drawn out tale that she just laid on her.

She could only imagine the thoughts that traveled and carried around in Andreah's psyche at that very moment. She definitely knew one thing which was for sure her slip up of mentioning her hometown of Baltimore.

Celeste definitely was gonna have her people all over it as Andreah uttered out, and finally said.

"Ah ummm (clearing her throat) well.. didn't take you as the women that was such and open book nonetheless I appreciate ya comfort and your openness to share that with me." Celeste grinned and did one of her most Devilish smirks that always made Andreah uneasy inside. Because she could never decipher for the life of her what exactly her grins and smirks truly meant.

As Celeste overlooked Andreah unaware of how uncomfortable she was making her feel. Celeste broke the silence and said "Hmmm only with people I love and trust which isn't many people girl." Back to the remote silence between the two as they marveled in their own thoughts.

Saved by the bell Andreah thought when she heard her phone ring. She jumped startled from the loudness of her ringtone by Tamia There's a stranger in my House which let her know it was a unknown caller calling her. She never answered blocked calls, but due to how tense this conversation was getting. She made and acceptation and excused herself from Celeste and said "Unblock your number and call back...ANDREAH... WAIT...DON'T HANG UP HELLO." She was about to cancel the call until the voice sounded all to familiar to her as she said "HELLO. WHO IS THIS..HELLO" the voice on the other line said" Andreah listen. stop what your doing and meet me in the parking lot at the Planet Fitness were we first met."

Not wanting to reveal her puzzled expression for Celeste to be able to detect. She continued to flash her a smile from 10 yards away. As she turned out of ear shot from Celeste and barked "O my God Atum is this you...how the hell did you get my number..." Before she could say anything else Atum quickly shut her down and said "look fuck all that now is not the time for all this back and forth shit you wanna live you high-tail ya asss over here ASAP and make sure your not being tracked if not enjoy ya meal with Celeste I promise you if will be ya last if you naive enough to stick around..."

The phone went dead as Andreah tried to say "wait a minute how did you know." Immediately realizing she was speaking to the faded dial-tone she hung up the phone and fought to adjust her composure as she turned around, walking back in the direction of Celeste. "Haaaahh OOOO Girl what the..." straddled she picked her head up realizing Celeste was an arm span width away from her. With a look of seriousness in her stare when Celeste asked "ummm you okay Andreah I sense that there is something wrong"

Taken back Andreah grew antsy with Celeste choice of words and her all of a sudden bold forwardness. She immediately heard Atum's voice in her ear in that diner parking lot fair warning her you have not the slightest idea how dangerous and deep shit can get for you'. Now heeding and believing in Atum's alerts she thought quick on her feet as she stared down with Celeste and said "damn it's that obvious huh."

Celeste instead of answering just continued to stare her down. Which made Andreah come up with a lic and say would you believe it my psyche doctor called herself cussing me out because I missed an appointment that I scheduled and had to come out of my pocket to pay for haaa that women something else." Andreah laughed boisterously trying to lighten the mood back to the original chatter and humor it once was.

Celeste turned on her heels and made her way back to there table, and said "hmmmm! agree women must be crazy to try to cuss out a women whom compensated her for a appointment she missed over a couple of weeks ago care to explain." Celeste now at the table centering her attention back on Andreah who was fumbling all over herself trying to keep the lie alive when she said "I know right and Darling you know I would love too, but I'm gonna have to make a rain check if I want to make it on time over to her office to get our script...you know these white folks don't play about timeliness."

Celeste smiled, but it wasn't a smile of joy, it was a masked smile of disappointment. But not wanting to make Andreah aware she charismatically said "Awwwwee hmmmm(she pouted like a spoiled little brat just when it was getting fun. well can't be to mad at you especially since you're going to get our goodies." They both now giggled like school girls from Celeste's playful manner she grabbed Andreah's filled glass of Champagne as well as her glass and asked "Dreah honey you trust Les right."

Andreah was wondering where that came from and didn't realize how much she recovered quickly. Wasting away some of Celeste's suspicion when she responded back with "BITCH WHAT.I should be asking the same question." The women stared off at each other for a brief moment until Celeste thought wise of the situation then said with a laugh "To trust Bitch... Andreah masking her sigh of relieve clicked her glass and said "To trust yea I like the sound of that right there ummm.."

Andreah knocked back the glass polishing the entire bubbly Celeste chuckled as she retrieved her glass walking back to their dining table as she said "I'll have my men drop you off at your car, and as for as work don't worry about Johnny Boy he'll heal someone owes me a favor anyway you'll be back at work by tomorrow trust me." Andreah shot back with "Thanks, but no thanks Les I'd rather be dead than going back to work for that piece of shit..."

Celeste laughed frightening her because it wasn't your ordinary cordial laugh. Of a close friend it was one of those laughs of a person that detected BS and wanted to set the record straight when she said "hmmm be careful what you wish for honey. Andreah paused then said "Come again" then Celeste said "I said who said anything about working under Johnny...ha ha you said it yourself that I practically service your whole entire staff or did you forget that quick."

Andreah smirked, but then came Celeste's men ready to have Andreah escorted out. When Celeste said "hmmm it pays to have connections girl, but you should already know that slick...Anhh you better get going baby before your late. You know how timely them white folks can be."

As Andreah was walking out Celeste's last statement gave her chills.

171

She fought with her conscious wondering if Celeste knew something she didn't. Her anxiety levels were flushed as she was actually overtly to excited to get out of there.

Back at the table with Celeste: she removed a Virginia Slim out of her bougie ass cigarette compartment and sparked it up. A waitress came to remove all the dirty dishes off the dining table and when the young lady went for the glass. Celeste grabbed her forearm with the strength of three men scaring the young waitress.

When she growled "Bitch bye..." that's all the young girl needed to hear to high-tail it on outta there while Celeste channeled her attention on the glass retrieved her phone again instant messaging Awode...while meanwhile on the other side of town.

"Please you guys please you don't have to do this. Whatever this is about I can make this right I swear... Pow! The sound of Awode's hook when it connected to Justice John McConnelly's jaw sounded like a gun erupted off in the quiet mist of the night. Atum cringed off the sound of the impact knowing that, that sound he heard was the bones of Justice McConnelly jaw shattering in two.

His assumption was solidified when Awode growled "white boy shut the fuck up talking about whatever this is about you can make this right well how the fuck you gonna do that if you have no idea what this is about huh." With venom Awode spat; as Atum sat back and watched him in rare form as Awode turned to him and barked "Yo A. Stop standing there looking stupid and tie this motherfucker up bruh hurry up." Awode threw the rope at Alum whom jumped, but did as instructed not wanting to receive the repercussion from Awode's crazy ass if he said NO.

Hours ago Atum recalled back to when he bent the corner hot on the pursuit trailing Awode. When he saw him tailing what appeared to be Justice John McConnelly dispersing into the parking lot to his car. Thinking back on it Atum was so puzzled behind the wheel. As he turned into the parking lot with suspicion. That as he passed the young man in the toll booth. Hooked a sharp right at 15 mph he rode approximately 10 to 12 yards and hesitantly stomping his foot on the brake.

There appeared Awode out of nowhere catching Justice McConnelly completely off guard. Smacking him upside the back of his head with the butt of his gun. Sending him sinking hard to the floor like an anchor dropping to sea-level.

Completely out cold Awode anxiously looked around trying to see if anyone was in sight. As he growled at Atum at the wheel what are you still sitting behind the wheel for cuz, get cho ass out, and help me grab this motherfucker." Atum frozen in fear; needed time to ready himself. Just weighing in all that just transpired.

Then in seconds he hopped out of his car and ran over to Awode to assist, who growled "man hurry the fuck up little nigga before we get 25 to life with your slow ass, grab his legs champ, come on." With a urgency they both hustled back quickly with Justice McConnelly in tow tossing him in the trunk of Atum's car.

While Awode threaten and barked orders at Atum to get his narrow ass in the car and get them the fuck out of there." Atum.. Atum.. ATTUUUMMM nigga snap out of it" Awode jabbed him in his solar plex causing him to lose his breath and immediately snap out his daze back into the apartment all three of them were present making him shout "pussy. GOD what the fuck moe why you punch me so hard."

Awode barked back "Nigga if you think that was hard motherfucker daydream again, and see what happens. Now tie this cracker up before I get mad." Atum matched his glare, but with no verbal debate went to work hog-tying Justice McConnelly who at that moment couldn't contain himself as he uttered out "Awweee come on guys please man can y'all at least tell me what this is about pleeeaaassseee..."

Awode smiled as he grew irritated off the sound of his voice and decided to silence it with Electrical Gray Duct Tape. Muffled jump off the tape as Awode listed into the air saying "Ahhhh finally bonehead here is now starting to answer the right questions." Awode circled around Justice McConnelly like defenseless prey then took a seat across from him.

In a love chair all to familiar to him as he continued on to say "Well Johnny let's see hmmmm where to began...Oh how about your weekend, how was it anything out of the ordinary now this is where you talk." He snatched the tape that was on his mouth. Disregarding the pain he inflicted on him ripping off his Stache and stubby chin hair as he pleaded crying "Ahhhh this weekend I ahhh I believe I was with my wif..."

Awode placed the tape back on his mouth. Then played along and said "I'm pretty sure Johnny ole pal your familiar with the ole saying "You Sir have the right to remain silent anything you say can, and be used against you in the court of law unfortunately you have no right to any attorney which believe me, and you can agree is a waste of tax-paying citizens dollars anyway." Without warning Awode removed a mini handle size metal sledgehammer, and with thunderous coordination slammed it down on Justice McConnelly's left pinky finger breaking it instantly.

The coiling howl from Justice McConnelly made Atum cringe and jump from Justice McConnelly's bounded restraints as Awode stated "Strike the first juror please your Honor the goons of the Southeast District of Columbia ask that this juror be removed from the panel. Sheriff you care to do the honors." Awode looked at Atum who appeared disoriented and confused as Awode reached into his back pocket and pulled out some wire cutters passed it to him and said "chop chop baby boy." Atum looked at Justice McConnely who continued to howl, scream, and plead.

Atum with his eyes traveled back and forth between a petrified looking Justice McConnelly, and the wire cutters. He was frozen in fear as Awode's patience was wearing thin and grew tired of waiting for Atum to make up his mind as he barked while sucking on his teeth Pssssshh such a shame...somethings you gotta do ya self." Awode walked towards Justice McConnelly whose eyes grew as wide as headlights wailing like a pig to no avail of no hearing.

With pleasure he grabbed Justice McConnelly's mangled broken left pinky finger and with the wire cutter proceeded to cut all the way down to the grissle of the bone. Hearing the sound of the agonizing screams, and fleshy tissue, meat, and bone being severed by the wire cutter. Atum's stomach became uneasy and at seeing the blood squirt from the severed finger that fell to the floor.

Atum vomited, but immediately darted to the connected bathroom to the master bedroom decorating the floor along the way to the toilet. Awode mumbled under his breath "Pussy.......I always knew it umm umm umm." He grabbed Justice McConnelly's pinky finger off the floor, and parted his lips to say "you'll have to excuse my partner Johnny, he's a sucker in a half, when it comes to this gangstas shit which is part of the reason I encourage his ass to tag along with me."

Although Justice McConnelly could careless why Atum was there as Awode continued on to talk. What he failed to catch due to the excruciating pain he endured. Was his master plan in play he planned to orchestrate in his favor by killing Justice McConnelly, and then pinning the murder on Madame Celeste's precious Atum.

Atum made it all to easy for Awode when his weak ass threw up all over the crime scene, and outside of the previous things he had touched in the apartment. It wasn't shit for him to do a thorough wipe down of the place and kill Justice McConnelly upon Celeste's orders. Then finish the job on Atum by taking him to a diner to grab a bite to eat. Then poison his meal.

Then from there write a suicide letter impersonating him as to why he did it and how he could no longer live with himself. Over the years Awode has been patiently waiting for his moment to come out of being Atum's shadow. In this dysfunctional family and business.

It troubled him how much affection Celeste showered Atum with than with him. When Celeste needed anything from international exposure, new recruits, A-Listing clientele, to a serious murder game on a job. Not to

175

mention taking the risk of trafficking sex slaves young males and females from France to Virginia bringing them from there to D.C.

Not only was he her go to guy, but he requested the workload with a smile. Now feeling under appreciated and still second to her Atum as he brainstormed. New thoughts entered in his mind.

Now as he thought bigger into his scheme of after he finished off Atum by framing him. Take it a step closer and also eliminate Celeste leaving the lucrative throne to him and his cousin Valerie A Devilish smirk littered his face as he shot back at Justice McConnelly "now where were we..that's right a juror was removed from the panel and if you continue to play dumb with me Johnny like you really don't know why we're here then we got 19 more jurors to go and that's including item prank ass hoes slick…"

Justice McConnelly immediately knew right then and there why he was practically beat to a bloody pulp and tickling the strands of death. Tears streamed down his face as he wished hours ago that he could be able to go back and changed what he did back in his office with Andreah. Awode doinked him with the severed bloody finger then barked "hmmm you play pussy Johnny Boy and you bound to get fucked Champ so let's try this again."

He snatched the tape off of Justice McConnelly's mouth again. Who now cried out and looked disheveled in the face as he pleaded "ple ple please man if this is about Ms Phillips I can explain." While meanwhile five yards away in the extended bathroom:

The sound of vomit splashing inside the toilet hitting the water. Escaped out of Atum's muscled chiseled figure as he fell next to the toilet on his side uncontrollably breathing rapidly. Hearing the gut curling wails from Justice McConnelly and imagining all over the brutal episode Awode was playing out, made Atum reach for the toilet again and practically hurl up his guts.

Coughing viciously now sitting up on his ass he was able to utter out "umuggghh come on Atum pull yourself together moe uuuggghh.." He looked around the decent size bathroom and the decor was feasible in a homely middle class way. Rising to his feet now standing erect he paused as he caught a glimpse of something that was all to familiar to his memory.

He walked over to the door were it was hanging freely on the robe hook and said "hmmm whose body do I remember seeing you on before." Speaking aloud with the expensive gown in his grasp. He pondered back in his mental rolodex until it hit him like a sharp right round-house "Oh Shit Andreah."

He dropped the gown and took a step back marveling in the new profound news. His mind was in a series of curiosity that was dosed with a entrenching flame of questions such as how did this gown get here? Is this her place? Were is she? Oh God her. Awode, and Valerie were at the auction, but wait that was in the premiere room wasn't it? Why are we doing this here?

His mind was on overdrive with question after question. He had not the slightest idea what to do, so he did what came to mind and bolted out of the bathroom and screamed "Awode stooopppp..." Awode turned around looking at him with the look as if he lost his mind as he barked "Nigga stop what...man park ya weak ass over there and shut the fuck up I'm almost done with this mother. Click Clack" the sound of Atum's 9mm Berretta captured the attention of all in the master bedroom as Atum growled "you make me repeat myself again moe the next sound you hear from this chrome is gonna split your dome nigga..."

Awode with his back still to Atum with the wire cutters in hand chuckled demonically. As he dropped the wire cutters down to the floor in the pile of nine fingers from Justice McConnelly, He turned to face Atum and began clapping as he said "well I'll be damn slim check you out little bruh how's it feel huh...holding another mans life in your hands having the power to do with it what you please."

Atum tried his best not to show his fear. He never shot a man ever in his life, let alone held a gun to one as he pleaded "Awode bro don't make me do this please let's just..." Awode cut him off, as he grew disgusted with Atum's pleading approach when he barked "Nigga Let's just what! Walk

177

out of here like this shit didn't happen. Wake the fuck up Atum welcome to the flip side of the coin in the game with ya sheltered ass niggas like you make me sic." Atum hearing enough, fire back with "man fuck you Awode are you serious right now bro, all this madness over some jealousy shit you got towards me, and Celeste manipulative abusive ass. Your sick you know that, if only you knew how much I wish you can have the privilege, on what you got fucked up in your head you believe I'm rewarded...

Awode laughed uncontrollably and hard so hard that it disturbed Atum. With his gun trained on Awode he spat back with "you seriously are stupid you know that... WOW growing up as kids I knew you were a little special and green to the game but you honestly believe this shit is about your position in that bitches empire. Nigga fuck you, and that scandalous whore this is about seniority and clout motherfucka."

Atum was lost and it was written all over his face, as Awode continued on to say. "Before that bitch came to Paris, and found me that whore was nothing more than some parking lot pimping Back-page water-down pimp surviving off of short-stays and golden showers on tricks maxing out on credit card limits in thrift stores, and Rainbow retail stores trafficking petty ass drug orders for radical militants in the pen. Who more than likely were getting high off the shit. With you as her prize-fighter raking in the most coin y'all wouldn't even have an Empire if it wasn't for me.I was the one that introduced her green ass to real playas out of the red-light district. I was the one that taught her how to finesse, prep, and turn a Foreign Exchange Student into a prize-fighting Ho...I was the one that got her to upgrade her profession into the International Market of Human Trafficking, put down a impeccable murder game to keep her hands clean and the fortress guarded and protected..."

Awode inched closer towards Atum making sure Atum's focus was still on his words as he finished off saying "And now I'll be the one to kill you, this piece of shit behind me, and bring down the most lucrative sex-ring in the land providing it with new management Me and Val the true polish playas of this game. so what do you think mama's boy how does that sound." Now within few feet away from Atum as Awode continued to creep. Atum was zoned in on him and allowed everything he said to fester in deep he had to admit although Awode was next level crazy he admired his drive, ambition, and loyalty to the game until the person he believe was his student, but now boss violated and now that same ambition once motivated in the interest of Celeste was now overturned and hell bent on seeing that very same women destroyed.

If only Awode was able to see how that same profound hatred he has for Celeste now Atum lived with that veil of pain and animosity fresh out of Foster Care as he said "hmmm sounds like you've been planning this shit for quite sometime now Awode there's only one problem." Awode smirked as he was ready to make his move counter-attacking Atum he slightly chuckled under his breath feeling as though Atum was oblivious to what he was about to do which made him sarcastically say "(Ha Ha) and what's that champ." Atum with all seriousness stated "ummm how do you get away with smoking a nigga that not only has the drop on you, but has been planning for the same thing, but has just been patiently waiting for his moment."

Barking of a dog close by could be heard distracting the attention of the men in the stand off Awode believing he'll never get another chance sprung into action at the gun "Pow..." the gun went off as the men began to tussle over the burner throwing down like there lives depended on it. There struggle and malicious brawl carried on for 2 to 3 minutes as they both now had control of the gun, and one was able to manipulate the trigger quicker than the other

"Pow..." a gut-wrenching wail sounding like a wounded animal escaping off the lips of no one other then AWODE. Atum with his gun now trained back on Awode. Who was sprawled out on the ground clinging on to life, not leaving nothing to chance he planted two more bullets in his body for reassurance and said aloud "never judge a book by it's cover Moe."

He remained stationed there savoring in the moment at the kill bewildering himself amazed at what he did. Reality kicked in and his motor skills shot from slow to panic as he looked around not knowing what to do. Awode's phone ringed and Atum mind screamed at him telling him to leave it alone and high tail it outta there, but his heart told him something completely different. Ignoring his judgment he kneeled down near Awode's corpse rummaged through his pockets and pulled out his Galaxy S5.

He was able to see that the incoming missed calls came from Celeste as well as the text that read "is it done darling." Atum was confused until he looked over at Justice McConnelly a fingerless mess, and walked over to him ripping off the tape barking "you got 15 seconds to explain why Celeste wants you dead starting now.

"Justice McConnelly was out of it mumbling over his words as he said "ple ple please come on man all I did was fondled Miss Phillips backside please Sir yes I was wrong, but not deserving of death...please Atum you have my word I'll make this right I'll hire Ms. Andreah Phillips back in my chambers better yet I'll speak with the other Justices, and do one even better and have her as a Justice on the First Circuit panel she's more than qualified just please don't kill me I'm begging you." Atum bark back "wait a minute hold up Johnny rewind that back what the hell does Andreah's assault got to do with why Celeste wants you dea..."

Atum paused as a light bulb clicked in his head and brainstorm back to the interest of Andreah years back when she first started to receive service from there agency. At the time Atum was never able to put a face to the mystery women Andreah. But he was fully aware of how important the women was to Celeste and the agency if she could be tamed.

Now after siting back and listening to Justice McConnelly babble on it all made sense now to him as he said aloud "Oh you Grimy, Slick, smart son of a bitch damn your good." Sirens could be heard in the far far distance gaining closer making the strand of hairs stand straight up on his neck and forearms. He grabbed his phone out of his pocket and called

Andreah it took a moment for Andreah to answer which agitated him on the 6th ring he heard a voice say "Unblock ya number, and call back…" he sensed she was on the verge of hanging up which made him spazz saying "ANDREAH…..wait hell don't hang up hello."

He could tell she was puzzled and possibly confused on the other line which made him check his GPS tracker he had planted in her phone the day he had his boy hook her up when he said "Look Andreah stop what you're doing and meet me at the Planet Fitness were we first met." She muttered off at the mouth which made him detect due to where she was at according to his GPS Tracker that she was right in front of Celeste. Knowing he was on borrowed time he sounded off in the phone saying "Look fuck all that now is not the time for this back and forth shit you wanna live bitch high-tail your ass over here ASAP and make sure you're not being tracked, if not then enjoy your last meal with Celeste I promise you it will be your last if you naive enough to stick around."

He ended the call and from there he proceeded to leave until he heard Justice McConnelly. Whimper in tears from the lost of blood and excruciating pain suffered and that surged through his body like lighten bolts. Stopping in his tracks cutting his eyes over his shoulder back in Justice McConnelly's direction now crying and whimpering louder

Atum with his gun in hand watched along as Justice McConnelly pleads "Come on Atum you don't have to do this man please I told you everything you wanted to know I promise I won't say nothing HELP HELP SOMEBODY PLEASE I'M IN HEAR HE'S TRYING TO KILL ME…...Come on man you don't got to do this HEEEELLLLPPPP SOMEBODY." This continued on for seconds more as the sound of the sirens gained closer, and closer leaving Atum with no choice as he said aloud out to Justice McConnelly his last words "I'm sorry Johnny, but you know I can't do that you leave me choice……….NO0000000000 FUCK YOU YOU BLACK BAST…Pow…Pow…Pow…

181

Chapter 11

Pimp Ordie

The Concierge up front of the stretch limo employed under Celeste spoke into the intercom and said as they cut the corner a foot away from the courthouse. Madam Phillips were coming up on your working quarters in approximately 25 seconds. She almost forgot the Concierge up front said something since she was so pre-occupied in her thoughts.

The car came to a halt in front of the courthouse. The traffic was still thick, but somewhat coming to a halt. Since the courthouse was closing and everybody was just now getting off work.

Jumping out of the car the Concierge made his way over to the back of the limo. He opened the door and before he could greet Andreah and extend his farewells. Andreah like an anxious puppy barricaded in a cage all day waiting for freedom.

Darting out of the limo with an urgency in her step. Before the Concierge could extend his warmest pleasantries and good-byes. The Concierge continued to watch her until her figure dispersed into the parking lot.

Once she was out of hind sight the Concierge signaled into his ear-piece and said the package is in pursuit..." Andreah blew past the valor at the toll booth. Who was used to her saying Hi and Goodbye. But as he saw her urgency and eager pursuit to get to her destination. He chucked it up as it was nothing and resumed back to what he was doing.

Andreah retrieved her phone and goes to her recent calls and cursed aloud. When she saw that he called from a blocked number. Running out of options she hustled over to her car. After searching for it in the spacious parking lot garage for a few minutes.

Able to locate it she then deactivated the alarm, but realized something was odd. Because when she pressed the button it actually activated the alarm instead. Puzzled at first she looked around but felt someone was watching her.

Noid and realizing the time was ticking she brushed it off and deactivated the alarm again. Now hopping into her car. As she brought the beast to life she hopped on her phone and speed-dialed a friend. When the party answered she fired off saying "hey Connie I need a huge favor."

Across the street from the courthouse staked out in an Impala listening to a Country song off the radio called (It was Meant to Be by Bebe Rexa). People were piling out to the streets from the courthouse and near facility storefronts getting off of work. Heading to the vehicles, ready to go home after a long day from a case of the Mondays.

The evening traffic in the business district was about to commence. As restless employees fasten there seat belts and get in there motor vehicles to head home for the night as Agent Meghan excitedly said aloud "O my God Chess look..." Agent Chesa wasn't a sleep, but she was resting for a moment as she snapped to and said "What...huh....damn...here I go."

Fully alert now Agent Meghan said to her "there's our girl right there coming out of that stretch limo and she moving fast too." Agent Chesa using her digital binoculars made a match at visual and said aloud "well I'll be damn she looks so much different in person." Agent Meghan fired up open the door ready to pursue until Agent Chesa grabbed her and pulled her back into the car and said "Whoa Whoa Whoa princess now what exactly do you think your doing and going."

Agent Meghan not appreciating being babied barked "what does it look like I'm doing Chess I'm bringing her in for questioning..." Agent Chesa politely cut her short and said "Ok bring her in for questioning where and under what grounds did you forget that quickly Meg that were going ROGUE..." Agent Meghan coming to her senses retreated her thoughts and shut the door slowly as Agent Chesa began to say there you go Meggie that's my girl now you using your head sit back and relax let her come to us trust me."

Andreah like a speed demon cutting comers all around the parking lot garage. Was now up to the toll booth with her ticket in hand to give to the valet man who with a warm smile said "Good evening Ms. Phillips how was your day today.." She didn't realize in her upbeat tone and manner deeply indulged in her phone call that she accidentally flagged him off. The young man was usually always flirtatious with her, but today he was able to read that something was off.

Choosing to be quite. He quickly accepted her ticket and activated the pole to be lifted by the press of the button inside the toll booth control panel system. "Hold on Hold on Connie somebodies on the other line."

She flashed over and said "HELLO." Atum with conviction said "are you at the courthouse yet." As the toll booth pole lifted, Andreah shot out of there a nervous wreck skimming the roof of her Audi against the pole that wasn't lifted all the way. In such a rush paying no attention to the young man and caught up in her phone call she barked over the line "I'm leaving now Atum, no more games now tell me what the hell is going on because this shit is starting to spook me the fuck out."

She hooked a sharp right onto the busy street almost causing an accident. As cars honked there horns at her reckless driving. Atum on the other line told her listen all the questions you got Andreah save them for when we meet up remember what I said make sure nobody is tracking. Andreah snapped not appreciating being short ended when she barked "BULLSHIT Atum. that's not good enough for me now how do I know for sure your not trying to line me up to get killed huh…"

Atum losing his cool shouted over her because bitch if I was trying to murk ya ass shawty I would've never murk the fool that was trying to set you up with a stiff one at your apartment. The line instantly got quiet, as both parties remained entranced off of what each other said. Atum was kicking himself in his own ass how he accidentally slipped up and said that over the phone.

Frustrated he said nothing more and hung up the phone. Which made Andreah screamed "HELLO...ATUM WAIT..HELLO..." She cursed at the top of her lungs and threw her phone in the passenger seat telling the voice automated car system the command "ALEXA play Keyshia Cole's track called I Just Wanted To Be Over."

"Look..... Look Chess there she goes" Agent Meghan roared with excitement Agent Chesa then said "She's moving pretty fast too she completely almost totaled that car." Agent Chesa turned on the car and smacked the car in drive as Agent Meghan said "Hurry Chess were losing her." Agent Chesa said nothing as she simply just looked at her partner and said "buckle up Meg it's about to get bumpy."

Keyshia Cole's hook to the banging track I just Want It To Be Over back around 07 and 08 when it came out popped off the surround sound speaker oozing out a crispy sound with Keyshia's vocals. As Andreah vibe to the melody trying to make sense of all that was going down and all that was being said. She couldn't fathom the thought nor wrap her head around Atum killing in her honor.

Barley knowing the man she was able to tell that he didn't strike, or come across as the killing type. Growing up on Baltimore's cast Side she seen things she wished she didn't, she brushed paths with people that fit that bill. Through her experience Atum nowhere near qualified, but if everything he said was true at the moment she didn't know what to do.

Her emotions were all over the place. Thinking in overdrive about all that transpired. With her relationship with Celeste, the small details of her enterprise, all the powerful and famous people she employs and service. Down to her short-term relationship with Atum and how it became satisfied through the shedding of blood.

She was raw and was oblivious to what relationship to feed on her emotions towards either Celeste or Atum. Running her fingers through her hair she didn't even see she ran a red light. She gained a little more further in distance until an all to familiar siren snatched the evening wind with Woop Woop...Cop Sirens."

She looked in her rear view mirror and sighed deeply getting even more frustrated as she barked "You gotta be fucking kidding me NOW WHAT urrrggghhhh." She drove a little more further in distance until she pulled over. On the side near the freeway that takes her to her psyche's office and the Planet Fitness Atum instructed for them to meet.

She smacks her Audi in park and goes into her glove box for her credentials. Unable to find it in there she then thoroughly checked her center console and the driver mirror flap. Then quickly remembered "Fuck my license and registration is in my purse, in the back of the trunk."

She went to open her door, but thought it wasn't wise of that when she said aloud "bitch wait bad idea you giving these crackers a reason." She took her hand off the handle then decided to retrieve her purse from the back compartment. Pulling out the armrest to the backseat to gain access into her trunk.

Rummaging through her trunk from the backseat she's feeling everything besides her purse. One thing in particular she feels is something she can't put a finger on. As to what it might be until she felt further and snatched her hand back immediately due to how ice cold the object was.

"Haaaaahhh what the Fu..." Andreah gasped in fear, but curiosity because her whole being screamed the worst, but her mind screamed to her to make sure." Andreah fearfully inched closer her hand back in the trunk. But this time climbed back there halfway to get a visual.

She hit the light in her car to decease the darkness in the trunk, once she did that her suspicion was quickly answered. When she faced off with an ice-cold lifeless corpse that was an all to familiar acquaintance. When she screamed "AHHHHHHH OH GOD NO NO NOO000...

She covered her mouth as tears blitz out of her eyes for her office daughter Leslic. When she cried out "OH GOD LESLIE NO NO please

GOD...NOO000." She heard a car door slam bringing her back quietly to reality. She muscled up enough courage to rummage pass Leslie's corpse in the trunk in search for her purse.

Every second that ticked was a footstep closer the Patrol Officer, who was literally inches from hearing his walkie talkie. In the nick of time found her purse and grabbed it. Then quickly lifted it up the backseat and shut it. Hustling back to the driver seat trying to buy time.

She pulling the flap down in her driver window doing her make-up. Within seconds a knock at her driver side window startled her. Rummaging her hand through her hair jumping into character she announced "Well Hello officer what can I do for you this evening."

She could tell immediately by his posture of this douche bag he was a stickler and possible asshole. She was never a firm believer in chance and luck. But today she wouldn't mind being favored as the Patrol Officer said "License and Registration ma'am."

She looked at him with a smile trying to get a read and a feel for the man. But he didn't budge nor flinch a muscle. She knew right then and there he was a full blown asshole and chances on scapegoating this traffic routine was slim to none.

Now panicking but refusing to show it on the surface. She swam her hands around in her purse buying time as she said "No problem Officer I have it right here. Do you wish to tell me why you pulled me over this evening." Her Dolce & Gabbana wallet was in clear sight of her purse. However, she idly wanted to buy some time to figure out her next move.

The Patrol Officer growled "how about I ask the questions here, and you just provide the answers ok now license and registration please ma'am." Disgusted Andreah ran out of options and immediately grew irritated with his assertiveness and shot back "ill what bit you on your ass here everything you need is here..." She hand him her wallet, he looked at it then grabbed it. He then scanned her whole entire vehicle, then retreated back to his cruiser where he punched in her information.

Seated behind the wheel pale face and flushed as if she seen a ghost. Her nerves were so shot as every idle second swelled away. That's when she heard her phone ring, which made her practically almost jump out of her skin.

"Honking of her car ho.....OH DEAR GOD" she looked at her phone and saw the caller was private number. Already knowing it was no one other than Atum she answered the phone with venom in her speech and screamed "leave me the fuck alone Atum you crazy motherfucka fuck you and your serial killing ass family I'm done. Dreah baby get done now." Atum screamed at the top of his lungs over the receiver until it was to late and then all she heard was heavy gunfire erupting fast from a machine gun "TAT TAT TAT TAT TAT TAT TAT TAT TAT TAT TAT TAT TAT TAT TAT TAT TAT TAT TAT TAT TAT."

The anonymous driver and passenger who were hanging out the side window with a AR 15, with a blue flag around his face completely Swiss cheesed the patrol cruiser and everyone in it. Oncoming traffic slammed on there brakes in horror off of the thunderous eruption of gun fire. The anonymous vehicle sped off tires screeching loudly in the streets.

The passenger as the driver blew it on the freeway connected to the ramp towards the highway. He emerged out of the sun-roof with the AR-15 in hand and lit up the whole back in and windshield of Andreah's Audi "TAT TAT TAT TAT TAT TAT TAT... Andreah screamed like a terrified toddler who had a bad dream as she remained low in the fetal position in her seat.

The anonymous car blew it up the ramp leaving no trace except for the heavy artillery littered all over the scene. Through the thickness of the chaos Andreah heard the voice of two women. Storming her way which she couldn't make out what they were saying.

She raised her head to make a visual and when she did she saw two planned clothe women running her way with guns screaming. Atum's voice over the phone screamed "Andreah... Andreah.....baby if you can hear me

Drive there coming to kill you." Her natural instinct to survive kicked in upon hearing Atum's voice. It ignited her to snap out of it and shake outta there as she slammed on the accelerator all the way up the avenue.

"Freeze Freeze FBI Andreah Violetta Smith-Bey Pow Pow Pow" Agent Meghan fired until her partner Agent Chesa barked at her "Meggie what the hell do you think your doing lower your gun now have you lost your mind." Agent Meghan cut her eyes at her and shouted "we got a 127 in pursuit and your asking me if I lost my mind what are we still standing here for come on." Agent Chesa shot back with and go where sunshine after her go ahead I promise you you'll be in the slammer by the end of the night.."

She pulled out her cell phone and called it in seconds later she could be heard saying "this is Agent Franchesa Liverpool Badge Number #242 out of the Homicide and Criminal Investigations Unit for the Bureau, we have a 127 in progress and an Officer down I repeat an Officer down requesting Paramedics and backup immediately at the intersection of exit 663 off of Washington Avenue over." While Agent Chesa was on the phone her partner Agent Meghan took in the horrific scene and replayed all that just occurred from the viewpoint of the passenger window of there Impala. Scratching her scalp running her fingers through her hair trying to piece everything altogether she caught a glimpse of an operable vehicle 15 yards north-bound with there turning signal on.

She was about to dismiss her visual of the vehicle until she caught a more thorough glimpse of the occupant behind the wheel kissing the air and winking his right eye. "haaaaahhhh yoooooouuuuu..Chesa we've been made!"

A 100 yards in the distance Andreah breaths heavily trying to will herself to calm down. She couldn't stop shaking for the life of her. The rapid gunfire that erupted back in the thickness of the heat. She constantly kept looking North, South, East, and West fearful of what to expect next.

Her nerves were completely shot. She wasn't expecting for Atum to still be on the line when he said "your in the clear babe..." His voice ping pang-ed off surround sound system more clear than receiving the call from just her phone. Screeching of tries as she slammed her foot hard on the break.

She swerved off the avenue smacking hard into a fire hydrant igniting a powerful jet stream of water in the air, deploring her air-bags upon impact. Dazed and borderline out of it, but aware and conscious. She hears heavy footsteps coming her way, but she is too disoriented to care or figure out if the pressure is friend or foe.

The prying open of her wedge shut door as he got wet from the powerful water pressure from the detached fire hydrant. Atum finally was able to improvise as he punched out the glass of her driver side window, and said "Andreah come on honey we don't have much time. "Still a little disoriented she mildly protested to no avail of working in her favor; Atum was able to delicately pulled her thick frame out of the busted window.

Secure her in his brollic arms and run off in the direction of his park truck looking around in a panic making sure no one was around and the coast was clear." "Lemme go lemme go I want nothing to do with this just lemme gooo..." She began popping and cracking him upside the head. Which made him release her momentarily from his grasp.

But not to far as he snatched her up tossing her over his shoulder like k=his very own prize as he barked. "Andreah stop it it's me I'm here to help please." A few feet away from his truck and now draped over his shoulder she lost it as she screamed aloud pounding away on his brollic back "HEEE LLLLPPPP HE'S TRYING TO KILL ME HEEEELLLLPPPP." Atum hurried quickly over to his truck open the passenger door and tussled her ass in.

He pulled out his pistol pressed it against her forehead and growled "bitch shut the fuck up before I change my mind what the fuck is the matter with you huh Huh." Andreah shut up immediately as she stared down his gun, meeting his menacing glare. Switching her approach now she began to plead with Atum begging "please don't kill me I I promise I

191

I'm no trouble I'm just a horny ass legal aid for the court that gets off on young men please...I'll do whatever."

He cut her off growing impatient with her pleading and barked "Ho ain't nobody trying to kill ya ass I never was now sit your ass back and shut the hell up." He shut the passenger side door behind her and quickly ran over to the driver side door He paused before he hopped in because he felt a chilly sensation creep up his spine. It made him wiggle, shake, and stretched as he checked his 3 and 8 o'clock shrugging it off. He hopped in his truck and sped off contemplating his next move.

Phone rings for 3 attempts the other party picks up, but doesn't say a word. The party that called speaks in French, but also in a code that couldn't be detected by authorities. As she says it's just how you called if Madam, but your not gonna believe this when I tell you the motherfucker tampering with the package is not a suite it's sadly one of our own, someone very close to the forbidden tree."

The women paused to see it the party on the other end was gonna speak. When she didn't she continued on to say. "I'm out here now surveying the scene and the tension is thick out here Madam I've been having eyes on the package ever since she left customs. Ole girl got a lot of fans because outside of family but now a foe tailing her she got suits on her radar now too, this is so bad for business my lady."

The other party on the other end couldn't hold her water no more, as she broke her silence and said in French. "I don't need you to remind me what's bad for business I need for you to be straight forward with me and factual now are you sure family was tampering with the package." The caller on the other end said "my lady I know this maybe a hard pill to swallow however you can bet your last dollar on it family just removed the package out of her vehicle strong armed the package into his vehicle and rode off into the sunset God only knows where."

The caller remained in her car approximately 15 to 25 yards away from the rubbish and debris that was left of Andreah Audi. As she heard sirens and paramedics plus the fire departments within the distance which made her smack her car in drive and blow out of there as she said "Madam have you heard from my king." Celeste allowed that question to ponder as she thought aloud, "hmmm your guess is as good as mine my chill hasn't answered his phone since I've contacted him on the legal work I needed for him to expunge for me this afternoon."

Celeste was talking about the hit on Justice McConnelly which was apart of her plan lodge against Andreah if she decided to play hard-ball and not play to Celeste's beat in her mischievous sex operation. The caller on the other end "Madam Celeste I'm worried that's not like him not to respond or return calls I think something might be..." Celeste cut her short and said "There there Chile let's not get carried away on this hot-line you getting mami's kitty to moist now for that."

The party checked herself and quickly apologized for her meekness. The line remained quite for a moment as both parties on different end from each other sat back intertwined in there thoughts. The caller said "so what's the next move my lady" Celeste with a napkin held Andreah's glass in her hand from earlier and looked at it with serious inquiry festering up a master plan.

She almost forgot to answer Valerie until she said aloud "for the time being swing by the package living quarters and see what you find, play your phone close because I'll be touching base with you soon ok. Valerie a worried mess replied "O ok Madam I love you forever and always" Celeste smiled on the other end of the receiver and replied how she replied to all her property except for one which was "I know precious we'll see watch ya body the line goes dead. Celeste with the glass still in her hand now twiddled it around in her fingers as she thought aloud "hmmmm it I would of know you would have been all this trouble I would left you alone a long time ago.

For a little over 4 years now ever since the day she saw a once a time timid, shy, reserve Andreah at Big Susie's Diner waiting for her lunch special. She knew from the first time she met her there was something about Andreah from the rest of the black sisters in D. C. Admiring the fact that she wasn't uppity and more or less trying to be like the white elite counterparts in the politics game.

She became intrigued with her even more and wanted to know more about the new black face in the game.of politics; but breaking the ice with her wasn't easy. She spent 3 years showering her with gifts that Andreah appreciated, but always returned, services for free that Andreah happily obliged and paid for every time. She even invited her to countless parties that Andreah every time respectfully declined, but extended much appreciation and thanks.

Andreah believing this would eventually in time slow up Celeste's eagerness; it only motivated it more to wanting to turn her out, but not to have her work, no the plans she had for Andreah was much much more keen to her master scheme of plans. You see only childhood friends knew about her obsession with Joe Conforte the Sicilian Godfather of Ho'n and Pimping on the most grander scale of American History. He started of with nothing literally; he came to the Bay area and became a cab driver driving locals around for chump change.

A lot of the locals he drove where call girls who he constantly would ear hustle on there bizarre sexcapades with random johns. One thing lead to another and the next thing you know he went from being there driver to employing them to turn johns in an underground play-pin he built called THE MUSTANG. The rest of the man's legacy was self-explanatory as he went down in the books as the Notorious Pimp that got away scotch free, and piratically pimped the Government out of millions while he lavished in it over in Brazil never having to worry about extradition whatsoever.

Everybody knew though Joe Conforte wouldn't of been shit without the retired DA with clout all around Clark County, Nevada and that's exactly why Celeste gravitated to Andreah so close knitted. When she found out Andreah was a legal aid to Justice McConnelly one of her A listing clients, she grew hell bent on getting next to her planting her seed. Her goal was simple have her climb up the ladder to where she would have enough juice to become a decision maker on law doing what Comfort did in Nevada what Celeste once to do in Maryland legalize prostitution.

She was enamored and troubled how her plan was crumbling between her eyes. Planting Leslie's corpse in her trunk through her whore Valerie while Awode murdered Justice McConnelly in her apartment was supposed to transpire while they were having lunch. She wasn't planning for Andreah to leave so soon; so, when she hopped up and said she had to go.

She panicked as she called Awode and Valerie both to see if the job was done when Valerie was the only one to answer. She knew something was wrong which was why she had Valerie track Andreah to see what's up, when Valerie told her in code what occurred and went down plus who was behind the aid of Andreah's rescue. She didn't want to believe it, but had to come to the struggling terms that her little world Atum might have turned renegade on her.

Thinking back to the day when she first brought Atum home from the foster care shelter in Laurel, Maryland. She smiled off of how innocent he was and how he had a birthmark on his left ear, where many teased him about it in the shelter. She found his imperfection absolutely beautiful and when she finalized the adoption paperwork, she couldn't wait to get him home.

Believing that by her bringing Atum home for her and Raw it would be able to equal to a son she was unable to give him biologically. Sadly, she learned that hard way that that was not one of her wisest decisions as Atum became more of a burden than a miracle. Since the paperwork was finalized and the only way in the State of Maryland to cancel such agreements would consist of a long-drawn-out proceedings.

She was stuck with a son that she loved and adored but couldn't complete the perfect family with Raw the love of her life she always yearned for and adored as a trouble kid till now. Dwelling on the trials and tribulations she made a much younger Atum endure up to maturity and continued further.

She was able to spot the triggers in him to possibly flip on her. "You Got Mail..." the notification came in as a alert which made Celeste check her phone for the new message. When she pulled the link up and clicked on the video that came from her whore Valerie of Andreah and her Atum. She was in tears watching the segment and dismissed what she once felt for Atum and refueled it with revenge and a whole entire new playbook to incorporate in her game plan.

Loaded with fury she scrolled through her contacts. Until she came across the one she had saved in her phone as Ms. Coverage. The line rang a few times until the other party picked up. An eerie silence could be heard until Celeste with authority barked "we need to talk now."

Chapter 12

We've Been Made

News Anchorwoman on Fox 26 News on the motel room TV screen..? and where live on Fox 26 News Good Morning my name is Denise Porter and where coming to you live out of the D. C. area with the latest news..." Andreah was glued to the TV screen zonked out of her mind half naked under the covers in the second bed of the motel room. Not missing a word on what the news anchorwoman was saying.

She barely got a wink of sleep last night from going back and forth between Atum spilling his guts about everything to her. Plus her anxiety getting the best of her from the gun play to all the murderous plots at hand. To say Atum spilled his guts would have been an understatement; he literally aired out his and Celeste's whole entire dirty laundry from the beginning to end.

He told her about how him and Celeste met at the foster care center and how he never knew his real mother. The information he had about his biological mother was that she was young at the time, suicidal and didn't want the responsibility. From there he went on sharing with her about his childhood with Celeste how everything was good until Raw who was like a father figure to him grew skates and left.

Celeste overtly depressed and financially in a jam not having no one to release her pint up aggravation and abandonment. Channeled it on Atum and from verbal to physical abuse, in time it graduated to sexual abuse. To committing petty crimes making prostitution there back-bone main income.

Atum held back no detail as he shared with Andreah his tragic days and moments bending the blade in the pimp game. Celeste turned him out at 15 making him service male and females. Shocked off of his instant success she made him step up a notch and scout a recruit kids at local middle schools and high schools.

Eventually as time progressed, and Celeste's under-age stable with Atum as her breadwinner and prize there clientele successfully matured. That is when the level of the game changed for her. Coming back from Paris with four additions to the growing sex ring, and a new blue print for converging over to Human/Sex-Trafficking Business on an International Scale.

He knew with this upgrade it was not only going to be a lucrative pay-day. But without question kick down the doors to dangers one could never imagine. Andreah was completely mind blown and in awe.

When she replayed what Atum shared about all the connections and International Agreements they had, with almost 20 plus countries ranging through three continents Europe, Africa, and Asia. These continents were the breeding grounds for her new recruits and scouts for purchase and sale in there ring to a clientele so elite they had Bill Clinton on speed-dial. There scheme was complex, but simple.

All of her International traffickers she brush paths with through Awode who was a run away male African Frenchmen whore with a bounty so large on his head that the Pope himself would flirt with the idea of collecting. He knew all the set-ups were the whores worked, where the low level pimps met all the way up to where the upper echelon of Bounty Hunters, who paid for the potential goods (fresh male and female flesh) to report back to there traffickers for a durable fee.

Who then resold them back on the open International Black Market, or work the poor boys and girls until the wrath of the game caught up to them. Making them become damage goods, and only worthy from that point a bullet to the dome. Business was excellent, but every trafficker overseas knew whomever could lock into the American Market there revenue would triple overnight easily.

As appealing as that sounded the task was not easy many had tried and each attempt was and upset every time. The U. S. had next level restrictions on importing, exporting, and trading plus with all the publicity sided towards there back and forth negotiation with China raising tariffs (taxes). The public exposure placed a serious hurting financially on the discreet bankrolls of traffickers who for years utilized Chinese conveyances of transportation to safely export there goods (human flesh) through an advised detail of customs that was paid off.

That all changed when Celeste came abroad after of course a thorough screening, and a murderous initiation for her to be eligible for her membership in the International Scale of the Sex Business. What she brought to the table was not only American young booty that made the royals thirsty overseas to purchase and solidify there Dual Citizenship in the U.S.A.

She also created a new line of travel safe enough for seasoned traffickers to consider since there underground Asian pipeline was out of commission. After test drives with there cargo extradited from there breeding grounds to Ally Territory for the U. S. which was France, Celestes political connections and means of transporting flesh through temporary Student VISAS, GREEN CARDS, and falsified work permits, worked wondrously since the age ratio on the males and females fit the bill raising no red flags.

This new route proved to be prosperous to all, and within the passing of years the Traffickers made so much money. They established so much trust with Celeste. They promoted her to being the Ambassador of the Americas appointing her and given her free-reign to sit at the table with the most elite in the business, behind the scenes only seen when they want to be seen...

"Andreah bay helloooooo yooouuu whoooooo..." Atum said as he saw that she was out there and did not show any signs of wanting to come back. Atum appeared from behind the motel room door bathroom with nothing but a towel on which made Andreah stuck on his washboard abs as she uttered out "Ahhhh huhhhhhh." Atum looked at her and couldn't help but smile as he repeated himself again saying "I said it's getting close to checkout time, and I was going to get us some breakfast before we hit the road would you like anything."

She pondered on what he said and before she could say no her stomach did the talking for her making Atum chuckle as he said "I'll take that as a yes come on get dressed we got a long journey ahead of us." Andreah now able to get her thoughts together raised up with the sheet around her and said "go where exactly and what do you mean we." Atum dropped his towel and was now butterball butt ass naked, walking around putting on one piece of clothing at a time. When he said "exactly what I said Dreah; we..but quite frankly if you think you can stand tall on your own by all means good luck the doors right there I'll give you a week at the most.

She glanced over at his naked frame, but shook that thought of pleasure and growled "I'm not the criminal here and you know that I had nothing to do with none of this shit and people are going to see that..." She stop talking because Atum laughed and added on to say, "hmmm I guess just because your a legal aid for years doesn't mean your a Johnny Cochran huh. Well check this out bay since you think you know what the people going to see allow me to shadow your worry with facts."

He paused for a moment then continued, "Check it out slowly The People of The United States of America vs. Andreah Phillips. Is going to see yea a middle-aged Black Women employed by the government with no record, whatsoever. More then likely you will cooperate about soliciting service from Celeste. Trying your best to convince them, about why all the bodies dropping around you.

Hell you might strike gold incriminating her, and the whole entire operation bringing her down on International Commercial Sex Acts. That is of course if they believe everything I have just shared with you. The Feds are going to state your mental history on the record, and shoot your credibility out the window. Overall the million dollar question is going to be is how in the hell are you going to explain not only the body in your trunk who happens to be your ex-co worker, but also the two bodies back at your apartment that's without a doubt crawling with suits right now,

How do you think the Feds gonna respond when they ID the bodies at your house. As one John Doe your very own boss and the other as a wanted illegal immigrant in several countries for murder, rape, and befouling of a corpse it's not looking to good for you An." Andreah snapped as she charged at him half naked screaming and swinging "fuck you you rotten son of a bitch you and I both know that, that's you and that scandalous bitch Celeste work I'm clean." Atum was able to gain control, and pin her down in a restraint.

On the motel bed violently shaking her growling "Call me what you want Moe, but you and I both know it ain't about what you know it's about what you can prove bitch. Now look you don't got to like me hell as a matter of fact when we get within 3 states distance from the city your more than welcome to find your own way. However as it stands I'm all you got. So pick your poison shanty time a ticking."

The news anchorwomen caught there attention as she said loud enough for them to hear. "This just in authorities are looking for an African-American women for question on yesterday's events traffic stop turned fatal ending in an Officer and K-9 dogs life in rapid gun fire. Footage of Capitol Patrol Officer Derek Wilitz from his dash-cam on his cruiser shows him engaging a pedestrian on the standard procedure traffic stop. Then extensive footage shows the over-kill execution style murder of Officer D. Wilitz and his K-9 on a first responding motorist phone who has asked to remain anonymous let's take a look your now watching the merging of both videos."

Stationed on the motel room bed they both sat back and watched the footage for the first time on the news. They stayed up all last night trying to catch it till the break of morning. Until there bodies gave out and needed some much serious rest.

Watching it made Andreah relive it. As she heard the guns erupt off making her cringe and jump in fear. The gunman then swerved off hooking around the ramp to blow it down the highway, as the passenger hung out the sun-roof opening up on the back of Andreah's Audi.

She watched on the news her drive off as the bullets lit up the back of her car. All the way until the picture cut off. Then a photo of Andreah popped up, and the news anchorwomen announced.

"Capital Authority and the U. S. Marshall Department are posting a reward for $250,000.00 for the capture of Ms. Andreah Phillips. She's wanted for the questioning of the fatal traffic stop that end in the death of Officer Wilitz and his K-9 Rockie.

The last trace of her was yesterday evening around the hours of 5 and 6 o'clock when she sped off from the scene, and totaled her vehicle a couple of blocks up north bound on Washington Avenue. Upon authorities, arriving there was no sign of Ms. Phillips, but after investigation of her totaled vehicle, detectives found a dead body in the trunk of her vehicle, stiff and cold as if it was in the freezer for weeks. Andreah Phillips is a middle-aged African American female in her mid forties roughly between 5'5 to 5 7, 125-130 lbs, fair built, black hair, and brown eyes.

Viewers are asked if anyone sees this woman to please contact us at 1-877-crimes-rus. Viewers with any information will remain anonymous. "Atum raised to his feet and continued to get dressed now with an urgency as he tossed her clothes at her, and said Now that you see how real shit just got I'll trust.... Atum didn't even get to finish his statement as Andreah threw on her clothes that Atum copped for her, and with urgency and pep in her step was speechless. Atum said nothing as he thought to himself "bout time you start using your head as they both moved quickly to hurry up, and check out. Andreah's phone ring making them both pause.

Andreah inched over to her phone, and peep it was Celeste calling through Facebook trying to Skype with her, on the new wave of communication the millennial's were doing. Atum signaled her to get dressed seconds later her phone rang again, but then also Atum and

Awode's phone rang too and when they both checked them they all said Celeste. They where boggled off of how she was able to do that until they peeped it was and I'm with a video clip link that read" a quarter million dollars is decent money for a runaway Ho can we talk y'all? Clueless on what she meant until they both seen the video of Atum pulling her out of the totaled car, and driving off. Another video clip came that read "if y'all call I promise I'll behave after viewing this clip, Atum cursed in the air because it was the clip of him leaving Andreah's house from what he presumed unnoticed.

The segment also of the clip reveals afterwards what Andreah's house looked like. After it was littered with cops, paramedics and forensics team specialist who made him scream." Valerie! Fuck yo. Shit. Sneaky crafty summa bitch."

He destroyed Awode's phone smashing it in the motel room sink mirror out of frustration. Andreah looked at him a little taken back from his furious behavior, but understood completely which made her upset. Respecting Celeste hand even more when she admittedly said "wh wh what do we do now Atum?" now fully dressed awaiting on orders like a subordinate Navy Seal.

Atum looked at her snatched her phone and called Celeste immediately. As he paced around and awaited till she picked up the line. He knew her all to well as he imagined her posture and amusement. He knew she received off them sweat as on the 4" ring she answered and said "Well Helloooo 00 Lil Daddy I'm so glad you where able to return my call at such short."

Atum snapped as he said "cut the shit Les name your price what you want." Atum placed the phone on speaker as Andreah caught the tone of Celeste's demonic cackle as she shot buck with Awwweeeee banay, bbee you think this is about money ha ha clearly you know me better than that." Andreah growing impatient with the badgering barked "well if it's not about the money Les than what is it, what do you want honey."

Celeste in an extra animated tone said "Oh hey girl isn't this a pleasant surprise I caught your work all over the news hmmm I didn't know you had it in you slick Aaayoo000." She giggled as she mimicked Cardi B the up and coming Diva rapper infamous quote. Andreah not finding Celeste's remark funny at all shot back with "bitch I'm glad you find this funny because I don't you know damn well this ain't my doing, and I'm going to prove it.

I hope you enjoy the rest of your days behind a wall. I know it all ho, I know about the International Connections. Political Protection, Celebrity and Elite Status Clientele, the murders, trafficking, and even the innocent babies you've scored and made sex slaves. You sick perverted son of a bitch.

So how you trying to play honey, if we go down you go down, or you let us know what you want and every bodies satisfied, you got 2 options." Celeste remained quite over the phone listening to Andreah's every single syllable, and word that jumped off her tongue. The silence was eating at Atum and Andreah as they wondered if she was still on the phone.

Until she said, with a thunderous clap of her hands that echoed loudly over the phone with no hesitation she said. "Well I'll be damn check you out Honey with cho bad self you got me all figured out don't you hmnunm.' The suspenseful pause in her speech made them hang on the strands of her every word.

The hairs on there necks and arms stood erect as she cut back in and said. "It's a shame, I had such big plans for me and you oh and I can't forget my lil daddy over there with you ahh yes yes Honey ummmm. Dreah baby you are looking at the very reason of why I am what I am today.

He ain't tell you? Andreah looked at him as he said aloud "Dreah babe we got's to go now hang up the phone." She attempted to, but Celeste spoke louder and said "Of course he told you for you to know all about my business there's no doubt in my mind he shared with you his deadly diagnosis of HIV or did he."

Andreah face became an instant pale as everything around her heighten her awareness. Atum began to snap over the phone with Celeste who received pure amusement and joy stirring up the trouble. Able to find an extended moment to speak she chuckled then said.

"I should of known; matter of fact who am I fooling I always knew yo ass one day would grow wise, and grow enough balls to plot a REBELLION against me, and run off with my richest, with the next bitch. Although I didn't imagine the bitch you'd choose, and shared our riches with would be your very own mother.." This time Atum felt like someone stabbed at his heart when he cried out

"WHAT DID YOU JUST SAY." silence took it's toll for a moment until Celeste spoke up, and said "Andreah Violeta Smith-Bey ummm ummm D.N.A. boy is a motherfucka Slim I tell you. You must take after yo Daddy boy because you don't look nothing like yo mamma."

Celeste burst into laughter as the party of 2 on the end receiver of the call looked at each other with distraught and painless years of confusion. Atum in his mixed emotional state was jacked and conflicted as he faced off with her not knowing what to do. Tears began to stream down his flawless brown checks as he searched for the words to say.

He finally uttered in a pain stricken whisper "tell me she's lying Dreah tell me...O my God it's true isn't it." Andreah's worst fears came true, outside of the mental anguish suffered from her childhood memories. One of her worst Top 5 fears was the possible day she'd might have to face her one and only child she ever had, and abandoned.

Now 23 years later here she is standing before the young man that shared a home in her womb for 9 months and just yesterday day night intimately explored it sexually. "Say something..." Atum snapped! Frighten she jumped and burst into tears saying aloud.

III was young.... I was a kid that was rapp........I'm sorry..." Before she could complete her pleading and crying in her sentence. Atum Lost it as he gripped her up by her throat. Snatching her completely off her feet pinning her up against the motel wall growling.

"Bitch…...What the fuck you mean your sorry do you have any idea all that I been through because of you do you DO YOU..." His death grip around her throat felt like the strength of a Diamond-back Guerrilla. Squeezing the soul out of her as she gasped for air trying her hardest to escape his grasped.

Atum grew blind with rage as he keyed in on finishing the job on Andreah. He didn't necessarily want to kill her. He was just so plagued by his childhood memories and abuse by Celeste

That since she wasn't there the only one he could trigger all of his pint up aggression on was the women responsible for the abandonment. Andreah was literally seconds away from death. As her eyes grew heavy and her arms gave up the fight.

It wasn't until Celeste had said something that triggered Atum snapping him back to reality. When she barked over the receiver "hurry Atum you don't have that much time left hurry." Releasing his grip instantly Andreah sank hard to the floor.

Disheveled coughing protrusile gasping and struggling to get air in her fiery scorched lungs. As she cried out "I was raped, I was raped please Atum pleaseeeee I'm sorry I was young I didn't know what to do...OH God I'M SORRRRRY SORRY SORRY PLEASEEEE HAVE MERCY." Her tears and pleading completely robbed him of all his anger and hatred.

Replace now with sorrow and empathy he now began to cry and wail like a motherless child. Cursing aloud atrocious remarks at the Lord threatening him to take his life. Saying he was a coward and didn't have the balls.

Celeste was all ears listening attentively to the travesty unfold in front of her through the phone. That she was the cause of as she sarcastically said "Ummmmm I hate to break up the family reunion guys, but hmm we got some unfinished business here we need to disgust." Atum heard enough as he rose to his feet and took the phone into his grasp "Fuck you bitch are business is done find a new fish, or adopt a new son I'm out, and don't bother trying to find me Moe you'll fail miserably."

Celeste this time grew tired of the games, and shouted "Nigga you out when I say you out motherfucker. Who you think you fooling slim Where the fuck you think you going to go with no connections or money.

Celeste always plays 10 moves ahead of you disloyal whores. Come on little daddy you smart enough to know mommy don't trust shit and keeps Hittas on the payroll you wouldn't last a week." Atum with pride growled "See that's were your wrong champ your not the only motherfucker that plans 10 moves ahead little do you know years back I've been planning for this day for the longest, and let's just say ya boy can retire off the coin I've been collecting and stashing."

Celeste crushed his hopes when she said "you mean them 2 accounts you got over in Paris 2 years back from that client that was a bankster looking for an American venture capitalist to inflate there peso Awwweee Daddy you thought I didn't no about that did you boobie."

Atum's whole entire facial expression changed as she continued to say "yeah just issued a lien on it roughly 36 hours ago; Awwwee boobie someone should of told you about them Latin Banksters baby they make America look like a kindergarten on levels of corruption.

Now if your thinking what I think your thinking good luck trying to survive off our books. Because once our clients get a load of this surveillance of you coming out of this bitches apartment. From icing good ole Justice Johnny you can kiss your memorable service with the upper echelon good-bye baby.

You and I both know A-Lister's like this, ain't jeopardizing M's over NO DELINQUENT BOOTY." Her thunderous laugh taunted his as it played with his psyche, pride, and ego. She knew it, and Andreah a few feet away from him sat back a mess, witnessing the malicious event at hand.

Growing passionate for Atum's sulking demur and furious with Celeste mind games as she growled. "I've heard enough of this shit fuck her Atum you don't need her, or that money you got me and my people baby let's go." Celeste, and her sarcasm, grew irate as she barked "Ahhhhh you again;

BITCH I thought this fool killed ya ass it's a little too late to play mommy now Hoc Atum what the fuck are you waiting for kill that bitch."

Andreah jumped to defense mode, and pleaded with Atum "Atum wait before you do anything sweetheart I'm not going to sit here and try to even think I'll ever be able to understand how you must fell and all that you went through because I don't OK. The waterworks was coming as Andreah pleaded for idle seconds to explain her case.

As she looked at Atum who shared the same passionate stare. Looking at him from that window of silence she seen her childhood love Jeff resonate in his features. Stuttering momentarily as she pulled herself together she blurted out "Na Na not a day goes by that I don't think about what I did to you, but sweetie you got to understand I was young, scared and rapp..."

Celeste ignorantly said "Won won won Wooooonnnnnn. spare us the sob story bitch the world don't give a damn about them tears, now it's like this because y'all don't got many options." Sirens in the distance can be heard gaining close. As Atum frantically rushed over to the window and pulled the blinds back scoping the activities outside.

As Atum growled "you grimy son of a bitch. You set us up your tracking us." Celeste not wasting, a second more shouted through the receiver "Sorry Boobie desperate times call for desperate measures now back to those options

Option number 1 you come home no funny business, and we work this out. I'll be willingly to even look past your disloyalty and let you keep that money under my terms. We go back to the ultimate goal making this money on finding a new bitch to dominate the White House.

Option number 2 you go out in the blades of glory with the deadbeat worthless piece of flesh of a mother of yours by D. C.'s Finest whom if I may add is on the payroll champ pick y'all poison toodles." The line goes dead as the sirens grow louder and Atum and Andreah have the face off of Life and Death. Atum looks at his gun that is 3 to 5 feet away from him, and approximately 3 feet away from Andreah.

Who knew even if she was to grab the gun. Atum would easily be able to over power her, and finish the job. She with no care, nor energy left to go on said "if your going to do it then do it I'm tried of being tried anyway. You'll be doing me a favor, and serving justice for yourself but just know Atum I never meant for any of this and from the bottom of my heart..."

Her voice cracked as she looked at him packed with unbearable emotion as she weeped closing off saying with tear-stained eye's. "1 I'm sorry Atum and I waited years to build up enough courage to come and find you and to tell you that I love you and I'm so sorry." He stormed over grabbing the gun taking aim as she feel to her knees continuously crying and now beginning to offer salaat in Arabic.

As she reciting the Fatijah a picture fell out of her pocket. That had Atum puzzled as he growled "bitch what the fuck is Allah going to do for you Ho I am Allah." His curiosity got the best of him. As he reached for the picture with the gun still trained on her until he seen the picture. That made his heart instantly flutter.

It was a picture of him and her when he was a new born. She was in hospital scrubs much more youthful with a fake smile. On the surface trying to hide her true emotions. At the time that was entirely to painful to release.

At first glance he had not the slightest idea what the photo was until he thoroughly analyze it, and discovered it was a much younger him and her. The sirens now could be heard bleeding through the whole entire parking lot. Causing a ruckus of disturbed motel residents to pile out to the parking lot being noisy trying to figure out what was going on.

Atum in an emotional rant growled "What is this. How did you get this Moe." Andreah continued to recite the Fatijah prayer in her teary-eyed stupor. Awaiting her fate that lied in the hands of her one and only son Atum.

Never once did she fear tempting the angel of death. Since as a youth a very young girl she was raised up with the terminology of knowing that

Death as Certain, but Life wasn't. She never knew who would be the man, women, or thing that on the day of her judgment would play God and do the Deuils work.

She just knew the day that it came, when she stared into the eyes of death she would be ready. Atum snapped aloud again and said "(cock back the gun) Bitch I'm ask you again now how the fuck did you get this picture." As if Andreah was completely ignoring him as she continued to offer and recite her salaat in Arabic.

As she came to the ending of her pray where she said "Assalam Wailiakam ra man to Allah Assalam Wailinkam ra man to Allah" she then further said "you'd better go son before it is too late don't worry about me I'll be fine." Loud commotion beyond the motel walls and door could be heard as idle seconds ticked away unaccounted for

Atum with a shivering palm and finger on the trigger panicked As he didn't know what to do, or what his next move would be. Decisions, Decisions, Decisions as the stares between mother and son prolonged until the sound of guns erupted outside. Which made 2 gun shots accidentally erupt in the small motel room making Arum scream "Nooooo00000000000 Oh God Nooo0o0000000000 Andreah stay with me."

Back at Central Office in the FBI Headquarters Downtown D. C. Ooooooouuuuu, that sick son of a bitch I can't believe I let him slip under my watch Oooooooouuuu." Agent Chesa sat back observing her fired up rookie partner Agent Meghan.

Pace back and forth frustrated beating herself up verbally over the fatal incident that occurred yesterday. She admired her spunk and pernicious desire to want to bring their culprits to justice. Sitting back observing her reminded her of a much younger version of herself back in the beginning when the wound was still fresh of the murder of her ex-partner and husband.

She reveled in her honest mistakes she made back then that she wished now she could of done better with the insight she achieved over the years.

The ranting of Agent Meghan increased in volume snatching Agent Chesa out of her zone when she hollered "Ches...are you even listening to me.: Agent Chesa now focused her attention on her partner then said "Yes dear I'm tracking, hell the whole department more than likely is to Meggie Jesus bring it down a little bit would you."

Agent Meghan reserved herself upon hearing her partners remark, but not before first saying "well excuse me its not everyday I witness ones of ours getting killed in active duty and the ones behind it ride away scotch free like pompous thieves in the night you seem to be too calm about this." Agent Chesa wanted to respond, but she decided to guard her tongue and take a deep breath. As she simply stated "It comes with the job Meggie it comes with the job.

Seconds blew by and the Captain waltzed in half surprised to see once again an Agent Franchesa and her partner together in his office. Pausing in his footsteps he didn't even bother to ask how they got into his office. Instead he just asked "(Sigh) To what do I owe the pleasure of seeing you two lovely ladies faces in my office twice in one week."

Agent Chesa began to part her lips to speak until her partner rudely fired back at the Captain with "Don't flatter yourself Cap had you listened to me and my partner earlier we probably wouldn't have an 187 on our hands of one of our fellow officers and his mutt you piece of..." Agent Chesa in shock jumped up and said "Agent Liverpool that's enough stand down." Then Captain Bonzer replied "I beg your pardon young lady."

Agent Meghan looked at her partner and Captain Bonzer both and dryly said "man screw this all you hot shots wreak of corruption I just watched a fellow officer get gunned down in cold-blood and the people behind it the same people me and my partner tried to forewarn you and that tortilla shell eating..."

Agent Chesa flared up and said "Agent Liverpool I am not going to tell you again stand down or." Captain Bonzer added "You know what, fuck all this back and forth shit I got a better idea turn in your gun and badge sweet lips you off the force." Agent Meghan froze as she studied the Captains face for sincerity then looked at her partner whose facial expression appeared more Devastated.

She trembled a little bit and thought about pleading and begging the Captain back for her employment in the bureau. Her pride plus her self-worth as a women was the only motivator that kept her in tact and dignified as she retrieved her badge and gun off of her hip and tossed it on the desk. Before she stepped of in the direction our of the Captain's office she growled "Hmmm good reddens and fine by me all you slimy pieces of shit is on y'all way to hell on a first class flight anyway.

I'm just looking forward now to when that day comes I can have the pleasure to sit there with the face to stare at y'all saying I told you so..." "She turned on her heels flicking her ex partner and the Captain off swinging her hips strong enough to make her booty bounce. As she slammed the door behind her loud enough to cause a raucous." Captain Bonzer was fired up as he attempted to pursue chase until Agent Chesa blocked his line of travel and said "please Cap just let her go she knows she overstepped her boundaries."

The Captain cut his eyes at Agent Chesa and with sinister sarcasm barked aloud "hmmmm you would know I'm sure." Agent Chesa balled her face up as he walked over to his chair to have a seat when she shot back with "What the hell is that suppose to mean Eddie." He reached for a cigar and clipped the butt before he fired it up and said "you know what I mean Fran so stop right there before you loose your job to your already on a roll with getting your partner suspended over your...

He paused as he almost accidentally said something he knew he would regret. But Agent Chesa fair from being slow picked up on what he was about to say immediately as she screamed aloud "run that by me again Edward." He sparked up his cigar as the smell of the vanilla scent smoke saturated the air.

As he now choose his words wisely, and said "that didn't come out right hold on, let me explain." Agent Chesa lost it as she screamed out "No fuck that Edward man the fuck up and grow some balls clearly you was about to say I'm the reason why that poor girl got fired because of me bleaching her thoughts with my decease husband huh that's what you meant right."

Captain Bonzer rubbed the stress lines in his forehead and mumbled "you need to calm down Agent." Agent Chesa cut him short as she growled back "Calm down, OH NOW IT'S AGENT HUN; wake the fuck up Eddie. For just a few minutes and seriously ask yourself who gives a damn." Captain Bonzer for the first time throughout there heated stand off remained quiet as Agent Chesa continued her rant with. "Why you bring me back Eddie huh, save me the sob story of because you felt bad because of are colleague at the Academy because you and I both know that's Bullshit." With no filter she pressed on saying "you brought me back in, not only because you know I'm the most qualified throughout are class, but even you believe deep down in your core, what's left in your heart for my husband, and your best man.

Something troubles you on his case of death knowing fully that that animal Celeste had help in accomplishing killing are guy." Captain Bonzer in his stern disposition stare at her with caution as his cigar continued to burn as Agent Chesa growled. "Quite frankly for years I played with the thought that you possibly might have had something to do with it or maybe you was covering for someone."

Captain Bonzer began to protest until Agent Chesa flagged him with her hand and pressed play on her recorder, back on the conversation days prior to when him and Commissioner Sanchez threaten him with the option of his pension or the roundabout speculation of Agent Chesa's new lead. Agent Chesa cut the thick suspense of the air with well since now that I know your not dirty your just scared shitless on loosing your IRA plan, now my approach is more concrete."

She tossed a thick file on his desk. Never breaking her stare as she awaited for him thoroughly to analyze the paperwork as she said "what you have their Cap is the school transcripts of both Andreah Violetta Smith-Bey and Commissioner Tatiana Sanchez. Thank God for yearbooks because Ms. Smith-Bey left shortly after the ending of the school year."

Nevertheless they still remained friends until the day of the fatal night. Were Andreah experience the lost of her love and perverted creep of a father. While little miss Commissioner Sanchez traces goes cold and she's never to be spotted in the city of Baltimore again."

Captain Bonzer now with this file in hand plus replaying back the event in his head, Talking to Commissioner Sanchez and how she quickly dismissed the photo of Andreah. As if it wasn't nothing.

The matter now made Captain Bonzer curious. As he thought aloud "why would she say she didn't know her or even consider.." Agent Chesa countered "your guess is as good as mine Cap, but if I where to guess whatever it is it's got to do with that boy Atum. Unless the bureau has any other promising leads we need to move fast NOW."

Across town on Independence Avenue cuff to a hospital bed by her ankle hooked up to a series of IV's and a respiratory system. (Beep Beep Beep...) Andreah blinks her eyes as she comes back from the dead and ques in thoroughly on her surroundings. She hears an army of voices outside of her room.

Debating back and forth the interest to speak with her and how it was Court Ordered. The on call-surgeons and nurses expresses there acknowledgment to the Marshall's and Capitol Authorities demands and orders. As it stands as the senior surgeon said "Sir with all due respect we take into serious consideration the importance of our patient and have no concerns with you gentlemen camping out here.

Overall due to our health-care policy I'm afraid we can not release Ms. Phillips to you." The commotion continued on for a little while longer. As Andreah hospital bed bound finally alert was able to come to realizing what was going down as she tried to sit up.

"Haaaaahhhhhh OH GODD" she uttered out, but quickly covered

her mouth and went back to playing sleep in her comatose state. The pain that jolted through her body was indescribable. As she did her best to adjust her facial composure in case anyone happened to walk in.

Sitting there in shock from it all her memory grew foggy. As she recalled pleading with Atum when he found out she was his biological mother. The news delivered by Celeste through the phone was breathe-taking because the thought of it truly wasn't realistic to her until that night Atum spilled his guts and she did the timeline in her head.

Her mind then jumped to hearing gunshots a total of 4, then after hearing the 3 shot everything got dark. She hissed mildly as she relieved the sustain shots she suffered through her hip and thigh bone. The thought of the shots electrified the pain she felt back on the surface.

When she attempted to move her right leg that sustained the shot. Her movements was restricted as her ankle was cuffed to the bed. Her eyes popped open like high beams on headlights as her mind jumped to the conclusion on what she remembered vividly hearing from the news.

"Capitol Authority is asking for a $250,000.00 reward for the capture of Ms. Phillips she is rumored to be armed and dangerous..." She remained still looking around plotting and thinking her next move not knowing at all what it might be. The time ticked away as if she had 24 hours to live and she was on her last leg.

She heard the commotion from earlier increase as it gained louder in volume and came piercing through the ER room door. The commotion was a mixture of professional laypersons from offices of law to officers of medical healthcare. Once the badgering Marshall was reassured and able to see the fugitive Ms. Phillips was sedated and detained.

The nagging surgeons continued to press on saying "Sir as you can see the patient is still sedated, detained, and clearly not able to even confine to the idea of what is even going on around her, now with all due respect you and your men please...must wait outside." The U. S. Marshall looked around then keyed in on the patient Ms. Phillips then back on the lead surgeon and growled to his unit set up checkpoint perimeters around the area. Make sure the grid is locked down, not no one in nor out without clearance you hear me,

His company received their orders and snapped into action. As told while there Commanding Officer now centered his focus on the surgeon and said, "The minute she wakes up Doc...I'll take it from there the surgeon's frustration could be read all over his face.

As he professionally said "Sir I told you for the hundredth time already she is not medically cleared." The agitated Marshall grew irate as he stepped up in the surgeons face and barked "now you listen to me dock like I said before when that bitch wakes up I could care less if the whore is crippled break out a wheel chair and a bunch of first aid wraps is fine with me However just so were clear when that psycho-pathetic cop killing scant winks a frigging eye-ball at you.

Mark my words she's coming with me, no if and's or buts about it." The lead surgeon looked back at his company. Who all looked petrified even though they all pretty much still had there surgical masks on.

He then centered his attention back on the U. S. Marshall and said "you know what Sir my apologies I've completely stepped out of line. I should've directed you and your men to my supervisor first and foremost he would know more thoroughly how to assist than myself if you gentlemen would follow me this way."

The lead surgeon escorted the officer and his unit out. As well as his surgeons and nurses present. He informed 2 nurses to stick around for intensive purposes and then no sooner than a second went by the room was quite as the 2 nurses checked Andreah's vitals. As they engaged in small chit chat.

Andreah in her fake comatose state of mind was all over the place. As she replayed back to herself all that was said amongst everybody in the room. She couldn't for the life of her determine exactly who the bone narrow by the book officer was that was treating her like the nation's most wanted criminal.

After listening to them emphasize her as a psycho-pathetic killer thirsty for cop and political blood. She knew her chances of getting out of there were slim to none. At that moment she began to think about Atum all the way back to the day when she had him and the weeks later putting him up for adoption.

The day she did that she remembered vividly because it was the day she had to make one of the most toughest decisions of her life. Her mind began to picture herself in motherhood. Changing his first diaper, reading him his first bed time story, all of the things that was foreign to her.

In her upbringing as a child that she wished, she could have shared with him. Unfortunately this wasn't her fate back at that time she was young, scared, befouled beyond repair plus inform by authorities about a green-light on her head from the criminal organization group that reign supreme in the streets of Baltimore called The BGF (The Black Guerrilla Family).

In her mental state at the time, she knew this was no life for a new born child. So she made what she believed to be the best decision for the baby with a better family. Then after time to think took the government up on it's offer and cooperate against the remaining BGF members.

In return for a change of identity and new life elsewhere away from the wretched nightmarish streets of Baltimore. Believing wholeheartedly what the government told her and there promises of support. On the verge of accepting defeat ready to get on with the next phase of what was in store the minute she planned on opening her eyes.

A voice that was all to familiar to her cut into the air and said "Ummmm yes is this the room of Ms. Phillips. The 2 female nurses said "yes it is and you are." With such case and finesse the women in hospital scrubs and surgical mask stated "I'm sorry honey it's been a little bit of a suspenseful day I'm Doctor Rosie Maldonado y'all relieve upon Doctor Sean Pasqucle's orders.

There's a patient in room 223 that had a little accident with his doughnut." All 3 of the women cringed as they imagined that uncleanly sight the Doctor Maldonado said "yeecaaaa sorry ladies duty calls I'll take over from here." The 2 female nurses shrugged their shoulders and made their way out of the room leaving the doctor to herself.

When the female nurses left the doctor looked at Andreah and then the door and locked it behind her. When she pulled her surgical mask down. A flushed face of concern soiled her mood as she seen her childhood friend hospital bound.

Commissioner Tatiana Sanchez top of her class in the academy, but once upon of time before the badge and the gun. She was a product of her environment and an infamous handler and shaker back in the city of Baltimore, what the natives called The Dru Hill Homes.

Days prior to this event she had received a call from her extensive 10 year partner in the lucrative human-sex trafficking business Celeste. Demanding for a hit on a person of interest. Thinking nothing of it Commissioner Sanchez did, and then forwarded the whole file over to Celeste that she desperately requested.

It wasn't until days after she had the pleasure to have the file presented to her again by her Captain Eddie Bonzer, that then she was able to analyze her photo more carefully. By adding 20 years plus maturity to the photo of Andreah. Had she not been through the vigorous trials and errors in the field undercover on top level priority cases.

She wouldn't of been able to master such a stern poker face. That even her colleagues and close family found trouble in decoding. Tears streamed down her face as she looked at her girl with guilt weighing down on her heart.

In her mind had she not been so distracted in pulling the blinds over the bureaus eyes. As usual cleaning up Celeste's thunderstorm of a mess. She would have been able to put a halt on everything avoiding all of this.

She made the idle mistake in the past. Releasing over her whereabouts to her father after a malicious assault. She'd be damn if she would repeat that karma over again as she cried out. "Adio meho na na no juelo pa Fi" which meant "Oh my God Honey this wasn't suppose to happen to you I'm soo sorrrrrryyyyy."

With a quickness in her 4 inch black heels tight black jeans white button up with her hair in a bun. Agent Chesa moved through the parking lot with a purpose and a smile thirsty to find her vehicle and to get moving. Agents greeted her as she passed and she politely responded back with enthusiastic energy.

10 to 15 yards away from her car she now hustled up quickly to get to her vehicle. She presses the button to deactivate the alarm, but her back taillights came on signifying the alarm was already disarmed. Finally at the driver side door she saw that her partner Agent Meghan was inside and without thought into it she opened the door and hopped in slamming it behind her.

The 2 where quiet for a moment until the suspense grew to heavy and Agent Meghan flat out said "Sooooooo what happened Chess did did it work." Agent Chesa sighed as she cut her cyes at her partner and held out this long stern stare. Agent Meghan almost began to water up, until she saw her partner smile handing over her badge then her gun and said "like a glove darling worked him like a frigging glove."

Agent Meghan released a deep sigh of relief. But playfully threw a jab at her partner. Who now was in a joy of laughter when she said "Ha ha ha Awwwweee Meggie I'm sorry to soon." Agent Meghan caught a mild attitude as she crossed her arms defensively, and said "Gee.....Chess you think."

Agent Chesa calmed down, her laughter slightly and said to her "Aw Aw Awweee Meggie it's ok mummy's gotcha I'm crazy, but mark my words I didn't get this far from being stupid." Agent Meghan began to ease up a little bit. As she shot back with well in the near future make sure your crazy game plans don't include me and my pension."

Before Agent Chesa could respond back her phone ringed focusing both of their attention on the incoming call. Agent Chesa's smile quickly erased off of her face as she saw the call was private. She attempted at first to not even answer it. Her instinct was screaming at her to answer it so she did.

Placing the call on speaker saying "Agent Liverro speaking." The voice of the man over the phone sounded all to familiar to the agents in the Impala as he came over the receiver clearly saying, "There's no need for you to trace this call Agent Franchesa surprisingly I thought about our last workout in the gym and for the first time in my life I'm actually interested in a sit down with you and your sexy little pig ass partner."

Agent Meghan took his remark out of complex as she truly thought he was referring to her body-type. As porky the pig when she said "O my God Chess did he just call me a sexy frigging little pig." Atum happen to catch what she said and laughed as he said "Yo shortie you really need to loosen the leash on your much more and let that bitch breath champ with her green ass."

Agent Meghan snapped, but was over spoken by her partner when she shouted aloud. "Now how do we know your not blowing smoke up are ass, or trying to set us up you must forget I've been tracking you kid for." Atum growing impatient rudely cut her short and barked "listen champ if I was blowing smoke up ya ass do you think I would be calling you right now with details about the most infamous sex ring in history,

Bitch when this is all said and done; Ho you fuck around and get a star in Hollywood you and ya little pup after I drop on you the bombshell of the century. This is bigger than the suit that lined ya bitch ass husband. We're talking International playing on a grandeur scale Baby how you want it now.

The mentioning of her husband being set-up by one of her own touched a nerve. Although she already knew and assumed for years the execution of her husband involving an extra hand of law enforcement. The words still stung as she barked "That man you referring as a bitch you low down sleazy son of a bitch was my husband and dead or alive your going to show some God DAMN re..."

Atum growing annoyed growled "Ho please save yo tears for the next dick that gives a damn (speaking about myself in 3d person as he says) bitch must of lost her mind talking this have some respect shit like niggas really give a damn about... Woosawww Woosaww A.ite bust it, baby it's like this you got 2 options you already know what they are so hear the terms.

Diplomatic Immunity first flight out of the country tonight and a half a mill in a Portuguese account within the next 24 hours. I'll call you in 2 hours with the routing numbers and the location to come pick up your prize and I shouldn't have to tell you no funny business." The line goes dead as Agent Chesa screamed "Atum wait hello. Atum" party has disconnected the call.

"Shhhiitt." Agent Chesa screamed in a frustrated tone as her partner said "should we call it in" Agent Chesa looked at her with a what are you crazy dumbfounded type of look and said "Call it in and exactly tell them what without authorization, standing, or backing just a strong lead and a hunch. How many times do I got to tell you Meggie we're on our own girl."

Agent Meghan paused as she aloud everything her partner just said marinate. It took her a little while longer than usual to respond. But as the words were forming in her head, she went out on a limb and said "So so Sooooo what do we do and how do we know he is for real in what he is saying."

As soon as those words jumped off her tongue it was like it couldn't be any more perfect timing. As an Instant Message came in to Agent Chesa's phone. She looked at her phone instantly as the message came in unlocking her screen saver.

She was confused at first, but gradually picked up on exactly what it was. As her partner with anticipation said "What what is it Chess is it him."

Agent Chesa looked at it more thoroughly and hesitantly said "it it look like monthly balancing statements of what appears to be..."

Her phone rung again with another Instant Message. But this time it said "what you have there is the annual statement of what our business did this entire year with a special thanks extended from the private donors of the US Senate, House of Representatives and yours truly the vilest bigots in the District that protect and serve there very own private interest for power and pleasure. Now this is only just a year worth of money laundering, evasive tax invasion, sexual favors, murder for hire, the list goes on. You want the remaining roster in the additional nine plus years of the most lucrative criminal enterprise in the land. That's been operating under y'all noses all this time. I suggest y'all high and mighty asses get cracking on my paperwork and ends I'll be in touch shortly with my instructions."

Agents Chesa and Meghan now with a full understanding of what they were in possession of. Now in bewilderment of all the names listed in the statement. Plus the large amount of the contribution most made as indication of charity.

Some donors were anonymous, while others were careless depositing in their Company Accounts, Trust Funds, and 501(C)3's and 6's. The level of criminal intellect Devised behind it all was dashing leaving Agent Meghan mind blown. As she said "well I guess that answers are suspicion."

Agent Chesa was at a lost of words it came as no surprise to her the level of criminality, But after years of tailing diligently trying to create and build a case out of thin air. For her now to finally have concrete facts instead of calculated theories.

The evidence in hand made her tremble with concern. As she gazed over the IM again with the discreet donors recognizing most of the names instantly. Fully aware of there powerful persuasion tactics, influence, and dangerous profiles.

So what's the plan Chess!" Agent Chesa allowed her words to linger in the air. As she herself tried to figure out the next move. Her body instantly grew twitchy, and uneasy from reading over for the second time the contents of the anonymous overseas Trust Fund.

At the moment she knew if everything Atum sent her was accurate. Every move she and her partner had to make from there on out. Had to be played with precaution as she uttered out "We wait Meggie we wait till he calls back with his instructions then we make our move..."

Chapter 13

C.I.A.

Back at the mini-mansion play pen of Celeste in one of the more nicer remote areas on the outskirts of the Southeast section Celeste called home:

Atum stands outside of the house in the stretched drive-way. A nervous wreck of a mess counting down the idle seconds left he had before he entered there abode. Feverishly pacing back and forth checking his Bulova Watch and phone.

He cursed aloud in the air screaming to himself "Fuck..I should've known them pig ass skirts would've pulled this shit Stupid motherfucker Moe...DAMN." Speaking about himself in 3d person he panicked as he began to see his insurance plan wasn't coming through. The last thing in life Atum ever considered doing was cooperating with the FEDS.

Presented with the opportunity when he was much younger when he witnessed his first murder. The interrogation he endured was brutal until Celeste came to his aide and shut everything down immediately. Acting as his guardian with counsel.

Able to walk out of there scotch-free and barely unfazed. Celeste gave him his very first Hard-knock lesson on what happens when players go left. The beat down she inflict upon him was so wicked; poor Atum couldn't piss correctly without discharging blood for months.

From that lesson the thought of ever considering telling never even registered till now. When once again he was plagued with life changing decisions. Atum predicted this day into manifestation 4 years prior till now.

Back when he spotted from the sideline there transition from nationwide ventures of prostitution. To the international scale of Human/ Sex Trafficking that along the lucrative journey provided wealth and liberties beyond ones means. Overall the dangers that followed where it seem the only one who cared out of there enterprise was him.

Made watchful Atum instead began planning his REBELLION from the stable working smoothly for Celeste's trust to penny pinch off the top. So when the shit got goofy he could grab his earnings and shake the spot. Hearing the news of Celeste being on point to his scheming and treachery left him Deuastated and raw.

He couldn't figure out for the life of him how she became awoke to his tedious chippings of donations from clients, contractors, and quest. Because his subtractions where literally no more than a $100.00 favorably over the 4 year period of excursion. When he heard her deliver the crushing blow that literally solidified his future from the simple swipe of a pen issuing a lien on his personal assets.

He had to take a deep breath and truly admire and recognize all this time he believed he was being cautious and slick. While Celeste was on her game the whole entire time instilling his confidence to carry on. What motivated Atum to be inspired in the bitch-made decision he was locked into now.

Was when he witnessed another side of Celeste black-mailing tactics he grew immune to over the years inflicted on others. Seeing it now first hand transgress against him fully aware her approach can get him a first class ticket to Pine-Sol Heaven. His rebuttal of cooperation lessened his feelings of guilt coming to the terms of being a rat.

As his phone ring with a notification from Agent Chesa stating "Your compensation for your cooperation has been wired to off-shore Trust you inquired upon our agreement. Now pleas forward over the destination of our meeting time and place." Atum lit up like a Christmas tree as he thoroughly deleted the text and proceeded to check his Trust account Online to make sure she wasn't blowing smoke up his ass.

The trickling process tool same time for the balance inquiry to pop up. Through it all once he seen the amount of #500,000.00 deposited by a sequence of encrypted numbers for security purposes. He smiled as he new respond back in a text "welcome to the league of extraordinaire players in suits and skirts Slick; man of my word here is the remainder of the 9 year plan, plus the coordinates to the play-pen see you soon." While meanwhile ducked off inside:

The heart grabbing lyrics of Keyshia Kole's Autumn single almost 2 or 3 summers ago Trust and Believe. Come bleeding out of her surround sound theater system hooked up in her master bedroom. As she dressed for the occasion of combat for her awaited quest of honor Atum her everything.

As she dressed in her black get up which consisted of her ACG boots, spandex cat-suit, gold ring brass knuckles, with her hair in a bun, Vaseline down for war. A tear trickled down her cheek as she thought of Atum and sadly knew that this day would come.

She sighed deeply as she recalled when he was a little boy scared shitless trying to adapt to his new life. In the beginning it was all good until Raw her pimp and supposably husband. At the time left them both for dead leaving them to find for themselves.

That day was the day of her turning point for the worst and where her Devised plan of turning out young male and female children as prostitutes. Sprang into action nominating Atum as her main attraction. Years had past since then and as much as Celeste coached herself over the years into believing her cause was just.

She never forced any of the turnouts (young male and female whores) into the life. Her conscience constantly reassured her daily that no matter how many sick falsehoods she used to justify her means. Wrong was wrong and she knew she brought this upon herself.

The renegade behavior of Atum as she cocked back her 9-millimeter and swayed and sung to Keyshias lyrics saying. "When we were together. I held you down and I gave you all of me...when I was around and even with all your excuses...they don't add up.. that it is easy to see you don't deserve my Love... You push me far... You brought me to this... Looking now at her security cameras watching Atum in there stretched drive-way she kissed the cylinder on her 9 millimeter and whispered into the centralized air "let the games began Little Daddy!"

Andreah like a bat out of hell. She was in hot pursuit of Celeste's play-pin. She had not the slightest idea if Atum would be there or not.

However, she recalled by when Atum shot her that Celeste growled over the phone for them to meet there. The trouble Andreah endured to evade her captors was the struck of luck at the right time. Commissioner Tatiana Sanchez or better known back in the blood-thirsty streets of Baltimore City Tati.

Entered into the hospital upon hearing the news of her childhood home-girl Andreah. Disguised in surgeon scrubs and practically spilled her guts in what she believed Andreah was in a hospital sedated state. Andreah heard everything and when I mean everything: not a syllable short of the word of the truth.

Andreah tempted to inform her she was fine. As the tears and worry of Tatiana's concerned troubled her. She was happy to hear a familiar loving voice after all these years.

Remained reserve as through Tatiana's tears. She began letting her inner demons fall off her lips starting off with her guilt trip on how her father Stretch was able to find her all those years at Jeff's house. Because of her which lead to the sexual assault and murder of her love.

From there Tatiana didn't stop she continued on as if she was in the confession booth and Andreah was the Madrina. Tatiana went on to say how when she heard of her delivery of Atum and that Andreah decided to adopt. It pained her to see Andreah consider foster-care.

So she tried to apply for the adoption. But was denied because she wasn't 18 years of age yet nor a stable legal consenting adult. This made her according to Tatiana inspired to join the profession of Criminal Justice.

Then later join the academy after hearing the news in the neighborhood of Andreah cooperating against the Black Guerrilla Family.

Pleading further Tatiana continued to speak on how she completely understood now of the name change. But still throughout her travels in the Bureau was able to keep tabs on young precious little Atum. Who was fine until she received the news from one of her trusted intel that her boy crush code name Atum was adopted by a women by the name of Celeste Ann Ezter smith.

Whose name of importance back then was a hi and bye discussion in the office. But nowhere near full-fledged missing family dinners and kids graduation type of case like it was now. Tatiana had not the slightest idea that Andreah was alert and conscious to everything she was saying.

Nor did Andreah bother to stop her as colleague and how she was the cause of it. Her reasoning behind her treasonous acts war meritable. But she struggled believing it as she spoke saying had they would of convicted Celeste for the Criminal Homicide on the Agent. It was without question Life or a Death Sentence.

Plus innocent Atum whisked off again into the system possibly losing her tail on him like she did mistakenly on her. She left out the additional aspect of the lucrative channel of profiting off of Celestes international scale of trafficking, Able to feed, cloth and employ back home her family. In the native grounds in the Dru Hill Homes.

Reflecting back on all that she heard in the emergency room from Tatiana her girl for life. She kissed on the cufflink key and said aloud. In a stolen vehicle of one of the nurses back in the mist "Hold on Atum baby here I come honey; here I come."

Across town on Vermont Avenue approximately a quarter mile away from the Secretary Building of Veteran Affairs, Agents Chesa and Meghan sit anxiously! Anticipating for Captain Bonzer to scan over there evidence thoroughly. Hoping it was enough to retrieve a warrant to pursue there suspects.

Out of all people the only one the women felt might support was him and not only where the surprise they were shocked when he even wired the money to the account. The idle seconds that ticked by felt like an entirety to the girls. Until they got the call they both anticipated for which made them both almost jump out of there skin.

Jittery and on alert Agent Chesa answered on the second ring and when she said "Hello", the Captain announced over the phone "Congratulations ladies you got your warrant await my signal to move. Agent Chesa acted like she didn't hear what the Captain last comments was when she said "what Captain couldn't make out what you said permission to move granted Roger that over and out."

She cut the line and with restrained excitement let it all out, as she said "Yeeeecesaaaaa hmmmmmmm finally the day has come." Excited for her partner, but immediately swarmed with a little uneasiness suddenly she hesitantly said "so were are we all meeting up at." Agent Chesa looked at her and laughed "Meggie what are you deaf? We just got granted with permission to move out. Ain't no meeting up nothing suit up."

Agent Meghan couldn't contain herself as she blurted out, and said "are your sure Chess...sounds like Cap was adamant about..." Agent Chesa blacked as she centered her attention on Agent Meghan and barked. "Look fuck Cap, and fuck whoever stands in my way of Justice tonight. I most certainly hope and pray you don't think for a second we were arresting these animals tonight."

Agent Meghan dumbfounded decided not to answer because deep down that's exactly what she thought. Clearly now she is starting to see her partner had other plans in store. As Agent Chesa pulled out her service pistol and said.

"Well since you answered my question with your silence. Allow me to reassure you that arrests are out the window I am sending that bitches corpse down with the fishes in the Potomac River. What you thought this measly piece of evidence was our meal-ticket.

Meggie please recognize game when you see it girl this evidence was nothing more the Atums pardon and our Death Certificates to kill this son of a bitch." Agent Meghan took everything all in, as Agent Chesa continued her ramble saying "(sighs deeply in frustration).

God I can't believe I was almost that stupid (light chuckles). By the time, that evidence is presented to a Grand Jury and the Justices on the panel. See that for the donations that were not marked anonymous happen to some of there very own cohort and colleagues.

The indictment is going to get tossed. While the hussie makes bail and that silver-tongue speaking bastard walks scotch-free on the governments account. Uh uh not this time Meggie that's skant and her smooth talking gigolo of a son DIE'S TONIGHT.. Screeching of tries!

Celeste.. Who dee whooo00000...Helloooo000000 you hear mah! Atum peeled through the house gun in hand like a Swat-Team member on the hunt for Celeste. It was dark as hell throughout the whole entire mansion and entirely to damn quiet. Atum thought for a moment no one was there until all of sudden.

Boom Boom Boom Boom shell casings can be heard dancing loudly on the marble tile floor as Atum retreated for cover in the Alexandria styled library hissing loudly in pain as he screamed. "AHHHHHH SHIT MOE...crazy bitch shot me in the ass AHHHHH FUCK CELESTE WHAT THE FUCK." Celeste came hustling down the hallway ecstatic; when she saw that Atum went into there study since the door was open.

She came up fast on the door to the invite of gun play from Atum. Doom Doom Doom...she hit the floor with a dive for cover behind her Macedonian Greek-style statute 612 feet away from the desk. Where Awode and Valerie were months back. Atum could hear Celeste wasn't to far due to her extended panting form the adrenaline rush of the gun shot sustained in her shoulder as she mutter.

"Heyyyy little daddy so glad you could finally join us boobie a bitch was getting lonely. She didn't want to give away her position and inform him that she was wounded. Pretty bad giving him the upper hand as he hollered.

"Getting lonely...US...bitch you really did done gone off your rocker this time. So this is were we at with each other now huh answer me sli.. Boom Boom." She army crawled from her position to the study-room door not before letting go in Atum's direction.

Atum braced himself for the rapid fire ducking when he saw her shadowy figure dart out of the study room. Down the hall where he previously came from. He let off at the door and through the wall with hopes of hitting Celeste.

Doom Doom Doom Doom Doom click click click..SHIT" Atum cursed under his breath, He was empty and had no extra clip to reload. Arising to his feet slowly he inched his way towards the study room door.

Once there cautiously with his gun in hand looked down both the cast and west direction of the hallway for his own security purpose. The glass shattered from the study rooms door not to mention the wall he shot through with hopes to clipping Celeste. Displaying through debris and rubbish on the floor of his failed attempt.

Inching down the hallway with an empty tool in tow putting on a serious bluff tactic. He screamed aloud with hopes she heard him say. "Bitch show yourself what the fuck you running for huh I'm right here baby what's up..."

Atum was now in the front foyer of the mansion. Were you come in from the front door. Surpassing the portrait of Angela Davis hanging from the wall.

He emerged from the side of the huge steps and got awoken from the rapid fire from Celeste. Who was in the middle of the Romanian Architectural style wrap around steps letting him have it. "Boom Boom Boom Boom Boom Boom..."

Celeste chuckles loudly as she watches her rounds tear through Atum's muscular physique. In a panic stricken attempt Atum hauled ass when he heard the first shot. Towards the Dinning Room on ones left if someone accesses inside the mansion from the front door.

To no avail being such an easy target to hit. Due to his size and physique which was a gift and a curse. Two rounds penetrated through his back exiting out of his chest.

Making the impact knock him off his feet. Pushing him tumbling to the floor choking on his own blood. Staining the dining room floor.

Clinging to life as he crawled across the floor trying to get out of eye shot of Celeste. Celeste as she sashayed down the steps with a murderous smile. She could hear Atum in the dining room crying hysterically and screaming plus wailing in pain.

She had to check herself because her curious angel of regret and concern she felt. Battled with her executioner deep within. To delay her lower self from confirming the kill emerged making her question her act.

Shaking it off, as she bend around entering into the Dining Room watching Atum crawl aimlessly to no destination of security. She walked him down and said aloud "D.C. was supposed to be ours Little Daddy hmmmm good ole sexy Dark Chocolate City slick. But you just had to be disloyal..."

Atum knew then it was over so instead of pleading and begging like a bitch. He decided to go out like a G and barked aloud "bitch who you fooling live in yo skin for once and be real it's always been about you always has and always will be no matter who you scorn, hurt, or kill." Celeste kicked him hard in the ribs making him curl up in the fetal position.

She pressed her steel toe ACG boot on one of the exit wounds of his chest. Now making him wince and growl in pain. Has he laying flat on his back, as she barked.

"Boy please......you a grown ass man making grown ass moves, half the reason why your in this mess, is because yo scandalous ass can't accept the right, and reality of your situation I didn't chose this game niggu..."

Atum cut her off by trying to spit in her face. But from his positioning and angel it only hit her stomach in her onesie cat-women spandex suit.

As he growled "you didn't chose the game, but you also didn't have to play at it either. Your sick Les and what's so sad is you know it. But you justify your means because of how you were brought up and raised... Well guess what bitch no matter how many innocent foreign and American kids you wholesale. To these sick perverted crackas in power it changes nothing. You still have to live with the dark past of rape, molestation, solicited for sex, not to mention having a mother rob you of something precious as.

Celeste snapped as she squeezed at the trigger growling loudly to finish Atum. When she realized no bullets discharged out of the gun he laughed a sigh of relief. As out of nowhere a silhouette of a feminine figure emerged swinging a furnace poker, used for the fireplace at Celeste hollering.

"12 shots Bitch..." Andreah cracked Celeste upside the back of her head sending her sailing hard to the floor grabbing the back of her head groaning loudly in pain. Andreah dropped the fireplace poker and ran over to Atum's aid screaming "O my God Atum...no honey please stay with me. Help is on the way. Talk to me baby please talk to me where does it hurt."

Atum continued to hiss in pain. As he now held onto Andreah's hand firmly. As she tried her best with her disheveled attire ripping pieces off to apply pressure to his inflected wounds.

Atum choking up on his flesh was able through extended breaths to utter out "Dre dre Dreah look out." his attempts was too late. As Celeste grabbed a handful of Andreah's hair. Rising to her feet now while keeping Andreah pined to her position on her knees next to Atum.

She wined back her leg with all her might and with the swinging momentum connected her knee to Andreah's face. Sending her swinging across the Dining Room floor in excruciating pain. Celeste growled loudly she got nothing to do with this Les leave her alone it's me all mee."

She snatched her leg away from Atum and barked back at him "Nigga shut cho Captain Save A Ho ass up this nosy bitch wants to stick her nose in grown folk business then she can die with cho shady ass." Celeste made her way over to Andreah.

When Andreah tried to rise to her feet. Celeste kicked her in her stomach sending her crashing back to the floor as she spat. "Welcome back Bitch let's see if I can finish the job ya bitch ass son couldn't do correctly.

Outside of Celeste's mansion decked off in their Impala, Agents Chesa and Meghan said a prayer as they got ready for battle. "Amen.…...Amen…" they both said as they unholstering there pistols while marking themselves with cross kissing their hands and pressing their foreheads.

Agent Chesa cocked back the slider on her service pistol unlocked her door then looked at her partner Meghan and asked "how you feeling girl." Agent Meghan took a deep breath and looked at her partner with honest and said "I felt worst, but hey I'm here." Agent Chesa looked at her then her fingers through Agent Meghan's hair in a motherly manner and said "Listen Meggie if this is to much for you…"

Agent Meghan's service pistol snatched Agent Chesa's sentence as she cocked her slider back and said "I know what I signed up for Chess so let's go get our guy." Out of the comer of Agent Chesa's eye it zoned in in the figure creeping up trying to gain access in Celeste's front door. Agent Chesa studder as she forced herself to spit the words out saying "isn't that… Agent Meghan finished her sentence saying "the Commissioner."

Back inside the cat fight continues. As Andreah attempts to swing and Celeste weaves out of the way and catches her in the mid-section then across her face sending her crumbling to the floor again for the fourth time. Celeste barks "damn Ho don't make it to easy violating her she spat on her battered body then landed a series of flying kicks.

Celeste went mad as she went black in a rage with intentions on kicking Andreah to death until out of the blue. "(cocking back of her gun) Back away from my girl before I redecorate your whole entire dining room all bitch."

The broken English threw her off until she turned around to face her

237

accuser and barked "Commissioner. Wah wha now how the fuck did you get in my damn house." Tatiana better known in her profession as the Commissioner for the Bureau Tatiana Sanchez Aka Ms. Hammer in rare form hollered at Andreah's battered body in her broken English. "Oye nan na it's Tati loca you ok Mami talk to me I talk back struggling in her attempts to recover she crawled over battered and bruised in the direction of Atum uttering out "I'm I'm girl perfect timing thanks for coming."

Celeste snapped "perfect timing... Tati. Sanchez you know this Ho." Tatiana with pride said aloud "before the FBI puta it was Dru Hill Homes motherfucker never forget that." Agents Chesa and Meghan in the nick of time emerge and Agent Chesa growled "Dru Hill Homes huh you hear that Meggie" then Meggie replied "sure did Chess all of..." was all the words she got out.

Until Tatiana out of reflex turned around and responded with rapid gun fire "Boom Boom." The shots she fired snatched poor young Agent Meghan off her feet flying three back in Celeste's dining room wall. Agent Chesa upon hearing the shots crouched low and began firing in the direction of Tatiana "Bow Bow Bow (gun shots erupting) O my God Meggie hold on honey stay with me."

The gun battle now between Commissioner Tatiana Sanchez and Agent Chesa escalated now taking it's course. While Celeste took cover and high tailed it out of there. Andreah still at Atum's side crying hysterically at Atum's still corpus.

Shook him anxiously screaming for him to stay with her and that help was on the way. Realizing her attempts where not working to revive unconscious Atum. She cried in a thunderous pain momentarily until that pain converted into rage.

She caught a glimpse of Celeste breezing past the kitchen connected to the slide-door leading to her patio and wine cellar. Andreah took cover slowly rising to her feet to avoid getting shot. Making her way to the slide-door she saw a wood-block that contained 6 sharp Kutoo cutting knives.

With no hesitation she grabbed one and ran after Celeste before she was able to escape. Entering through the slide-door leading her to a spacious cherry maple wood patio. If you go one way it take you out to the back-yard. But the other way would take you back into the house into one of her entertainment rooms.

A dimmer of light the beamed from the house onto the fresh mowed lawn of Celeste spacious back-yard. Showed Celeste running across the land holding her wounded arm trying to hustle up to her doc to board her boat and get out of there. Andreah with every bit of energy she had left took off after Celeste before it was to late.

15 yards away from each other Andreah screams as her with the kitchen knife in hand "CELESTEEEEE STOOO0OPPPPPP." Celeste paused but not because of Andreah screaming at her. A helicopter from a slight distance away was coming in fast. But made matters worst for Celeste. When she saw the tail of the chopper said the CIA.

The man on the intercom said "Chandler Ann Smith the 3rd this is the International Sex Trafficking and Terrorist Unit of the CIA We have a warrant for your arrest on the counts for 45 counts of Human Trafficking, 12 counts of Inter-State Commerce, 24 Counts of Corruption of Minors and 3 counts of murder for hire, your place is surrounded and were giving you simple instructions to surrender failure to comply you will be shot right on the spot."

Then men and women now surrounded all throughout her back-yard and now by her docks with the FBI in the company suited and booted. Had Celeste mind blown as she spun around bewildered looking at all the suits now aligned in her back yard. In a circle debuting her and Andreah for all to see.

As more Agents from both the FBI and CIA spilled out of her mansion securing the area. Celeste looked now over at a reserved petrified Andreah with the knife in hand. Now realizing it was over all she could say aloud was "Who are you…"

Andreah now teary eyed said aloud "Celeste please it's over just do what they say and..." Celeste snapped and yelled again "Bitch who are you." Andreah now balled loudly with the waterworks coming down harder as she said softly "Ah ah A mother that cares."

Celeste filled with rage wasn't trying to hear it as Celeste stormed at her direction barking loudly. "Ho stop lying you a fucking BOOM BOOM BLAAAAAATTTTTT BOOM BOOM BOOM BLAAAAATTTTTT NOO00000000000000000..Ms. Phillips darling wake up honey wake up HAPPY PLACE HAPPY PLACE."

Andreah darling Hey Hey relax darling your fine...Hi it's Doctor Gasper remember me." Andreah looked around frantically with a thunderous beating heart trying to will herself to calm down. Sweating protrusively; as Doctor Gasper went to retrieve her a glass of water and a napkin.

Gulping down the water she breathed heavily then said "Oh God how long was I out." The Doctor caringly wiped away the sweat with a napkin then with a motherly smile said almost a good hour in a half Ms. Phillips. But we made good progress today my dear and I'm so proud of you."

Doctor Gasper rose to her feet and proceeded walking over to her counter to make notes of there session for today. Andreah's eyes followed Doctor Gasper and smirked with a smile how she did what she always does. Which was make her notes type up Andreah's prescription in her computer then printed out and give it to her.

Instead this time when Doctor Gasper turned around to hand her the slip Andreah surprised her when she respectfully said "Oh thank you Doctor Gasper, but the won't be necessary I've decided to take you advise with the whole route on Holistic Healing." Doctor Gasper gave her and up and down look then smiled while warmly inviting her for a hug and saying "O my Goodness...Dreah... Look at you...come here and give some I'm so proud of you sweetheart."

Andreah embraced her for a hug and said aloud "thank you Doc I really appreciate it! just think it's time you known. I know I've been driving you mad plus I think I'm going to take this time for myself I've bout had enough of Chocolate City for one life time. I need a vacation..

Doctor Gasper being noisy, but also in good spirit's said aloud "Awwweee no Andreah your leaving so this is our last session we were making such good progression over the years, Andreah smiled than went into her purse retrieving her card then saying aloud "when it's time to roll darling it's time, but rest assure Doctor Gasper I won't be far here is my card you make sure you keep in touch now."

Doctor Gasper accepted her card with a smile, but her smile erased off her face when she saw the contacts that was enlisted on the card that said "Sexy women making Deals in Lollipops & Heels." Doctor Gasper said aloud puzzled then Andreah rebuttal with reassurance saying "yes my dear all clients matter even the ones who most importantly value Confidentiality. When Doctor Gasper heard Andreah say that she already knew exactly what Andreah meant which left poor old Doctor Gasper raw and exposed.

Instantly Doctor Gasper began to replay past sessions with Andreah. In the very beginning and immediately became petrified from Andreah's Deducted calculation. The rise to the position that once upon a time belonged to Celeste when Andreah said "dear God Doc are you ok; you don't look so good."

Deep in Doctor Gasper's subconscious "Excuse me Ms. Smith (A CIA Agent responds) Andreah responds, sorry wrong girl my name is. The Agent cut here off Ms. Andreah Violetta Smith-Bey born June 18 1971 in Baltimore, Maryland to the parents of Clarissa Stevens who changed her name to... Andreah cut him short looking around a nervous mess Ok Ok Lord God what's the point of a name change if idiots like y'all shout it out for the whole world to hear.

What do you want? The Agent said we have a problem... Andreah said sarcastically, we call 911 isn't that what taxpayers pay y'all to do...

The Agent sternly replied; it's not the simple please get in there's a lot to discuss..." jumping further into her conscious "For goodness sake I've been sitting here for almost an hour for my order...Andreah snapped... The targets name is Chandler Ann Smith or better known as Celeste Ann Ezter

Smith we have reason to believe that Ms. Smith is responsible for the most lucrative human trafficking International Sex ring in the land right under the public noses...the Agent said; carry on damn y'all act like y'all ain't seen an angry sister before there's nothing to see hear...Celeste said aloud in the Diner.

Madam Celeste has been in business on this remote scale to our knowledge for the past 15 to 20 plus years. She's calculated, highly intelligent and connected thoroughly with powerful foreign counterparts. We've spent the last 81/2 years trying to find, but she is diplomatic guarded by our own who also is untouchable.one Agent said.

Ok so your telling me this why...Andreah rebutted; Grilled Chicken Caesar Salad with a diet Coke right... Celeste said to Andreah who said; uh ye ye yes...Ms. Smith. We know about your requested services of Celeste's requested young men for pleasure trust me when I tell you my superiors think I'm nuts, but...

The Agent said then Andreah cut him off saying, but...they wasn't lying to you your fucking insane if you think in anyway I can help... I didn't get your name... Andreah said then Celeste chuckled, and said: My name is Madam Celeste darling.

But if you happen to forget its on the card I just gave you. Well maybe your right I just might be crazy, but maybe the mother of this abducted child would consider, this young man doesn't happen to look familiar does he...

The agent responded; pictures of her first interactions with her son Atum. From the part till the end glitched throughout Doctor Gasper mental Rolodex. Up to when the accident almost occurred: O my god baby is that you...

Andreah said then Atum confused said, I'm sorry Ma'am I'm afraid not ah my name is Atum I believe we met... Pull over this fucking car right now let me out NOW.... Andreah spazzed then the CIA agent calmly said; Ms. Smith please were going to need for you to calm down this is a very serious matter...

Andreah shot back with; Calm down serious matter! Boy I tell you; you people got a lot of hairy balls. Ones at that to drag my son into y'all twisted plot of justice y'all are un-fucking believable. the agent said; Ms. Smith your son has been adopted by this monster almost 15 plus years ago not to mention many other children.

Adopted to graduating her minuscule prostitution ring. Into the grander scale it has become you have to believe us. Hold up wait! Look I'm not too good at this, but ah thank you for you know...

Andreah said to Atum as Atum countered back with; Nah I don't know you. Thanking me for what... Andreah says to the CIA agent; and what if I would consider you know assisting you gentleman like I did before what exactly would you need from me to do...

Glitches of Andreah getting an invite for Celeste to attend her conservative party. Jumping back form the events that transpired at Celeste's house up to the Garden of Eden sexcapades with her, Awode, and Valerie. As the CIA agent said, We've studied Celeste for years now.

What we were able to determine was close associates that we were able to get next to her. Who are still alive at least say she was enamored with the figure by the name of Sicilian Mobster Joe Conforte. Joe Conforte was what some would call the Godfather of Pimping.

But how he made any of that possible was through the ADA of Clark County. You fit the bill of what we believe Celeste is looking for. To do what Conforte did in Las Vegas in our nation's capital... More glitches of Andreah in and out of the Courthouse. Then it jumps to her with her brunch with Celeste. Then Andreah says to the CIA agent, but I'm just a legal aide to the man.

She provides service to I'm not a DA... Then the CIA agent said, that's great because she doesn't need to know that... Andreah said; why is my conscience telling me the way you making this sound is not as easy.

As is sounds... glitches of the events of the gruesome murders deployed by Celeste, and her company. As the CIA agent said, that's because it's not going to be a walk in the park Ms. Smith. This is not a game.

If you consider this you'll be going up against one of the most calculated criminals of this day and age. Any mistake could be your last. Glitches of Andreah's abusive childhood, and dilemma.

Including one segment of her as a mesmerize child wishing to be like the beautiful men and women in the Ebony magazine. As she said back to the CIA agent: look if I'm going to do this. It's got to be my way, and my way only...

One agent wanted to interject until the main one silenced him, and said; As for us... Then Andreah said listen all that undercover shit, and me being in y'all system. Absolutely not if she has power like that.

She could easily mark me from a mile away, and I'm not wearing no wire. So y'all better think of some hi-tech gadget for hacking, and recording purposes... Glitches of the heinous shootout from the traffic stop with the D.C. authorities, and the quarter mile up the road apprehension from Atum.

As the CIA agent said: hmmm any suggestions... Glitches of Andreah frantically driving away terrified then purposefully totaling her car. She quickly wrote on a sticky note that said call CIA agent Tashier.

Then stuck it on Leslie's dead corpse. As she peeped Atum coming to her aid quickly. She says to the agent: well a phone can get easily damaged, and a ring can get easily misplaced hmmmmm... Glitches of Atum dragging her across the interstate. As she looks around and catches Valerie recording the whole entire thing. She smiles as she thinks to herself (gotta love this sneaky lil Ho).

Then performs aloud for the camera screaming help he's trying to kill me HELP... Andreah says to the Agent: I got someone in mine. But she's not going to be cheap, but it's worth it... The two agents looked at each other. Then the main speaker said; let's hope you're right... Andreah looked back at them with a smile, and said, you have nothing to worry about...

The other agent said; Sir if I may. I think it would be wise for us to place surveillance, digital cameras throughout Ms. Smith's apartment.. Glitches of the wicked torture, and murder of Justice McConnelly by Awode and Atum played out.

When Andreah respond back to the agent; I have no problem with that at all. As a matter of fact that's an excellent idea.... Then the senior agent said; fair warning Ms. Smith, and be advised we have a protocol at the agency where if one of our operatives gets made, we have a distress signal for safety precautions..

Andreah responded back with; which is... back at the off the grid motel with her son Atum. In panic as she hugged the TV, awaiting for the news of the events that occurred. While Atum spilled his guts about him, and Celeste's whole operation.

She masked her smile as her picture popped up on the news, issuing a reward for her capture, and labeling her armed and dangerous... Andrea smiled in laughter as she shot back at the CIA agent with; really $250,000.00..

The CIA agent shrugged his shoulders then said WHAT.. you got the message didn't you. The other agent blushed as Andreah freshly said: Boy you better ask about all this right here. A bitch got that million dollar Oooookkkkkkurddd (Cardi B cat call)...

The main speaker said joking Cardi B's cat call; Oooookkkurrrr... Andreah's facial expression said it all as she responded back with; Oooo00owww will work on that... The other agent said; Ok now that we know their route.

We still don't know her inside help. It then jumped to the standoff at Celeste's house, Were Tatiana her childhood home girl saved her life..

Andreah lied to the CIA agent, and responded; Sorry no leads... The CIA agents looked at her then themselves, and felt she was lying but decided not to press the issue. As one asked until Andreah cut him off and said, listen white boy if you think Celeste is going down without a fight think again.

Her mind is already made up. The only going out she's doing is in a body bag. So if I were you, I would tell your men to suit up, and stake out at her mansion, and wait for my signal.

The men looked at each other. Then one said, Are you suggesting a KOS Ms. Smith, and exactly how you plan on that. Celeste dead doesn't put this case to bed.

Did you forget about them traffickers overseas... Andreah heard enough as she shot back at them firmly stating: No, I didn't forget them traffickers. Yes, I'm suggesting you kill that sick son of a bitch.

You don't need her you got me dumb asses. The CIA agents looked dumbfounded as Andreah picked up on their confusion and barked. Check it out y'all this ain't checkers; it's chess.

You bring her in on charges if you want. You're going to make a laughing stock of your Agency. Getting y'all asses handed to y'all in any courtroom y'all try her in.

The bitch for Christ sake services the whole entire Cabinet of the Presidency. You'll be lucky if that Ho even gets a Martha Steward bid. Now, if you spank that Ho, you done crippled the bitches whole entire American operation east of the Eastern seaboard.

Eliminating the suspicion of the foreign traffickers if they catch wind of if she is booked. Come on, think like a criminal guys, this is a Multi-Million Dollar business. If you was a trafficker, and you get word that one of your Ambassadors in one of your prize zones just got pinched.

What's the first thought that's going to go through your mind.... The CIA agents sat back. aloud what she said to sit and marinate then one uttered out; well I would wonder if she could hold water. Andreah jumped back in with, exactly but if she was dead hmmm dead men don't talk baby, and this Ho ain't Jesus...

The agents remained in silence, taken back at Andreah's decisive calculation. She continued on to say, business must go on. The only thing them players is worried about is whose next up to fill the seat.

If y'all had half the brain I believe y'all did. You would use the only meal ticket that bitch has left. Which is this fresh fry looking bitch...

The CIA agents looked at the picture of Valerie. Whom they acknowledged as Andreah's safety net throughout the whole operation.

As one agent said; you have a lot of trust in this women Ms. Smith... Andreah smirked, then with conviction said; gentlemen don't mistake trust with fear... fear I can control, but trust...

Trust is a mother fucka, and there's too much money to be made. To be pussy footing around. So what's it going to be boys huh times a ticking.

Images appeared of Celeste with a wounded shoulder running through her backyard. With hopes of a some getaway until she peep she was surrounded by the FBI and CIA's finest. In tactical gear at a stand off.

With Andreah's baffled-heart racing. As the CIA agent said; and exactly how you expect us to explain to the media this KOS request of yours. Andreah pulled out a Virginia Slim Long and sparked it up.

Inhaled then exhaled deeply and said: Please y'all been killing niggas wholesale since crackas done even know what an America was. Figure it out I got faith in y'all...

Images of Celeste played out as she got lit up like a Christmas tree (An assembly line of guns erupted) as she laid flat, and dead upon impact as Andreah close with the CIA agents with;

Andreah looked at the picture of Celeste when she was a male by the name of Chandler and smiled with a smirk. Looking at his autopsy the agents asked "hard to believe huh" Andreah looked at them then back at Celeste autopsy report and marveled in the lustful suspenseful journey endured with her for years. She wouldn't admit it to them, but deep down she never would of thought Celeste was every bom a boy before her change.

Out of all the swinging dicks present in the secluded car. She knew no matter how many may have thought they knew Celeste due to years of watching her. No one knew her better than the very own women who played little sis to her for years.

Waiting on her moment to pounce when the time presented itself. Then she could assume her role in her absence as the Americas new Ambassador. With nothing more to say she ended her response to the agents remark with "Hmmm in today's climate absolutely not...Hell pussy been running and influencing the world the only difference now is we move from behind the curtain to the stage "I'm looking forward to be doing business with" you gentleman in the promising future until then I'll be

IN TOUCH
Catch The Finale in Andreah's
CONTINUATION
Lollipop N Heelz
"Sexy women making deals"

Additional Pictures

ALL ART WORK IS AVAILABLE FOR SALE

Through the website <u>www.theribellyon.</u>
<u>com</u> or email <u>groglb2018@gmail.com</u>

Please make sure to check out the game and
prizes monthly on the website

The Ribellyon & Rebella Rez

Thank you for your purchase......More to come

Printed in the United States
by Baker & Taylor Publisher Services